Cocoon

a novel

emily sue harvey

THE
STORY PLANT

The Story Plant
The Aronica-Miller Publishing Project, LLC
P.O. Box 4331
Stamford, CT 06907

Print ISBN-13: 978-1-61188-036-6
E-book ISBN: 978-1-61188-037-3

Visit our website at www.thestoryplant.com

For information, address The Story Plant.

First Story Plant Printing: March 2012
Printed in The United States of America

dedication

*T*his novel is dedicated to dear friends, Kay and Gerald Turner, who showed me the world of steroid psychosis through their eyes: Kay, by experiencing the Cocoon itself, with all its nuances of nothingness and desolation and, at times, terror; and Gerald, by exercising blind faith, commitment, unconditional love and fidelity throughout the ordeal. Your exemplar inspires and buoys others to reach out and believe for the seemingly inaccessible.

And to my longtime friend, Billie McGregor whose triumphant battle with bone cancer beckons to those whose prognoses strike dread in one's heart – and admonishes them to "fear not." And though the characters and settings are completely fictional here, no other name seems to "fit" this story's character except "Billie Jean." Like real life Kay and Gerald, Billie is an icon of valor and cheer.

You are each true heroes. Thanks to you for your willingness to be transparent and generous. By doing so, you give hope to others.

acknowledgments

Cocoon's setting and characters are fictional. Paradise Springs is my "Brigadoon" and the colorful characters my dream circle. I loved the energetic creation process of this story, one that vacillates from darkness to light, from the fringe that separates them.

As always a deep, heartfelt thank you to my Story Plant publishers, Peter Miller and Lou Aronica. I am grateful to you for your faith in me and the fact that you turned me loose to pen six novels since 2009's release of *Song of Renewal*. Thanks again, Lou, for navigating me through sometimes rough waters, but most of all, for allowing me to be me.

A writer's greatest gift.

In the wider world, I am beholden to a larger network of friends than I can ever thank by name. But some rise to the top: John and Charlene O'Blenis, and Suzy Banzhof Nelson, always offering, with candor, valuable input, and Frieda Baird, who generously and spontaneously shares with me her wealth of holistic wisdom.

Eternal gratitude to Lee, my patient husband, who spends many a lonely evening as I sequester myself in my study and write the hours away – you remain steadfastly supportive and encouraging.

Thanks also to Daniel Isaac ("Laughter") Cooper, one of Michael and Susan Cooper's "miracle" children, for your grace and good humor when I tragically misspelled your name as "Danielle" in my novel acknowledgments for *Space*. I should have been noodle-flogged for not catching that in the proofing! I appreciate your great attitude, dear one.

Be blessed now, reader, and enjoy the McGraths's perilous, heart-warming journey!

prologue

"*Yee haaw*." Zoe's dark head fell back as she let loose her cry of jubilation.

The dance team leader, countrified stunning in her full-skirted, crinoline-petticoated clogging regalia, triple-, rock-, and brush-stepped as the hoedown music wound down and her dance partner, teen son Peyton, twirled her.

Seana, her mother, dancing in formation nearby, caught her breath as she spun out of the final twirl. Her matching mauve print, knee-length gingham skirt billowed out like a gently falling parachute as Barth's arms and hands skillfully reined in and steadied her halt. Then, hand in hand as one, the group of twelve took an elaborate bow to the whistles, stomping, and *woo-hoos* of the Paradise Springs populace.

Their lively performance officially launched the annual Paradise Springs Summer Festival. The Paradise Cloggers were the star attraction along with Danny Day and his Foothills Ramblers Band.

Though a quick mid-afternoon July shower had popped in to cool things down a mite, the dance exertion produced sopping perspiration.

"Here." Barth slipped a clean handkerchief into Seana's hand as the clogging team dispersed to enjoy festival attractions. Tantalizing food aromas filtered through the air as folks's noses led them to John Ivey's Tarheel Dog booth.

Retired USAF John's Concord, North Carolina BBQ was a favorite thereabouts, along with all-beef hot dogs and a range of sausages from spicy Italian to Cajun to German-style bratwurst.

Seana made a mental note to later feast on the North Carolina-style chopped BBQ with John's inimitable home-made sauce. She also noted they were grilling hamburgers to specification.

The aroma would have made her salivate had she had a drop left in her mouth to dredge up.

She carefully blotted moisture from her brow and returned the handkerchief to Barth, still catching her breath, smiling into his admiring eyes. Right now, behind the thick lens, they were Cocker Spaniel brown. Other times, glasses removed, they were more – well, not wild exactly, but she figured they probably had been in his younger days. Perhaps fervent was a better word for them.

When they were alone, minus the lens cloud between them, his eyes darkened and sparked a range of emotions that pushed exciting, long dormant buttons inside her.

Barth rubbed his neck and groaned. "Not as young as I used to be." He rotated his shoulders and stretched his back and long legs, still catching his breath. "I feel at this moment imminent mortality." He then removed his glasses, efficiently handkerchiefed the foggy lens, then slid them back on.

Seana felt a strong sweep of affection as he stuffed the deep mauve cloth – compliments of seamstress Sadie Tate – into his back pocket. A purely masculine gesture that tweaked something in her that made her feel even younger and more romantic. Something she'd not felt since long ago high school days of pep rallies and cheering at football and basketball games, with Ansel watching her like she was a candy bar and he was starved for a sugar fix.

She tamped down that direction of thought, reminding herself that this was now.

Barth's black Western outfit with silver buttons and tiny piped, mauve trim fit him well. White tap shoes clinked as he shifted his weight restlessly, reminding Seana, again, of the youth they had not spent together.

"I wish I'd known you when you were younger." The words slid out, despite her efforts to stifle that impulse-penchant of hers. It had not been divinely destined, after all. It was a childish, obsessive curiosity that had seized her.

Then her eyes half-mooned.

"Imminent mortality?" She laughed aloud. "Not that bad, surely."

Barth's head of salt-and-pepper, full, wavy hair moved slowly from side to side. "Not surely." He took another gulp of air, blew it out, and slid his arm around her shoulder, guiding her to a nearby booth sporting fountain drinks and an array of packaged quick treats from Fred's Grocery.

She glanced at his profile, with its full gray mustache. On him, it looked good. Doggone good. Matched his hair and his dark complexion.

Handsome dude he was. If you let the thick glasses just blend. But then, love was blind, wasn't it? A nerdy, aged Clark Kent was what he was. She grinned. That nailed him.

Seana ordered a diet soda and downed half of it before coming up for air, this time ignoring Barth's troubled stare. She looked at him. "What? This one time of drinking artificial sweetener won't kill me."

Barth shrugged and skeptically eyed the other sugary selections, whistling softly. "Got any water?"

"Sure," Fred Johnson, the local grocer, replied rather grumpily, yanking a paper cup from the counter.

"Hey, here's five dollars for your trouble." Barth winked at the short, red-haired, ruddy-faced man, then doled over the contribution.

"Thank you!" Fred beamed, filled the large cup with ice, and covered it with water.

Barth drank thirstily, emptying the cup in three pulls and discarding it in a handy garbage can.

"Zoe!" Seana called out to her daughter. She grabbed Barth's hand and tugged him along, shouldering through the festive crowd to where her statuesque daughter, Zoe, stood chatting with friends and her Happy Feet Dance Studio clients.

As they approached, Seana caught Zoe's eye and saw the warmth fade from the finely honed features topped by a burst of thick raven hair – her Cherokee Indian heritage through her late father's lineage. Her great-grandmother had been full Cherokee.

The crystal-blue eyes were vintage Seana. What a beauty she and Ansel had created. A bittersweet longing pierced her, then floated away on an invisible soft dulcet note.

Right now that blue turned to ice chips when they rested on Barth. As usual, Barth seemed oblivious and offered his huge, guileless smile. But Seana knew that it took courage for Barth to forge ahead in romantic pursuit of this rival's mother.

"Hi, Zoe. I sure hope we were up to snuff tonight," he ventured.

Zoe's nod was condescending. Dismissive.

Seana grinned at Barth. "Hey, your adoption of Southern slang is quite good. Very good, in fact, for a doggone Yankee." The two of them laughed, though no one else joined in.

"How'd we do?" Seana ignored Zoe's coolness, jumping into the chilly waters with both feet. What the heck? "Did we mess up too bad?"

In a blink, Zoe turned professional, looking the part with her slicked back ebony hair, nape-tethered with a rhinestone barrette. The clogging dress's fitted bodice and puffed short sleeves looked great on her. Zoe, with her long thinness, lent style to anything she wore.

"No. You did great. In fact, I'm very proud of the performance."

"Didn't Barth do good?" Seana couldn't help it. The words spilled out. How dare Zoe ignore Barth, who'd worked so hard for this festival performance? "He's not been doing it as long as the rest of us." Only for the past five months, actually. "A danged miracle is what he is!" Seana smiled up at him, pride radiating from her.

Zoe's gaze slid to Barth. *The interloper*, declared her slit-eyed appraisal. Barth, whose ingenuous patience would have put off a lesser opponent, failed to dent Zoe's steely scrutiny. Coldness crackled with the hauteur lift of chin. And the thought flitted through Seana's mind that one thing God hates most is a proud look.

Now, standing before her, was the reason.

"You gave a good performance, Barth."

The words fought their way from Zoe's straight, tight lips. The arrogant cast of eyes reduced the words to mere crumbs.

"Hi, Zoe. Great performance with the team." Tim, Seana's tall, sandy haired son appeared with his daughter tucked under his arm.

"Nana!" Ashley, their thirteen-year-old perfect child, rushed into Seana's arms, nearly knocking her over with fervor. "You were soooo good tonight, Nana. You can really, really clog! I want to learn now. Can I, Dad?"

"Sure, honey."

Seana clutched her sweet, usually shy granddaughter against her bosom, breathing in her fragrance, a fruity blend undergirded by vanilla. She basked in the welcome splash of unrestricted love.

Good-natured Tim held out his hand awkwardly to Barth, who grasped it and pumped enthusiastically. "Hi, Tim. Great to see you. How's the real estate market?"

"Good to see you, too," Tim muttered, glancing uneasily at sister Zoe, who stood stiffly, staring off into space. "Oh, can't complain about business, despite the economy shift."

Polite. Distant. It all registered with Seana. Hurt perched

on the periphery of her emotions. She held it back with everything in her.

Barth's smile remained intact. "Nice festival. I'm impressed. By the way, where's Sherry?"

"Oh, she's somewhere hereabouts." Tim scratched his head
and looked around aimlessly for his wife. Definitely ill at ease,
Seana silently noted. Hurt now dangled precariously close.

Barth was remarkably resilient. His optimism was tough
and thick as a cement slab. So was his inclination to being
"chatty," as her family privately pointed out, a thing they didn't
exactly cotton to. Their stop-and-smell-the-roses, chill-out
Southern mindset required ample silent lapses.

In other words, every moment didn't have to be filled with
prattle, however intelligent.

But Seana had spent many a silent, lonely night with no
one to talk to. Now, she fancied Barth's gregariousness. He
was well-read, a walking fountain of knowledge. And he loved
to share with those he perceived in need. The end result lately
was that he sometimes aggravated his project of the moment.

Barth's good heart was, in this instance, his worst enemy.

Seana had told him that he was overstepping with the family so he gave her permission to simply tell him when he grew
too verbose or intrusive, and he would tone down.

Seana shook her mind loose of the uncomfortable analyz-
ing. "Yes. Where *is* Sherry?"

Ashley raised her head from Seana's shoulder and said,
"She's probably at the book booth. She loves to read." She slid
around to Seana's side and linked arms with her.

Silence settled awkwardly over the family scene.

"Say," Barth reared back and cast a baleful look at Ashley. "How about me? I danced my fanny off, too!" He did a
little shave-and-a-haircut-two-bits step, spread his arms wide
and bowed.

Ashley dissolved into giggles, blushed, hesitated, swaying from foot to foot, then rushed to throw her arms around
Barth's middle. "You were good, too."

Seana breathed a sigh of relief. Leave it to Barth to rescue sanity and civility.

Zoe lifted herself to full height, gaze averted. "Well, I'll leave you guys. I want to browse a bit. See you later." Her mincing footsteps on concrete, enunciated comically by shoe taps, took her from view in seconds flat.

Seana turned her attention to Tim, who looked more uncomfortable by the moment. "How about coming by the house for a while later? I know you're going to fill up on John's famous barbecue, but I've baked a chocolate cake with fresh strawberries for dessert," Seana ventured hopefully.

"Umm …" Tim scratched his head and frowned, still furtively watching the crowd for a glimpse of his wife. Tim rarely ever had refused Mom's chocolate cake, no matter how last minute thrown together.

"Please, please, Dad?" Ashley coaxed, batting her eyelashes sweetly.

"Uh, I don't think so, sweetheart," he addressed Ashley. Then Seana, "Actually, we've already made plans, Mom..."

"What plans?" Ashley whined, disappointed.

Tim looked at her, agitation leaking through. "Your mom has a new restaurant she wants to try in Easley."

Ashley's face brightened. "Then Nana and Barth can come –"

"No," Seana injected, smiling at her precious granddaughter. "Barth and I are going to gorge on all these Tarheel food selections. Sample as many as we can. Then we want to just chill out tonight, sweetheart. We're tired, you know? Some other time."

"Yeh," Tim brightened. "We'll do it another time. Let's go find your mom, Ashley. Later, Mom, Barth?"

"Right. See you later." Barth smiled and waved them off.

Tears pushed behind Seana's eyes as she turned and collided with Peyton, her tall, dark, and handsome grandson, dressed in his own black country clogging outfit. Zoe's oldest son, at sixteen, was the most agile and proficient of the clogging team.

"Nana, you did wonderful." He looked down at her, steadying hands on her shoulders, his gaze loving her so much it buoyed Seana's beaten-down heart. She hadn't realized how shredded she felt until he pulled her into his arms, his beautiful dark head laid atop hers. She embraced him and felt his hand gently patting her shoulder. "Love you, Nana," he murmured.

Seana swallowed back a lump the size of Oklahoma in her throat. "Love you, too," she whispered. "Very, very much."

Barth waited until they'd stepped back from each other before offering his hand.

"Hi, Peyton."

"Hi, Mr. McGrath," Peyton murmured politely. Then he waved to some friends nearby. "Gotta run. We're all going to chow down on some Tarheel burgers and dogs."

"*Barth*," Barth called after him. "Call me *Barth*."

"Sure thing, Barth," Peyton called over his shoulder as he dashed away.

For the first time, Seana saw just a glimmer of pain in the Cocker Spaniel eyes. Or did she? Those thick lenses could be deceptive.

She prayed he would not be hurt by the family freeze. She held out her hand and felt his large, warm fingers interlace with hers and squeeze gently.

Seana loved this man.

She grinned up at him. "Let's go have some good Southern chow – that is, if you can tune out all those additives and forget how unhealthy some of it is."

He grinned back and inhaled the wonderful smells. "Woman, what's unhealthy? Let's get at it."

chapter one

aybreak's lifting velvet curtain soothed Seana as she
sat on her back deck, one that stretched the length of
her sprawling bi-level ranch house. Brutus, her faithful four-
year-old red Lab, sprawled out next to her lounge chair, relaxed
yet alert to every nuance of insect life and birdsong.

The eleven-room structure sprang from the crest of a twen-
ty-acre farm, situated just barely outside the town limits of
Paradise Springs, population two thousand. Its second-level,
smooth wood balcony embraced her both with its comfort and
incomparable cedar fragrance.

With its familiarity. Its continuity, when so many other
things in her life had changed.

Seana inhaled deeply of honeysuckled air as the first sliver of sun peeked over the mountains, pushing back lingering
primrose and lavender and painting the sky first pale gray, then
azure. Coffee's sweet aroma brought her to here and now. She

sipped thirstily, holding the liquid on her tongue, closing her eyes, and relishing its taste.

July's early mornings here were wonders to behold. Paradise Springs nestled in the South Carolina foothills, near the North-South Carolina border. Ansel had chosen the site wisely and built well. Not only from her deck but from each floor-to-ceiling window wrapping the back of the beautiful structure, Seana's eyes feasted on the distant blue Smoky Mountain range. The upper South Carolina terrain thereabouts was one of graceful rolling hills and valleys.

Seana's late husband, Ansel, had built it for her in the early days of their marriage. Had three decades actually passed? Incredible. She smiled and sipped her aromatic coffee. This was her dream home and had served them well as they raised their two children, Zoe and Tim, and on into their empty nest years until Ansel's death seven years ago.

His lengthy bout with cancer had allowed him time to set his finances in order. He had left Seana and the children well provided for. The farm was paid off years ago. Ansel's prudence and investment savvy had, in the end, ensconced Seana in debt-free comfort.

His love still, after he'd been gone for so long, reached out to her and spoke of his selflessness, evidenced by the legacy he'd left her. Ansel would forever remain a part of her heart. That certainty surrounded and embraced her this morning, and tears misted her eyes as she breathed a prayer of thanksgiving for all her blessings.

Then she reached for the fruit she'd earlier prepared, a mixture of sliced strawberries, local peaches, blackberries from her own back yard, a shaving of banana and, topping it off, a big dollop of vanilla yogurt. She spooned a generous scoop into her mouth and bit into the succulent, sweet fruit. Mmmm.

It didn't get any better than this.

Brutus's noble head lifted only slightly to acknowledge her feast before lowering again to the floor. Seana's son, Tim, had purchased him from a search-and-rescue friend after Brutus's early retirement due to a shoulder injury that caused a slight limp. And though it disqualified him for the sometimes harsh requirements in SAR, he could run normally, as their resident squirrels and neighboring cats soon discovered. And Billie Jean, her widowed cousin, too.

Seana caught his tea-colored eye and smiled. "Good boy."

Her bonus was a couple of enthusiastic tail sweeps before he floated into drowsy canine oblivion.

An ear-splitting whistle pierced the stillness, jerking Brutus's head up to full attention. He sat up and looked at Seana, a question in those intelligent eyes.

"Go on," she said, and he tore into a run, paws clicking loudly as he loped down the steps to join Seana's cousin, Billie Jean, on her morning run around the property. Widowed Billie Jean resided downstairs in Seana's rambling structure, an arrangement that had served well since Ansel's death.

Seana grinned as she watched the two disappear over the hill; Billie Jean, a compact, energetic woman with rich chestnut waves harnessed by white sweatband above running gear of red, sleeveless sweatshirt and shorts. White Reeboks kicked up dirt tufts with Brutus loping astride.

She took another long sip of coffee, and sighed.

The aloneness, Seana's companion for so long, now seemed almost elusive.

Almost. It was still difficult to completely let go of Ansel. He'd been the strength and solidity of their relationship while she'd been his "muse," he'd always happily insisted. He'd let her be herself, with all her whimsical romanticism and free-spirited giving to and loving the entire populace of Paradise Springs.

All that changed when he died. Seana had to grow up, to a degree. Tamp down her childlike abandonment to life. Suddenly, she was at the helm with her children.

She and Ansel had set their younger child, Zoe, up in her ballroom dance business after she became enamored while studying dance in the high school Governor's Fine Arts program. Vibrant Zoe had found her niche. Happy Feet Dance Studio became a favorite hangout in Paradise Springs.

Entire families, drawn in by Zoe's economy family package deals, signed up in droves. Even children became proficient in fancy footwork. Smart girl, Zoe, knowing that if she could captivate the kids, the parents would land in the palm of her hand.

It was there, in the roomy yet intimate ballroom, that Seana and Ansel had spent the majority of their down time. They'd enjoyed dancing, but most of all, they loved the way it drew not only their family but other families together.

The coziness of it, plus the invigoration of dance, was intoxicating.

Tim, older than Zoe by two years, finished Clemson University with a degree in business. Upon his father's death, Tim stepped into Ansel's shoes. Seana had signed the lucrative real estate business over to her son, figuring that since she and Ansel had blessed Zoe with her dance facilities and capital to get her started, their gift to Tim evened out the two siblings's playing field.

Ansel's vast real estate rental and lease holdings, managed by a professional firm, remained Seana's legacy. He left Seana free to simply enjoy the fruits of his labors.

But all the wealth in the world didn't keep away heartache.

Following Ansel's death, Seana experienced a loneliness such as she'd never imagined possible. For years she remained convinced a part of her heart had been surgically removed and would forever leave a gaping, raw void where romance once thrived.

And then, she met Barth. Against all odds, she met him when she least expected to ever again *feel*.

&

That Monday night, Seana had settled down in a chair at Happy Feet Dance Studio, chilling out. Tired after spending a good part of the day at son Tim's Howard Real Estate office, helping his wife, Sherry, with some paperwork.

She'd discovered how rusty her office skills had become. "I've got to take a computer course to brush up." Seana blew out a frustrated breath and gazed at Sherry as she sat at the computer. "Everything is changing in cyberspace."

"There's going to be a computer class at Tech in a few months. I'm thinking about taking a refresher myself," Sherry said, stapling some forms together that the collator machine had just spit out. She reached down to give Seana a hug. "Thanks, Seana. You're sweet to bail me out of this paper jungle."

"Glad to be here for you." She glanced at her watch. "Oops! Gotta get over to the Studio."

So there Seana sat that Newcomer's Night, one held periodically to welcome new arrivals to town and maybe infect some more locals with dance fever. Zoe depended on her to help greet those who wandered in. Too, Seana knew it was to get her mom out of the house.

Seana covered her mouth to hide a huge yawn.

She was weary and – lonesome. In a room full of happy, dancing people.

Lonely.

Seemed ridiculous. But there it was, like a daggum Grand Canyon chasm gaping before her.

Then she saw him. A newcomer. A stag. Most folks thereabouts came in twos and sometimes more.

Ambitious Zoe's coupons for two free introductory dance lessons littered the entire town to lure folks in. New resident Barth McGrath took the bait, moseyed into Happy Feet Studio and planted his long length in one of the folding studio chairs as far back into a dim corner as he could manage, fidgeting at his white starched shirt collar until he could stand it no longer and pulled off his paisley tie, folded it, and slipped it into his navy blue blazer pocket.

Seana witnessed it all that Monday night, fighting a tug

at the corners of her generous mouth. Her tiredness dissolved. He looked about as lonely as she felt. Next thing she knew, she migrated toward him.

Tall and lanky as a Western cowboy, he looked so ill at ease and so nerdy she felt sorry for the man. But that only lasted until she looked through those thick lenses into eyes the color of roasted chestnuts and saw the vulnerability lurking there.

That he was sort of attractive behind those frames, in a decidedly rugged way, was the next thing to register.

"How about we show these folks how to dance?" she heard herself saying to him and was rewarded with a slow smile as he arose. The smile produced dimples as he swallowed her hand in his big one and in a blink had her moving with the music.

He was remarkably graceful on the dance floor being as how he'd never had formal lessons, he quickly informed her.

"I'd never have known," she said truthfully.

"Of course I spent a lot of time dancing years back," he added. "I really liked the disco era. Gave young folks places to go to simply dance. Like this one. Nice place. Who owns it?"

"My daughter, Zoe." With blatant pride she pointed out her lovely brunette offspring, partnering with the town jock, Scott Burns.

"That her husband?"

"No. But not for lack of his trying." Seana grinned up at him. "He's Paradise Spring High's athletic coach and is determined to win my Zoe. She's a challenge, something Scott cannot resist." She whispered theatrically, "It's in his blood."

Barth chuckled, nodding his head. "I see."

Scott's pursuit of the wary, slippery-eel Zoe was by now what Paradise Springs's legends were made of. Big, strapping, available Scott was all-American good-looking, with his butch haircut and muscular physique.

Scott was at his best in contest. In this one, Zoe was the prize.

Thus, the drama played on.

Barth the newcomer was light on his feet for someone his

size. And he was a quick learner and adventuresome, to Seana's delight. She hadn't had a good partner since Ansel and was excited to have someone so compatible, both physically – he was tall but so was she at five-eight to his six-one – and they both loved music and the pull and challenge of dance.

Yup. Seana felt herself relaxing and enjoying simply being, like she had not since Ansel's passing.

It felt good.

ಌ ಞ

In those next two hours, she discovered other things the two of them shared in common. One was a love of anything literary. The other was music. The gamut from country to classical. He was a musician, actually, played piano, saxophone, and guitar. And though Seana's knowledge in holistic studies and health foods did not compare with his, she was fascinated by his expertise. He wasn't neurotic, just smart about good health choices.

"Where's your home?" she asked. "I can't quite place your accent."

He looked at her long and hard, then chuckled. "Anywhere and everywhere." When Seana continued silently waiting for a more thorough response, he shrugged, then added, "I'm originally from Canada."

So that was why she'd not been able to discern his origins. Still, the dialect sounded a bit familiar.

"What brought you here to Paradise Springs?"

"A friend of mine lives here. He's been trying to get me here for a long, long time."

"Oh? Anyone I know?"

"Keith Melton."

A splash of pleasant surprise. "My pastor. Small world, huh? How did you know him?"

"College pals." He didn't elaborate.

"So that's where I've heard the dialect before."

It was like a door opened into a bright, new world for Seana. Oh, it wasn't an overwhelming love-at-first-sight thing. Not at all. Barth was first and foremost a new, interesting friend. A fun companion. They began going out together.

With him, Seana felt that long abandoned child within her slowly rising up once more.

At first her daughter Zoe didn't seem overly impressed with Barth one way or another. Which was not surprising. Zoe was not easily impressed. Period. Seana, after all, had not been romantically interested in a man since Zoe's father had died.

Tim, her son, was polite and characteristically friendly – yet Seana sensed his reservation. A wait-and-see one. His wife, Sherry, remained non-committal but polite. Granddaughter Ashley, now thirteen and shy, clammed up at first but – with Barth's winsome coaxing – then opened up and chattered like a magpie, endearing herself to him.

And to Seana. How she loved that little sandy-haired girl, a composite of Sherry's delicate features with Tim's soft brown eyes – Ansel's legacy – and gentle manner.

Barth was the perfect prescription for the loneliness that had beset her in recent years, since the children married and started their own families.

Their own lives.

కుండి

Barth.

Brutus's bark of delight snapped Seana back to the present. The Lab lumbered up the deck steps to her side, panting and plopping down beneath her chair to cool down. She heard Billie Jean's door close downstairs. And she was alone again with her memories.

Barth.

Warmth trickled like warm summer rain through her as she remembered their time together last night. She'd invited him home with her after Paradise Springs Summer Festival. How had she ever not seen his beauty?

Today, five months later, Seana gazed mistily at the blue mountain range from her deck, took a deep breath, blew it out and grinned, resisting the urge to fan her face.

My oh my. She rolled her eyes. Who would have thought it? After all these years, she was in love again.

Never would've believed she could love again after Ansel. How she'd loved that man. And to lose him had been excruciating. He would forever occupy a part of her heart. In retrospect, she admitted the dark odyssey had taught her lots of good things. It taught her to treasure each day as her last. And she learned that when one door closed, another one, divinely opened, would offer up equally wonderful opportunities.

At the time of Ansel's slide into eternity, however, she'd felt that no good could ever trail such loss.

But time and the help of the good Lord had brought her through.

She shook her head to clear out the sad memories, arose, and gathered her dishes from the patio table. In the kitchen she rinsed and loaded them into the nearly empty dishwasher. With her being the lone diner there, dishes didn't collect quickly. At one time, that little observation had decimated her.

Not any more. It would not be so for much longer.

She tucked that knowledge inside her cozy, little heart niche reserved for Barth.

Brutus's clicking stride took him to his water bowl where he lapped for a full two minutes, quenching his thirst from the long run. He came to her and nuzzled her until she gave him an affectionate rub between his shoulders before trotting away to settle onto his den pillow.

Her cell phone, lying on the nearby granite counter, vibrated into a lively patriotic rendition of "God Bless the USA."

She looked at the ID. Barth.

"Good morning," she trilled like a school girl as joy, like helium, filled and lifted her.

"Good mornin' yourself," drawled a Canadian Clark Gable voice, raising goose flesh on Seana's arms and neck. The scrumptious kind.

"Hi," she murmured, suddenly breathless. The huskiness in his voice curled her insides. She rolled her eyes on that thought. Lordy. She had it *bad*. "So you're fully recuperated from last night's festive excitement, are you?"

"Absolutely, except that ice cream vendor who decided to have his own version of Hooters waitresses to serve folks. Some citizens didn't particularly take to that, did they?"

Seana burst into laughter. "That was too, too much for Sadie Tate. I can still hear her telling that man in no uncertain terms that his helper had better put on more clothes or she'd see that his booth would be shut down. Said she'd never saw an outfit like that. Feisty little thing. Her little, crooked fingers were flying, texting the news over her newfangled cell phone."

"But he did have long lines until that happened, didn't he?" Laughter tinged Barth's unique, un-Southern, citified drawl.

"That he did," gurgled Seana. Heavens, but it felt so good to laugh ... most of all to have someone to laugh with.

"See you tonight?" His query was husky, hinting of anticipation.

"Yes. Here? I can cook if you –"

"I'm gonna take you out. Seven?"

She grinned. "Can't wait."

After they hung up, Seana had to descend back to Earth. This thing with Barth was a powerful ride of emotions. Whew! *Lordy! Feet, behave yourself. Settle back down.* She turned to go to the den and nearly bumped into her daughter.

"Zoe." She was about to embrace her when Zoe swept past her.

Seana planted hands on hips and turned to watch her. "Well, hello to you, too. I didn't hear you come in."

"I know," Zoe snapped. "You were too caught up with lover boy." Her back, ramrod straight made her five-ten look even taller as she stalked into the den and crossed the room to gaze out the window at distant blue mountain ranges as though she wanted to dynamite them, bringing Brutus's head up as he gauged her temper.

Her garb consisted of funky apparel from the Sassy Rags shop, today gaucho-style blouse and felt vest over calf-length matching floaty skirt. From beneath the earth-tone ensemble sizzled sexy brown boots with skinny heels, now tapping impatiently against Seana's shiny hardwood floor.

"Zoe, why do you feel this hostility toward Barth? You don't know a single thing about him that should –"

"That's just it." Zoe spun from the window and glared at her mother. "I don't know a single thing about him. Zilch. Just who is this man who comes out of nowhere?"

Seana's nose did a slight flare as she fought her rising temper. "He's a wonderful man who makes your mother happy, Zoe. That's who he is."

Zoe moved to within inches of her mother, her gaze oozing cynicism. Her long, ebony hair, so like her father's, framed a pale oval face whose deep blue eyes, so like Seana's, revealed that she'd seen too much of the world too soon – a view that came at too great a cost.

How Seana loved her, this dynamo female child of hers who had carried her own load, plus her ex-husband's baggage over terrains too rough, at times, to forge. Zoe had almost single-handedly raised her child to adolescence and done a fantastic job of it.

Who stood squared off before her mother, challenging her, hating the man Seana loved.

Seana reached out to touch her arm, only to have it snatched away. "Are you going to find out who this man is? I've asked him and get this runaround –"

"It's none of your business. Maybe that's what he feels. You know he senses this resentment, Zoe. He's not blind." Seana hated the shrill note that crept into her voice, but she couldn't help it. This was her life, dadjimmit.

"None of my business?" Zoe's eyes filled with indignant tears. "You're my mother, for crying out loud! I love you very much."

Seana's heart began to melt and she started toward her, but Zoe's back-off stance stopped her dead in her tracks. Zoe's gaze narrowed. "But what I want to know is this. Are you going to marry him?"

Seana stared at this beautiful, wild creature standing before her. Like a lioness protecting her cubs. Only this time, it did a flip. The cub was protecting the lioness.

Seana shook her head free of the crazy image. She took a deep breath.

"Zoe, Barth proposed last night," she said, steeling herself to settle this for once and for all. "I said yes."

Zoe looked as though she'd been struck. "Mama, you can't mean that! Why don't you wait –?"

"I'm going to marry him. Soon," Seana repeated gently but firmly. "And there's no use in trying to talk me out of it." How her heart hurt that she should have to be so – so radical.

And she felt a twinge of resentment that Zoe forced her into this militant stance.

"What is he bringing into this marriage, huh?" Zoe's voice trembled with indignation. "Nothing. That's what. You're giving him a meal ticket, you know. He doesn't have a job or anything."

"He'll soon be helping Pastor Keith out at the church. He's a wonderful speaker and musician, Zoe. You should hear him play –"

"Gotta go." Zoe swept past, eyes straight ahead. "You're making a huge mistake, Mother. A really huge mistake."

The door slammed behind her. Seana stood there, frozen in shock as she heard Zoe's car roar from the drive.

How her heart bled. Just when she thought she'd found happiness again, along comes this – this jealousy thing with Zoe. It had to be that, didn't it?

Zoe had been Ansel's little girl. Those two had been tight. And since his death, Seana had been both mother and father to her children.

But didn't she have a right to love again?

After all, Barth was everything a woman could want in a man. Wasn't he?

Despite the dark past he'd shared with her. A past she could not reveal to her children. Not now. Maybe never. She remembered something F. Scott Fitzgerald once said: "Family quarrels are bitter things. They do not go by any rules. They're not like aches or wounds; they're more like splits in the skin that won't heal because there's not enough material."

Would that be the case with Zoe and Tim? Would they – if they discovered the whole truth of Barth's past – have enough mercy and grace, the material of forgiveness?

Seana wasn't willing to risk it.

She deserved happiness and Barth represented everything she desired in life.

Then in a heartbeat, confidence filled her. From deep, deep inside her, the feminine intuition well sprang up and filled her with certainty.

Barth was the man she loved. He was the man she would marry.

༄༄

Seana couldn't repress a grin as she climbed from her silver 4Runner and spotted the beauty shop's sign, *Homecombing Queen Beauty Salon, Joanie Knight, proprietor.* Her pal Joanie's joke was that she hadn't been the high school homecoming queen like Seana, but darn it, she *would* be queen in her own hairstyling kingdom.

"Hey, Seana," Joanie called out from behind the shampoo sink. "Grab a seat. I'll catch up in a jiffy. Got a little late start, what with the long night at the Spring Festival and all. Nearly clogged my legs off, but oooh how much fun it was. I won't be long catching up."

"No problem." Seana settled into one of the crimson-padded white wicker chairs lining the soft pink waiting area of the Homecombing Queen Salon. A quaint jungle of assorted, vibrant greenery, strategically arranged, brought together the warm feminine hues in a way delightful to the eye.

Seana picked up a Ladies Home Journal from a white wicker table and began flipping through it. But she couldn't arrest her thoughts to the pages. Couldn't get past the shock of Zoe's earlier, vehement objection to her engagement to Barth.

"Hey," Joanie's assertive voice scattered Seana's thoughts. "Barth's a real hottie, when he takes off those specs, Seana. Smooth as silk on the dance floor, too. Things getting pretty serious, huh?" Her astute gaze required a response.

Seana didn't mind this from her lifelong girlfriend. She smiled and nodded.

"That's good to hear. I was afraid you'd let 'im slip away." Joanie, blonde and Kewpie-Pie cute in her white uniform and platform sandals, winked one of her eyes, enhanced from day to day by colored contact lenses. Lashes long enough to fan away flies framed her orbs, which today sparkled like green emeralds. Her blonde curls, heaped high atop her head, loosed long, slim tendrils to frame her porcelain, perfectly blushed cheeks.

"Like she's done so many times before," joined in Sadie Tate, seamstress extraordinaire and town gossip. But Seana loved her anyway. She was harmless. Most of the time. Just loved to talk. An hour early, as usual, Sadie'd slipped in and took the chair next to Seana, already playing with her ever present Smart cell phone. This time at Joanie's was one of Sadie's most fruitful social connections.

"I never met anybody before who appealed to me," Seana said, laying the magazine aside. And she had not, despite all the matchmaking attempts of Paradise Springs's locals.

"So this time's different, huh?" Sadie gouged, pocketing her phone for more crucial fodder. Her raisin-black, piercing eyes glittered with anticipation. She crossed her spindly legs, poking from beneath a bright Hawaiian floral shift, and angled more toward Seana, sending whiffs of *Tabu* to Seana's nostrils. A pleasant, spicy floral fragrance, one that sent Seana's yesteryear melancholy spiraling. Back to when she'd worked at the downtown five-and-dime store.

"Um-hmm." Seana turned and smiled at her, seeing only childlike curiosity. In turn, Sadie's eyes warmed and her vivid red slash of a mouth curved into a smile. "That it is," Seana said.

Sadie's swollen, rheumatic fingers reached over to pat Seana's hand. "I'm glad for you. I truly am. You had a long, hard time of it with Ansel and all. It's time for you to get on with living."

Seana stared at her for a moment, seeing only genuine care. Sometimes, Sadie went beyond caring and into meddling. Not today. "Thanks, Sadie."

At her station, Joanie's small hands flew hummingbird swift in plastering Louann Melton's red hair onto smooth rollers and in a blink depositing her under the hair dryer. Pastor Keith's wife waved at Seana from beneath the hood, then blew her a kiss.

Seana responded in kind. Such giving people, the Meltons. They had, through the good and bad times, been there for Seana. And now, that bond included Barth, a bond that went back to Barth's and Keith's boyhood days in Canada.

"Seana, you're next."

At the shampoo sink, Seana and Joanie decided to add a few more blond highlights to Seana's thick light ash brown hair the next time. "The silver threads are about to overtake, honey. The blond highlights will camouflage that," Joanie whispered in her ear. Then, "How's Zoe taking things?"

Seana's heart skipped a beat. She blinked up at her from proneness as warm water sluiced over her scalp and through her hair. "What do you mean?"

Was Joanie psychic? The thought flitted through her mind like a startled cat.

Since she'd been seeing Barth, Seana and Joanie's intimate chat times had dwindled from cozy house visits to once-a-week salon time, such as this. Not intentionally. But Barth had consumed her prime time.

Joanie's fingers, strong as a brick mason's, massaged and

lathered. "I can tell she's not happy about you and Barth. Last night at the festival, she watched you two like a chicken hawk ready to swoop."

Seana sighed and closed her eyes. She trusted Joanie, had been a client and friend for years and years. Knew Joanie's makeup and had never known her to be unkind or unwise. Had, many times, confided in her. Never had those confidences been betrayed.

And she knew, too, that Zoe had probably indicated to Joanie while getting her own hair done that she didn't like Barth. Zoe was not subtle by any stretch of imagination. Probably hoped Joanie would tell her mama what an idiot she was.

"She's not happy, Joanie. I don't know why, but she doesn't like Barth."

Joanie rinsed as avidly as she lathered, and soon, Seana's hair squeaked when toweled. While ushering Seana to the styling station chair, she quietly continued their discussion, careful not to allow ever-vigilant Sadie to overhear. As an extra precaution, she turned the radio on to the local pop music station, loud enough to muffle their discourse.

Resigned and bored, Sadie took out her cell phone again and recommenced texting.

Joanie expertly snipped and shaped Seana's hair into a shorter, fluffy style. "*A la Monroe*," Joanie murmured seductively. "Give Barth a little ol' thrill."

Seana laughed, flushing with pleasure at the thought as Joanie fluffed and plumped the damp hair, gazing appraisingly in the mirror, gauging the balance and shape of the end result. Satisfied, she reached for the curler trolley and angled it close.

"Know what I think?" Joanie's hands flew from curler bin to head, comb-parting, sectioning, fingers flipping hair over curler, tightening, rolling, pinning. "I think she's jealous, Seana. You've always been such a good mother and she's never had to share you. Never. You've always put those kids first. You have nothing to apologize for."

"Hmm. True." Seana sighed and took the counsel to heart.

"I don't know. It seems to go beyond simple jealousy, Joanie. I can't exactly define it."

Yet, at the same time, she knew that Zoe's probing of Barth's past had a lot to do with her anger. But that was a subject she could not share. Not even with Joanie.

Comb-parted, lifted, curler-flipped, turned, pinned. "Maybe she's just plain got an issue of trust. Y' know?"

"Trust?" Seana's ears perked.

"Yeh. You know, she's had the worst experiences with men I've ever seen. And hey! I've seen quite a few bad examples, including my own." She rolled her eyes and swiveled the chair to access another hair section for manipulation. "Zoe's such a strong force to be reckoned with that she attracts these guys like gnats to peaches. They're the ones who want a tough woman to take care of 'em. Zoe fits the bill. She ends up doing everything, carrying the whole danged load."

"That's a good reading, Joanie." Seana felt again that jolt of regret that her daughter's genetic hardwiring had, in one sense, set her up for matrimonial defeat. Zoe's take-charge, no-nonsense drive had predisposed her to be the family leader. That was okay, except that very same tendency made her a target for lazy, and/or passive male breeds, like her first husband, and her ex–longtime boyfriend Corey Adams.

"Too bad about Corey," Joanie muttered. "Pretty good guy, just commitment-shy."

"Yeh." Seana sighed, feeling the same as Joanie. She'd liked Corey. "Five years is a long time with a guy who feels he can't leave his mama."

Joanie laughed. "A great son but would make a lousy husband."

She pinned the last curl in place, snatched a net from a drawer, and had it tied over the curls in a heartbeat. "Too bad you didn't have five Tims," Joanie said, laughing. "He's a dream, isn't he?"

"That he is," Seana agreed, surging with pleasure at the mention of her son. Her treasure. "My son's been so *there* for me. Oh well, you know all about that, Joanie." Seana felt herself steered to the dryer seat, plunked down, and head-tucked beneath the dryer hood in four breaths flat.

Click. Forced air attacked her scalp, slowly warming.

Joanie leaned and murmured in her ear. "Tim is a godsend, like his daddy was. Always there in time of trouble. I'll never forget when he came out in an ice storm one morning and over to the salon when I called you hunting for someone to help. He was my Sir Galahad a' fixing that busted, frozen water pipe for me. Saved me a queen's ransom in water damage."

Seana felt the rush of tears behind her eyes as she smiled up at her friend. Her confidante. Tim was, indeed, a godsend.

His love for her made this transition bearable

But as wonderful as Tim was, he, too, held reservations about her relationship with Barth McGrath. "Oh, he'll come around," Barth reassured her repeatedly, apparently not worried about the coolness all about him.

With all her heart, Seana hoped so.

∾

"Now, you have fun tonight, y' hear?" Joanie called after Seana as she swung through the door on her way out.

"I hear you," Seana called back, laughing, feeling marvelously buoyed thinking about the upcoming dinner date. Ninety-degree heat slapped her in the face as she impulsively dashed to the other side of Main Street to more closely examine the little black dress in Sassy Rags Shop's window display. It was love at first ogling.

"I've gotta have that dress." Seana burst through the glass entrance, relishing the smack of cool air while pointing to the display. Chelsea, the proprietor, popped up from behind the counter, juggling hangers and boxes.

"Hi, Seana," Chelsea beamed at her, rushing to a rack displaying a range of sizes in Seana's selection. "Size eight, right?"

"Right. But I still better try it on."

She did, careful not to muss her hair. "Absolutely perfecto," Chelsea exclaimed, hands on voluptuous hips as she checked her from every angle. Seana thought how Chelsea, now a good twenty-five pounds fluffier than in their school days, still looked appealing. Still danced light as a feather with the clogging team, too. Her sense of style was unparalleled hereabouts.

"Box it up. And while you're at it, add those gold earrings, necklace, and bracelet."

"Anything else? Must be a heavy date, honey," Chelsea drawled and cut her heavily kohled, silvery eyes at Seana, creating a dramatic Cleopatra persona with her onyx pageboy bob and artful makeup.

"Absolutely." Before the mirror, Seana held the earrings to her ears and tilted her head, warmed by her friend's obvious delight in her romance. "Love them! Oh heck, you just as well throw in those little black sling heels, size eight narrow."

While Chelsea pulled them out and placed them on the counter, she asked, "By the way, how's Billie Jean doing? She still feeling off kilter?"

Seana's cousin Billie Jean had been having some health problems. Without other immediate family, she'd jumped at Seana's invitation to move into Seana's downstairs quarters after Ansel's death. "To keep you company and to look after you," Billie Jean had insisted. They soon had the lower level kitchenette upgraded to Billie Jean's needs, and she was able to maintain her autonomy.

Seana had enjoyed the company of the adventuresome, full-of-it Billie Jean.

"Oh, she saw a rheumatologist last week. Waiting on blood test results. In the meantime, she's taking anti-inflammatory medication. Meloxicam, I think."

Chelsea hung the dress in a protective plastic carry bag. "I'm glad she's seeing to it. I've been worried about her."

"She appreciated the homemade fudge you brought by. Just what she needed to perk up her taste buds." Seana's eyes misted and she blinked it away. She had banked down her concern to the best of her ability, but it raised its head at times, over-powering her.

"Give her my love."

"I will. Thanks, Chelsea."

"I like those light highlights in your hair, by the way. And the softer, younger style. But then you're already beautiful, Seana." Chelsea spoke matter-of-factly while bagging the shoes.

Seana felt relief to leave the subject of Billie Jean's health. "Thanks, Chelsea." Then she huffed softly. "Look who's talking. Hey, you looked pretty spiffy in your clogging outfit. Still got the ol' glamour."

Chelsea fluffed her hair, did a Mae West provocative pose and drawled, "An' honey, I always will as long as there's hair color and makeup."

Seana burst into laughter. "Ah, Chelsea, you won't do. Seriously, you can still shake a pretty leg a' dancing, too. That's not changed." Their ties ran deep. She, Joanie, and Chelsea had gone to Paradise Springs High together all those years ago.

"And you were the Homecoming Queen," Chelsea reminded her as she slid the jewelry into a little fancy box with a red bow on top. "And popular cheerleader captain. Your beauty came from the inside out." Then she pealed with laughter. "Would you just listen to our lil' ol' flatterin' tongues! Almost as much fun as our school pep rallies, huh?"

"We did have fun, didn't we?" Seana's laughter ebbed. She sighed, feeling suddenly melancholy for the old days. Her emotions these days had turned to goulash.

She almost laughed aloud at that turn of thought. Had nothing to do with Barth. No sirree, Bob.

"Yeh. I miss those times, too." Chelsea walked her to the door, gave her a big hug, and waved as Seana toted her bounty back across Main and drove away.

Seana checked the time. Three hours to go before Barth would arrive.

Butterflies flapped like helicopter propellers in her stomach, as they had not in years.

She could hardly wait.

ی ی

"Shall we take my car?" Seana offered as she slung her dainty black purse strap over her shoulder, admiring her fiancé's finely cut figure in sharp, casual attire of black slacks, matching mock turtleneck, and a tweedy white-and-black sports jacket.

"Not unless you would prefer we do," Barth drawled, his gaze still sweeping appreciatively over Seana. "Wow," he murmured. "That little dress sure fits you nicely." He slowly shook his head, dark eyes twinkling behind softening lens. "Real good."

"Thanks, Barth." She smiled at him, feeling as beautiful as his eyes judged her to be. She also felt as young as she had thirty years ago. No, even younger. Like in her teens.

Her well-heeled steps were light as she set the security code and shut the door behind them. She could smell her *Armani* fragrance wafting about her.

"Let's just go in your car," she said as they crossed her front rock-laid entrance that evolved into a brick, circular drive. Somehow, Seana sensed that Barth's ego might react if she insisted on driving her infinitely more luxurious vehicle. Yet … he'd not so far displayed any sign of insecurities.

"Sure," Barth stepped confidently up to the passenger side of his clean yet seen-better-days '89 Mercury Villager. He opened the door with a flourish, and Seana slid into one of the most well-kept relics she'd ever seen. Its meticulous condition smelled of wax and leather, surprising her anew.

Just as other aspects of Barth continued to fascinate her.

His intellect was astounding. And his articulation, spoken in his unique, deep timbre, captivated her.

"Penny for your thoughts," he said as he turned the ignition key. The engine instantly sprang to life. Seana smiled. He kept that automobile as finely tuned as a Cape Kennedy space shuttle.

"Mmm, just enjoying the moment." She rolled her eyes at him and watched his features when their gazes connected and he slowly drank her in. Her gaze held when his turned back to the road ahead. In the headlights's glow she studied his finely chiseled profile. Full, thick hair barely brushed his turtleneck and her fingers, already acquainted with its texture, itched to feel it, roll it between her fingers, and shove her hands into it.

He looked at her then, and the impact shot through her like a Taser.

"Barth?" she murmured, breathless.

"Hmm?" His attention veered safely back to the road.

"Let's elope."

He stomped on the brakes … then let off. He angled a long, searching look her way. "What did you say?"

Seana smiled. "I said, 'let's elope.'"

He took a long, steadying breath. Looked at the speedometer, slowed to a legal speed limit, and slowly shook his head. "Do you mean that?"

"I've never meant anything more in my life."

"When?"

"How about right now? Tonight?" Her heart was pounding with excitement. The sheer spontaneity of it thrilling her to her very bones.

Barth cut her another searching look. "Let's talk about this over dinner. Okay? I'm very much in favor, by the way." Then he smiled at her, dimples punctuating a wide, face-splitting vote of affirmation. "Very much so."

❧

They ended up at the Mater and Onion Buffet on the outskirts of town. "I don't want waiters interrupting us," Barth insisted when they made the choice of a back booth. "That okay?"

"Absolutely," Seana agreed wholeheartedly.

Actually, this was *the* eating place of Paradise Springs,

where in the evenings, the lights muted and Jet, an amiable transplanted Filipino keyboard artist, played soft background music for diners. As usual, Jet struck up Seana's favorite request, *Embraceable You.* The entire staff considered Seana family because, all through the years, this had been her second home when dining out. They had grieved the loss of Ansel, but because Seana had now moved on with her life, Barth, too, was added to their fold.

"Hi Donna," Seana greeted the hostess with a quick hug and was escorted to a corner booth where privacy reigned. Donna winked at them, took their order for iced tea, and departed, leaving them to precious privacy.

Barth took a deep, long breath, blew it out, and leaned forward, arms resting on tabletop. He looked directly into Seana's eyes. His were solemn. "Why do you want to elope?"

Seana blinked, leaned her arms on the table, and narrowed her gaze. "Do you not want to?"

"Oh, I think it's a wonderful idea. The best I've heard lately, in fact. I just wondered why the sudden urge to – run off?"

She resisted the urge to bristle. It was, after all, a logical question. "Well." She wet her lips nervously, hoping he would get it. "I just don't want my family to ruin one of the most beautiful times of my entire life with their – less-than-charitable attitudes. Why can't they just let me be me, make my own decisions concerning my life? I always show them utmost respect when they face decisions such as this."

Her impassioned revelation tugged Barth's mouth into a gentle smile and his large, warm hands captured her cold ones. "Look, honey," he murmured, his fingers warming hers with gentle caresses, "we'll do what will make you happy. As for the kids, I believe they'll eventually come around."

The words were becoming a mantra, but the hope in them still kept her afloat.

"I hope so, Barth. I really do. This is breaking my heart, their not being supportive in something so important to me. I don't understand." She swallowed back the painful, throbbing lump lodged in her throat and felt the burn of tears behind her eyes. "I'm sorry," she whispered. A tear splashed over and trickled down her cheek, then another as she pulled one hand free and groped for a napkin.

"Sweetheart, don't worry about a thing," he murmured, gently taking her napkin to blot the wet streaks on her cheeks. She saw a glistening behind the thick lens. He blinked it back, cleared his throat, and said, "This will all work out in the long run. In the meantime, looks like we've got things to do. Where do we start?"

Seana's heart suddenly soared, despite the gloomy pessimism of her offspring. Barth's common sense, masculine approach was just what she needed.

"Let's go to the courthouse early in the morning," she said. "In Anderson. That way nobody will know."

She grinned. "At least not until we want them to."

� �

The civil ceremony, performed by a handy judge, was short and sweet. Afterward, Seana and Barth drove to the mountains and found a quaint little cottage for the honeymoon night.

"I don't want to be gone long enough for our absence to become conspicuous," Seana insisted. "Not yet. I want this time to be ours."

"Anything you want," Barth agreed, his generous mouth curving into that endearingly crooked smile of his that calmed her fears and made everything seem okay. "Unless you want to explain why you lost your mind and ran off with that Canadian scoundrel."

She laughed as he'd intended.

They went out to dinner in nearby Asheville. But neither was very hungry and soon returned to their honeymoon lair.

The cottage was perfect for their short hours of freedom to love and discover new delights in each other. Their courtship had been somewhat chaste yet filled with promises now fulfilled. The chemistry was explosive, as Seana had known it would be.

"You know, I find myself even happier that both Zoe and Tim have their own lives, rich full ones," Seana said as they lounged in bed that evening. Satiated and at peace. "At one time, not too long ago, I felt somewhat abandoned at times. Of course, that was selfish thinking because, after all, isn't that what parents want for their children? Rich, productive, independent lives?"

"Definitely." Barth gently brushed a stray tendril from Seana's cheek, causing a sweet stir deep inside her. "You're a wonderful mother, Seana," he murmured huskily. "The best. Don't ever forget that. I wish I'd had kids but it didn't happen. Betty wasn't able to, and I think that's one reason why –"

"Don't," Seana rolled over into his arms, wishing away the torture she saw in his eyes when he delved into his shadowy past. One he'd shared with her. One they dare not share with her children. "Don't go there. Let's not let anything intrude just yet. This is our time, dear Barth."

She turned her lips to his and he dipped to their warmth and comfort.

He lifted his head and gazed into her eyes. "Our time."

chapter two

"The thing about family disasters is that you
never have to wait long before the next one
puts the previous one into perspective."
– Robert Brault

"Ahh," Seana sighed two days later as the two newlyweds lounged in adjoining recliners on the deck at
home. "If only it could last. The exclusiveness. The beautiful
time of getting to know one another on a deeper level."

She and Barth simply continued their normal relationship
before family and friends. Barth had in the past, on occasion,
stayed at her house all night, taking one of the guest rooms,
not unheard of for folks their age.

Paradise Springs was a fairly open-minded place. Fairly.

"They know you for who you are," Barth often reminded her when she had appearance-misgivings. And it was true.

Though she knew it had to push his patience at times,
Barth acquiesced to her present wish for secrecy. He could
have ranted about her cowardly procrastination. But he didn't.

"Only demand I make is having my wife in my bed."
Barth's dark gaze pinned her and she felt the impact of his
territorial declaration.

"Thanks," she whispered and reached over to take his hand.

"For what?" His eyes swept over her in sweet ownership.

"For loving and nurturing me. I haven't felt so – *treasured* in many years."

"You're very welcome." His deep timbre rolled over her skin and she felt goose bumps rise. How she loved this man. How his very male protectiveness thrilled her.

How long it had been since she'd felt that snuggly warm covering.

From his nearby roost in the sunshine, a vigilant Brutus gave a guttural WoRuff, then trotted over to Seana and nudged his snout into her hand, then burrowed his head there for her touch.

"Okay, boy," Barth threw up his hands in surrender. "I know jealousy when I see it."

Seana laughed and pulled Brutus's head over her lap and gave his fur a thorough scruffing. "There's plenty of me to go around."

≈≈

"Seana, you look different," Louann Melton, the pastor's wife – an abbreviated, five-two, red-haired image of the movies's Nicole Kidman – hugged Seana in the church vestibule that Sunday morning as they left services. She leaned back and peered intently into Seana's blushing face. "Kinda like the cookie jar bandit."

At Seana's near startled response, Louann laughed. "Not that bad. But pretty close. You and Barth named the date yet?"

Just then, Seana's blond hairdresser buddy, Joanie, grabbed and pulled her in for a big hug, rescuing her from Louann's curious probing.

"Hey, darlin'." Her voice dropped to a conspiratorial whisper. "You have fun on your trip to the mountains?"

Seana's mouth dropped open. She reared back to gape at her friend. "How –"

"So it's true?" Joanie giggled and whispered, "Don't know

how she does it but Sadie Tate said she stopped by Fred's Grocery Store the other day and Fred said when you lovebirds stopped by the Texaco station he spotted suitcases in the back of your car. Sadie added it together and came up with the idea that you and your man was a' sneaking out for a tryst."

Shock speared Seana. "Well I never." She pushed back umbrage and opened her mouth to placate Joanie's curiosity, at the same time wanting to throttle Sadie Tate for her nosiness. And tale-bearing.

"Never mind." Joanie shook her head. "You don't have to tell me anything you don't want to, honey. I know Sadie's imagination's quite lively, doncha know? Well, I've gotta run 'cause some of us are goin' over to the Mater and Onion for their Sunday Buffet. You and Barth want to join us?" Her huge eyes, today a peculiar but lovely shade of lens-enhanced amber, appealed sweetly as the long, thick lashes blinked once, twice ….

"Er … not this time. I've already prepared some chicken salad for lunch. Thanks anyway for the invite. Another time?"

"Sure." The open smile flashed as she squeezed Seana's hand.

"Oops!" Joanie collided with brawny, strappy Scott Burns, Paradise Springs High's athletic coach. His big hands reached out to steady her, but his eyes were on Seana. "'Scuse me?"

"Sure, Scott." Joanie pivoted to rush out to join her lunch party.

Seana watched Joanie's classy red dress disappear from sight, feeling like she'd been rammed in the middle by *el Toro*. Were she and Barth that transparent?

Did everyone suspect them of being loose? Immoral?
A tryst?

It took her a moment to realize that Scott was talking to her. "Huh?" She blinked and focused on the intent, strong, all-American features looming over her. "I'm sorry, Scott. What did you say?"

"I didn't see Zoe today. Is she sick or something?" Though he tried to hide his distress, he didn't do too good a job. Seana's heart flailed toward him with his unrequited romance aspirations. He needed all the sympathy he could get in his pursuit of the remote Zoe.

"I haven't spoken with her in the past few days, Scott," Seana replied sympathetically. "I have no idea why she's not here."

"Thanks," he mumbled and ambled away, his wilted stance a sad sight to behold.

"Seana!" Pastor Keith swooped up in his flowing, black clerical robe, looking anything but dignified with his little boy impish grin. Sunrays spilling through stained glass highlighted his near-platinum hair. "It's so good to see you. You know, you're really good for Barth. Have I told you that?"

"A few dozen times," Louann reminded him as she zoned in, catching the last sentence. Louann smiled mischievously at her verbose husband.

"And vice versa," Barth inserted over the pastor's shoulder, grinning from ear to ear. "Least she tells me I am."

"Oh you are," Seana said breathlessly, just now recuperating from Joanie's revelation of their blossoming notoriety. Unbeknownst to kind-hearted Joanie, the news had been a real hard kick punch.

"Say," Seana said impulsively. "If you two don't have plans for lunch, why don't you come over and share ours? My chicken salad, according to Barth, is quite tasty." Besides, she needed their steadying company.

"The best," chimed in Barth. "Yes, why don't you?"

Pastor Keith and Louann looked at each other and briefly, quietly conferred about lunch plans or lack thereof.

"We would love to," Pastor Keith addressed them. "And thanks."

❧ ❧

The Meltons were easy to entertain. Actually, Seana concluded as she and Louann did final fruit and salad preparations in Seana's big kitchen, she didn't have to entertain them at all. They belonged to that select niche of friends who simply flow, their presence lending itself to warm camaraderie and sustenance.

"Come on, Brutus," Barth called out the door. He'd let him out a few minutes earlier to relieve himself and run a few rounds. Brutus appeared, panting and wagging his tail happily and taking advantage of time to cozy up to friends for a good back scratching and tummy rubbing.

"Brutus." Barth pointed to the den, where a corner cushion still provided a view of the kitchen, and being the well-trained canine he was, Brutus immediately trotted over, curled up, and soon dozed.

They dined in the cozy kitchen nook with its glass table and long windows framing a background of distant blue Smoky Mountains. The larger, more formal dining room simply wouldn't have embraced them as intimately, Seana decided, as she and Louann poured iced tea and took their seats with their husbands.

They joined hands and hearts as Pastor Keith gave thanks.

Conversation flowed pleasantly, spontaneously as they ate. Barth and Keith reminisced over their school days and first disastrous sermons in Homiletics class.

Barth laughed uproariously. "My tongue was so thick and dry I couldn't have worked up a spit if my life had depended on it. I'm much better at music than preaching, I can tell you that."

"Oh, you did fine," Pastor Keith said, taking a generous portion of chicken salad.

"Liar," Barth burst into fresh laughter. "I listened to the tape."

The pastor's shoulders shot up in an elaborate shrug. "What can I say?" Then his laughter joined Barth's.

"Chicken salad is delicious." Louann smacked her lips playfully, drawing appreciative laughter from the hosts. "The onion, chopped pecans, and sliced grapes hit my taste buds just right."

"Barth adds a few extra chopped herbs, too. They boost the flavor."

"By the way," Louann turned serious, "how's Billie Jean?

She's not been at church for a couple of Sundays, has she? I haven't seen her, but she could have slipped out past me."

"She's hardly come upstairs these past weeks." Seana rose to refill tea and ice. She didn't share her apprehension that perhaps Zoe's dislike for Barth had gone viral, infecting Billie Jean.

"She's having some medical issues," Seana added, concern flushing through her.

"Oh?" Louann was instantly alert. "What kind?"

"Billie Jean hasn't said much. You know her."

"Do I." Louann's eyebrows shot up then she laughed.

"She did say something about protein showing up in her blood tests – during a routine exam. Now she's going to see a specialist for more tests."

"Hmm." Pastor Keith shifted in his chair and leaned forward on his elbows. "That sounds kinda serious."

"Just what I was thinking," Barth said.

"Well, let's hope and pray for the best." Seana smiled, pushing back dark forebodings.

"Absolutely," Pastor Keith rubbed his hands together. "How about playing us a song on the piano, Barth? Something like – Moon River."

After quick teamwork in cleanup, they migrated to the den.

And soon, they were all singing along with familiar tunes, both old and new.

The time passed too swiftly; before long, they were readying to depart.

"Honey?" Barth's eyes captured Seana's across the den, a question glimmering in their mahogany depths.

Seana nodded. It was time.

Barth cleared his throat. "We want you two to be the first to know that we're now married." Barth went on to explain to his closest friend the whys and hows. Seana added the details of her children's hesitant acceptance of Barth, soft-pedaling most of it.

"However," Barth nodded with confidence, "they'll both

come around in time. I understand how difficult it can be to lose your beautiful mother to a stranger. They'll just have to get to know me better."

Seana looked at him, heard the hope in his deep voice and saw it in his eyes behind the thick lenses. Her heart struggled to believe what he said. He almost made her believe in magic. Surely, with time, Zoe and Tim would accept Barth for the wonderful man he was.

Wouldn't they?

"Well, congratulations are in order." Pastor Keith burst from the sofa, closed the distance, and pulled Barth into a bear hug while Louann captured Seana in a long, warm embrace.

"This is wonderful news," Louann said as she collected her purse. "So your children don't know yet?"

"No." Seana dropped her head for a moment and then looked steadily at her friend. "But I'll break the news in the next day or so."

Louann looked at her for a long moment, her eyes clouded, then, in an instant, her smile cleared them. "Kids can be funny about these things. We've got two married ones, you know. They can get a mite territorial at times."

"No joke."

They both burst into laughter.

After they waved the Meltons out of sight, Barth and Seana looked at each other and smiled.

"Two down," Barth said. "Two to go."

Seana's smile evaporated. "The two most critical."

❧ ❧

Seana came upon an idea. On her computer, she designed bold scripted letters that stated: DO NOT DISTURB THE NEWLYWEDS.

"What do you think?" she asked Barth after she printed it out on eleven-by-fourteen paper and boldly taped it to the front door.

"Cowardly, huh?" she added, squinting and hunching her shoulders.

"Nah." Barth looked at it, then nodded. "Not bad. A touch of drama. And humor ... I think."

"Whatever. I'm tired, Barth. It's wrung me out – all the controversy, all the ...." Seana shrugged limply, her heart heavy.

"Hey." Barth's finger lifted her chin and he smiled at her, dimples etched and eyes aglow. "Come on. You're bigger than all this junk."

As she gazed into the steady gold-flecked mahogany, she felt the flow of his strength and optimism invading, filling, and splashing over.

"Darn right." She dusted her hands together and nodded.

They went back into the house and Seana closed the door firmly against misgivings.

୶୨ ৩৯

The next morning, as Seana put on coffee, Billie Jean tromped up the den stairwell. "Hello?" she bellowed. "Anybody home?"

"Come on in!" Seana rushed to hug her cousin. "I've missed you, girl. Where you been?" Actually, Billie Jean looked like she'd been through an agitator wash cycle and hung out to dry. Seana bit back a hysterical comment.

"Aw, just chilling out." Billie Jean's usual hardy appearance hid behind wan features today. Her rust-hued curls had turned to frizz and dark circles underlined her tired eyes.

"Sit down." Seana motioned to the bar stool. "Tell me what the last tests show?" She took a stool facing her.

Barth came in, fresh from the shower, still barefoot in clean jeans and blue pullover. "Hi, Billie Jean. Long time no see."

"Yeh," she murmured, not looking directly at him. "Been busy."

Barth read the averted eyes and body language. Rejection.

He also saw Seana wilt with disappointment. Well, darned if he was going to buckle under to it. He sauntered to the den, softly whistling Moon River.

The doorbell pealed. "Will you get that, please?"

"Sure." Barth slipped on loafers, ran fingers through his still damp hair, then stuffed his pullover into his jeans. He jogged to the door and opened it.

"Hi, Zoe," he forced himself to say pleasantly. "Come in."

Zoe brushed past him. "Where's my mother?"

"In the kitchen. Go on in and have some break –"

Her abrupt dismissal as she brushed past him, a silent *whoomph* of one, left him blinking and scratching his head. Looked like he had his work cut out for him just coaxing some civility from this prickly child of Seana's.

And it hit him like a sonic blast: *Zoe was also his child now.*

Lord help him.

"Hi, Zoe." Billie Jean cosseted her coffee cup, still avoiding looking at him.

"Hi," Zoe grunted, plopping down on a stool.

Seana snatched a bowl from the cabinet and poured Cap'n Crunch cereal.

"You're not going to eat that, sweetheart," Barth said and went to the fridge for eggs, cream, cheese, and some fresh herbs he'd recently grown and harvested from a small herb garden out back.

"Oh?" Seana looked at him with mixed emotions glimmering in her blue eyes. He smiled with what he hoped was winsomeness.

"You need protein, not sugar. Remember?" They'd recently had several discussions about depression feeding off sugar.

Seana sighed and nodded. "Yeh. I do. You're right." She dumped the cereal right back into the box and put it away. She sat back down at the bar, folded her hands, and looked at Zoe, who sat across watching the exchange with tamped-down features.

"Well, don't you want to congratulate us?" Seana ventured. What the heck?

Zoe blinked. "Congratulations." The word came out flat. As flat as her blue eyes.

Zoe swung her gaze to Billie Jean. "Did you know?"

"When I read the sign on the front door." Billie Jean shrugged tersely, studying her coffee as through a microscope.

Barth observed as he whipped up a bowl of egg whites, then added cream, herbs, and grated parmesan. He saw Seana deflate. Her courage still flapped valiantly, but, underneath, he saw her vulnerability and her hurt that family didn't celebrate her happiness.

His heart sailed to her. Time to react.

"Thanks, Zoe," he responded pleasantly, getting Seana off the hot seat. Zoe shot him a cold look as he turned back to pour the onions into heated olive oil. The skillet was hot enough to begin sizzling without cooking too quickly. Barth was fussy about things like that. Loved good, healthy food. Well-seasoned and well-cooked.

He felt very ill at ease, however, in the cold, tense kitchen atmosphere and began to softly whistle, a thing that – during the worst of times – helped him deflect tension.

Zoe grunted something unintelligible as he whistled, and he felt her disapproval like the sting of a wasp.

Too bad. But he began to hum softly, hoping that wouldn't be as offensive to his newly acquired daughter.

He stirred the sautéed onions, lifted them out, and added them to the egg mixture, along with the other ingredients. He added more olive oil to the skillet, then dolloped a generous portion into the pan.

The foamy mix soon evolved into a succulent, aromatic omelet.

He scooped it onto a plate and added more grated cheese and diced, ripe, fresh tomatoes, also from his small garden out back. He presented it to Seana with a flourish. "Madame," he placed it before her, along with a fork and napkin. "All you need is some orange juice." He sauntered to pour some into a chilled glass and set it beside her plate.

He turned to Zoe. "Shall I fix you an omelet?"

"No, thank you." Zoe didn't even look at him.

"You sure? Wouldn't take but a jiffy," he entreated. He really wanted to break through that armadillo shell. For Seana's sake, he really cared.

"Absolutely," she replied in a clipped, icy tone.

"Billie Jean? An omelet?"

"Nah. Not hungry. Thanks anyway."

"Oka-ay." Barth rubbed his hands together and turned back to the stove. "I'll have one then."

Zoe turned her attention to Seana, who, Barth was certain, knew Zoe had something to say and wild buffalo wouldn't stop her. She was dead on.

"I just don't understand why you two up and sneaked off to get married. Why didn't you let us in on your plans?"

Seana bristled. "We didn't *sneak off* to get married. We simply eloped, Zoe. We did it because I didn't want to face ugly scenes that would take away from the happiness I feel."

"So it didn't matter to you how it made Tim and me feel? And Billie Jean. We were totally left out, Mother, like outsiders. Even Joanie knew before we did; thinking I knew about it, she mentioned in the beauty shop how happy you were. She heard it at church after you told Pastor Keith and Louann." She snorted. "How do you think that made us feel? Huh?"

Seana looked at Barth, who shrugged. They had not, after all, sworn the Meltons to secrecy.

"Hey, gotta go." Billie Jean slid from the stool. "Another doctor's appointment. See you guys later." Her swift departure punctuated the tension.

Seana sighed heavily and Barth felt her desolation. Yeh, he did, right down to his toes. And he also felt helpless to help her when Zoe despised his very presence, not to mention any counsel spilling from his lips.

"Zoe," she murmured, "I wouldn't have hurt you and Tim

for the world. Nor Billie Jean. But you're bound and determined to not like Barth. How do you think that makes me feel? And him? I love him, Zoe, and you're not willing to accept him."

Barth scooped his omelet onto a plate, feeling like the reluctant voyeur. He was distinctly out of joint, but now that he was married to Seana, this was his problem, too.

He sat down across from the females and picked up his fork, no longer hungry. But he forced himself to go through the motions of eating. They didn't need another kaput family member right now.

Family member. Like it or not, he and the riled she-cat seated across from him were family.

"Accept him?" Zoe spoke as though he weren't there. "Do I accept things the way they are? Yes. Do I accept that you're starry-eyed crazy about him? Yes. Do I trust him? No."

"I'm sorry you feel that way," Barth spoke up, a bit testy by now. "Have I done anything to offend you, Zoe? If so, I'm sorry."

"The only thing you've done to offend me is to take over my mother's life like you're doing. For crying out loud, you're even controlling what she eats."

"Zoe," Seana intruded. "I like that he –"

Zoe sprang to her feet. "I know, Mom. You like everything about him. I get that."

"You just need to get to know him." Seana stood, and Barth watched her seeking desperately for some middle ground. Even a smidgeon of conciliation.

"That's just it, Mother. I don't know him. He comes out of nowhere, with nothing. I ask him questions and he dances around straight answers and –"

"Ask me anything you want," Barth stood, too, determined to get past this impasse. "I've hidden nothing."

Yet, he knew there were boundaries he could not allow her to cross. Not now.

Zoe whirled on him. "No, you just haven't revealed anything substantial about your past. I don't trust you." She shrugged tightly and flattened her mouth into a cynical line. "Just who are you?"

"Stop it!" Seana's voice rose in a way Barth had never heard. "Zoe, I think you should go for now. I'm not going to allow you to attack Barth this way. He's a good man and I love him."

Zoe grabbed her purse from the back of the chair. "Oh, I'm going, Mother. And I don't know when I'll be back. If ever." With that she marched from the house, chin thrust out, leading the way.

Seana fell into Barth's waiting arms. "I'm so sorry, Barth," she sobbed. "So sorry."

Barth, feeling as inept as he ever had, held her close, rubbing her back and shoulders. "It'll all work out, honey," he crooned. "They'll come around." He knew the words were empty. Even to him. But he had to say them. "Just takes time."

❧❧

"Seana?"

"In the kitchen, Billie Jean," Seana called from the sink later that day, where she was rinsing, blotting, then bagging newly harvested herbs to freeze for later use. She labeled them carefully in Zip Lock bags: rosemary, parsley, basil, oregano, cilantro, dill, sage, and thyme.

They were better fresh, but the crop was so plentiful, she didn't have the heart to waste them. She'd decided to share them with Zoe, Joanie, Billie Jean, and Chelsea, then freeze what was left over for her own later use.

The rash on her cheek began to prickle again.

"Hi, Sweetie." She pulled a wan Billie Jean into her arms for a big hug. "You've been so absent I was about to send out a posse to find you. Lordy, I've missed you." The five-five female was not as robust as she'd been a year ago. Those shoulder bones poking Seana from beneath her cousin's baggy shirt were a lot sharper than Seana had ever seen them. The former glowing skin was sallow and the gray eyes, dull.

"Missed you, too, you dad-blasted traitor."

"Ahh, that's the girl." Seana laughed and held her back for a better look. "Why, you're so skinny you don't cast a shadow."

"Thanks a lot, Seana," she said dryly. "You keep up that talk you'll give me the big head."

"Come on and eat some of this vegetable soup we made for lunch. Got some corn muffins, too." Barth had directed her to freshly ground corn meal with no additives, and, despite her misgivings, Seana found the golden muffins quite tasty.

"Nah. Not hungry. Just got back from the doctor." Billie Jean sloughed over to the bar and climbed onto a stool. "Maybe a glass of your iced tea."

"You got it." That was one thing Seana would not forfeit – her Southern sweet iced tea. She did agree to using stevia with a small amount of organic brown sugar and discovered she couldn't tell it from processed-sugar sweetened tea. She poured a hefty glass, placed it on the bar, and took a stool opposite Billie Jean.

"So? What happened?"

She was astounded when Billie Jean dissolved into tears. Alarmed – extremely alarmed, she rushed around the bar and gathered the quaking woman in her arms, crooning and trying as best she could to calm her.

"Please, Billie Jean, tell me what happened?"

The haggard face lifted, tears streaming like summer gulley washers. "It's the Big C!" she croaked and shook her head from side to side. "I'm not scared. It's just so dad-blamed unexpected."

Seana felt the breath knocked from her but drew her close and held on tight, weeping herself, as Billie Jean rode the rapids and finally hiccupped her way back to composure.

That's what frightened Seana the most: this was so uncharacteristic of her stoical, sometimes even flippant, cousin. Billie

Jean could joke her way out of an Al Qaida standoff. At least she could out-BS anyone Seana had ever met. No. This was serious.

"Are you sure?" Seana rasped, her breath coming back in spurts and her heart beating fast and heavy as jungle tom-toms.

Then an amazing thing happened.

Billie Jean visibly bucked up, dried her face, and blew her nose soundly. "Yep. Sure as shootin'."

"Where?"

"Bones. In my stupid bones. Mama always told me to drink up all my milk and take my vitamins and dang if they didn't cop out on me after all." She gave a sharp huff of a laugh, her eyes lackluster.

"Yeh," Seana nodded, trying to smile. "Aunt Jessie was a vigilant mama."

The back door banged shut. "Oh, hi, Billie Jean." Barth deposited the basket of tomatoes on the floor next to the sink. Then he took a second look and his smile faded. "What's wrong?" he asked, his voice gentle, making fresh tears burn behind Seana's eyes.

Billie Jean looked him in the eye, unflinching. "I've got bone cancer, Barth."

"Dear God," he muttered, went over to give her a big, comforting hug, and then pulled out a bar stool across from her. Behind the thick lenses, Seana saw concern glimmering. "That's tough, sweetheart." He took a long pull of air into his lungs, visibly shaken. "What's the prognosis?"

"Oh," Billie Jean took a deep drag of tea, "they said it's incurable but treatable."

Barth sat there thinking for long moments. Then his features lifted. "Well, that's definitely positive."

"You think?" Billie Jean's reply was laced with a trace of optimism.

Hope.

"Sure it is." Barth helped himself to some iced tea and sat down again, his thoughtful expression intense. "Look. We've got some studying to do."

"And some serious, ballistic praying," Billie Jean added, a twinkle beginning in her gray eyes.

"You bet," Barth agreed, grinning.

"You know, Barth," Billie Jean thrust out her flat bosom and squared her shoulders. "I needed that one conniption fit. I won't have another. This ol' girl's gonna beat the stuffing out of the Big C. He don't know who he's tangling with." She let out a victory *woo-hoo.*

"Here's to Billie Jean's victory." Barth raised his frosty glass.

Two more lifted to clink in agreement.

"To victory," they chorused.

❧

True to her word, Billie Jean faced the following weeks and months like a trooper.

She came ambling up the stairs on a frigid December morning, following her morning run. Her nose was still red and she was briskly rubbing her hands together to warm them.

"Got any coffee?" she bellowed.

"Come on in. There's plenty." Seana hustled to pour a cup and slide the cream toward her.

"I know," Billie Jean raised her hand to Barth. "No sugar."

"Right. Sugar feeds disease." Barth sipped his coffee, watching her in a concerned way.

"You getting plenty of rest?" Seana asked, nibbling a veggie omelet.

"Heck. I sleep like the dead," she assured Seana. "What's that rash on your cheek?"

Seana reached up to touch it and shrugged. "I didn't know it was still there. It usually comes and goes. It doesn't hurt. Or itch that much actually. Maybe it'll go away again. Some kind of allergy, probably."

"Try some calamine lotion," Barth suggested, closely examining the rash.

"I will."

"Dang, but it's cold outside." Billie Jean shook her head of unruly chestnut curls. "I'd be surprised if we don't see ice before the week's over." She sniffled and cast Brutus a look of scorn.

"Wimp," she snarled at him across the den.

Brutus licked his chops and burrowed even deeper into his warm, pillowed bed. He'd foregone his morning romp with Billie Jean. Smart dog, thought Seana, and smiled to herself.

"How's the chemo going?" asked Barth.

"Okay," Billie Jean replied and took a huge slurp of hot coffee. "Thalidomide twice a day. Along with my 375 milligrams of aspirin to keep down blood clots." She shrugged elaborately. "So far, so good."

"You're blessed having been diagnosed so early with the multiple myeloma." Barth got up to refill cups.

"Yup." Billie nodded in agreement. "No holes or cracks in my bones. At least not at that time."

"Your walking is going well, too," Seana added. "I'm proud of you, Billie Jean, for your upbeat attitude."

"Well, the doc said that whatever I do, just don't stop exercising." Then she laughed heartily. "Last time I saw 'im, I said 'doc, don't ever use that F word again.'"

Seana peered at her, a little shocked. "What?"

Billie Jean chortled. "Doc asked if he'd said something dirty. I said , yeh, you did. You used 'FALL.' You told me that whatever I did, to not fall."

They all burst into laughter because one day after that medical warning, Billie Jean had tripped and fallen on the stairs, fracturing her ankle. "I'm just now getting back to brisk walking each morning. But I'm comin' along just fine."

Seana warmed to the camaraderie in her kitchen.

Yet, she wished her children would visit. Neither had visited in the past weeks and months.

Barth caught her eye and smiled, bringing his dimples into play. She wondered again that he could read her so easily.

He knew her heart. Silently, he pointed to himself then to her and winked. She got it.

She smiled back.

Together, they would make it.

≈୨ ९∾

Seana heard the doorbell ring that Saturday morning and rushed to answer it.

She spied Zoe's automobile through the window and her heart sped up as she flung the door open.

"Peyton!" she squealed and hauled him into her arms. That Zoe wasn't with him was disappointing, but not enough to dampen her joy at seeing her grandson.

"Come on in, darlin'. Long time since you visited."

"Mama let me drive her car over here while she's doing some makeup dance lessons at the studio." His long lankiness still surprised and delighted her.

They slid onto the den sofa together, looking at each other in wonder. "I've missed you, Nana," Peyton said in his deepening voice. A man.

Yet, still so much her little boy.

"Ahh, Peyton, I've missed you, too. I know we see each other at church, but it's not the same as quality visiting time. How's your mama?"

Peyton shrugged. "She's – mama. You know." He looked uncomfortable.

Seana nodded. "Yes. I know. I miss her, too."

The silence settled thickly. Then Seana perked up. "Go play me something on the piano, honey. Something Christmas-y."

Peyton smiled, shrugged, and sloughed over to the piano. He sat for long moments before he started playing Seana's favorite holiday tunes.

"Oh I love that," she murmured, laying her head back and closing her eyes as "I'll Be Home for Christmas" rolled off his long artistic fingers then modulated into a fingery version of "O Holy Night."

Suddenly, the notes grew so full and rich her heart seemed to expand, and when she heard Peyton's surprised chortle of laughter, her eyes sprang open. Barth had quietly entered and slid onto the piano bench, joining Peyton at the keyboard. Ten fingers now flew over those ivories, sometimes crossing over each other until they crescendoed and came to an impressive finish.

"Know this one?" Peyton immediately swung into a rousing rendition of "Jingle Bell Rock." During it, he and Barth switched places twice without any discernable note gaps. This happened through three more lively holiday selections until, exhausted, the two halted the concert, looked at each other laughing, and high-fived each other.

"Say," Barth looked at Peyton. "You got time to go down in the woods and help me find a tree for Christmas?"

Peyton hiked up his long arm, peered at his watch, and nodded. "Yeh. Mom's got several lessons to make up. Couple of hours at least."

"That should do it." Bart slapped him on the back, and Seana heard them laughing as they bundled up and headed out the back with Brutus trailing them.

She knew that Barth had not included her in the tree hunt because he wanted a male-bonding time with Peyton. How like Barth to find the icebreaker in the current arctic standoff. She sighed as she watched her two guys disappear into the forest, wishing Zoe were as open-minded as her son.

❧ ❦

Happy Feet Dance Studio bustled that night with holiday cheer. Reds and greens emblazoned by sequins brightened up every nook and cranny of the place. Two large trees laden with tons of ornaments and lights illumined the place. Holly-based

Yule candles centered the white-clothed tables and painted everyone romantic and festive.

It was still a week before Christmas, but Zoe had so Yuletide-spritzed the décor that one had to, in self defense, get into the spirit of things.

Seana and Barth had spent the afternoon trimming the freshly cut fir. Peyton had been a big help, Barth told her. They'd loaded the nine foot tree into the back of Barth's pickup – one that Seana had recently insisted on purchasing for his gardening activities – and hauled it to the house where the two men set it up in the den amid much grunting, huffing, and puffing.

Zoe had cornered Seana at church to express her disapproval of Barth's extravagance in demanding a pickup, at her mother's expense, she'd added. And though Seana had pointed out that it was she who'd insisted they needed the truck for farming, not Barth, Zoe was not mollified.

Seana pushed away the troubling thoughts and focused on Barth and Peyton securing the tree on its stand, still struggling with the sheer bulk of it, amid much laughter and silly jokes about imagined hernias.

After Peyton left, Seana had marinated in the lingering warmth of his visit.

Barth had insisted that they continue to attend the dance studio evening parties. "Zoe needs us to support her, whether she knows it or not."

Seana agreed. So tonight, they'd dressed festively and arrived to find the place full. First person Seana encountered was Joanie, dressed to the sparkly red fingernails in a sequined, green pants outfit and gold dance slippers.

Barth migrated over to chat with Fred Johnson, the grocer, who wasn't very fond of dancing but came to please Elsie, his wife.

"Well look at you, Joanie!" Seana grinned and was rewarded by a twinkle of Christmas-y emerald eyes, the tint of the day. The two hugged and Seana spotted Zoe across the room, resplendent in a form-fitting silvery pants suit. Her long ebony hair was loose except for the front and sides, which were pulled up and tethered atop her head with sparkly silver ornaments.

"Like it, huh?" Joanie whispered as she caught Seana's pleased response.

"I do. Did you –"

"My handiwork. Wanted to give Scott Burns a little thrill, dontcha know?"

Seana chortled. "It worked. He looks like ol' Brutus at a barbecue cookout." And heaven help her, he did, as he hovered near Zoe, who barely glanced his way.

About that time, Zoe's gaze collided with Seana's. Zoe quickly schooled her features and made her way over to her mother. "Hi, Mom."

"Hi, honey." Seana wanted to throw her arms around her daughter but the solid wall of resistance was up. It was in Zoe's stance, thick and impenetrable.

Manilow's "I Wrote the Songs" rolled from the speakers and partners began to pair off into a sedate foxtrot. What with all the ages and degrees of dance expertise, it proved to be entertaining.

"I was thinking, Mother," Zoe looked off as if studying the crowd for their dance technique. "I want to have the family Christmas get-together here at the dance studio this year. It's already decorated." She looked at Seana and shrugged, her expression bland but challenging. "For a change."

Change.

Seana swallowed soundly, willing her emotions away. They'd always had the celebration at her house. Always, because as the kids had always said, "It's home."

Now, even that was disputed. A sharp arrow pierced her heart. "Sure." She nodded and forced a smile. "Fine with me."

Zoe looked at her for long moments, like trying to decide something.

"Mom – I resent calling your house, only to have to go through Barth to get to you."

"But, honey, he lives there, too." Frustration flailed inside her.

"I know," the reply was crisp. "But I called and asked to speak to you the other day and he said you were taking a nap. I told him it was important and he said he couldn't disturb you." She threw up her hands. "He refused to let me speak to you. I don't have access to my mother anymore. It was important or I wouldn't have called."

"I'm sorry," Seana said. "But Barth is sort of – protective. I haven't been feeling well lately and he's insisted on my having more rest." She didn't mention that stress over the family situation was the main culprit.

"He doesn't have to protect you from me," Zoe fairly hissed. "And when I'm trying to talk to you, he's always there, hovering, injecting his own thoughts and – just intruding."

As if fate were conspiring with Zoe, Barth appeared at Seana's side, smiling and ridiculously clueless. "Hi, Zoe. Nice party."

"Thanks." The reply was clipped. Cool.

"Dance, Zoe?" Scott Burns appeared at Zoe's elbow, his attractive face intent.

"Sure." Without preamble, Zoe slid into his arms and made his night as they lilted away to the beginning strains of Elvis's "Blue Christmas."

Seana would have laughed had she not felt so rebuffed just then. Zoe usually put Scott off, so this little interlude had certainly worked in his favor.

"Dance?" Barth smiled down at her, dimples flashing.

She stepped into his arms and danced away from the stinging hurt.

❧

The family met at Happy Feet on Christmas Day, but it wasn't the same as in years past. Both Peyton and Ashley seemed subdued, whispering in Seana's ear, "I liked it better at your place, Nana," making her feel infinitely nostalgic.

Some comic relief was provided when Ashley wanted to show off her progress with clogging lessons. Peyton partnered her with a routine they'd practiced for just this occasion. The hoedown music and lively steps and turns had them all tapping their feet and clapping. Seana's eyes misted with pride.

The performance was lively and entertaining. "I am so impressed," Seana told Ashley afterward and gave her a big hug and kiss on her flushed cheek.

"Hey! I made her look good, dontcha know?" Peyton teased, and Seana gave him equal time and affection.

But the overall ambience of the gathering was disappointingly cool. The place swallowed up their little clan, leaving room for an army, like their voices echoed in the space. It was dispirited. Like everybody was simply going through motions. Zoe's influence hovered over the entire scene. Not surprising, thought Seana, considering her daughter's assertive strength of will. The impact definitely watered down the usual holiday cheer.

"I felt definitely shut out," Seana said on the way home.

Barth was silent, but Seana felt his letdown.

Then suddenly, he said, "We *were* shut out."

"Yeh."

"But they're still coming to terms with the changes."

Seana knew he was right, but Zoe had had months to adjust and, still, she lingered in a perpetual state of suspicion.

"Barth, I think I'm going to take a weekend and go somewhere with my daughter. A mother-daughter time, if you will. She feels – well, she feels pushed away. I want to somehow reach her."

Barth was silent so long Seana didn't think he was going to answer. Then, he said quietly, "Go ahead, honey. It can't hurt. And it just might help."

So Seana later called Zoe and proposed a weekend girls's getaway.

"I'll check my calendar, Mom, and get back with you."

Though Zoe tried to sound distant, Seana heard the thawing in her voice.

She smiled.

�⋚

Their trip took them to the little North Carolina mountain town of Brevard. The mountains took Seana back in time to life with Ansel. This had been their retreat when life had gotten to be too much. Here, they and the children took time out to relax and become one with creation once more, when the entire world's cares and baggage seeped away and peace flowed in and filled the gaps.

They rented their favorite suite at the Marriott, then went out to dinner. The first night, they avoided discussing anything controversial, focusing instead on each other and memories of bygone days. The next morning, they were up early and went shopping, selecting small gifts for the kids.

Midday, they picked up a huge sub sandwich to halve and headed back to the air-conditioned suite where they propped up bare feet and ate, listening to cable's Sirius Escape music. "Mmm." Zoe smiled, lolling her head back on a cushion. "I'd forgotten how relaxing times like this could be." She sighed. "It's nice that Peyton is old enough to entertain himself." Then she snorted. "And beyond that, I can trust him to stay out of trouble."

Seana nodded and smiled, then washed down her bite with diet cola. She'd defiantly bought the cola, remembering how Zoe had accused Barth of controlling her life, even down to what she ate and drank.

Sure, she knew the chemicals in diet drinks were not healthy, according to medical reports. But she didn't want to prove Zoe right by refusing when Zoe had stopped at the hotel drink machine and asked, "Diet cola, Mom?"

Seana had recognized the subtle challenge and it saddened her to no end.

Now, she refused also to comment that Barth had invited

Peyton over to their house to spend the weekend. "No need in him being alone," Barth had insisted.

Peyton had accepted and the two guys had been hunched over fishing gear when Seana had left with Zoe. "I wonder if they've caught enough fish for dinner?" The words slid out before Seana could curb them.

Zoe didn't comment, but she didn't go all rigid like usual. So Seana began to relax. "Barth is a great fisherman, actually. Peyton seems eager to learn some of his tricks. He usually catches a hearty supper's worth."

Zoe smiled tightly, then glanced at her watch. "Let's catch a movie."

HBO offered an assortment of shows. They ended up watching a rerun of *E.T.*

"Mom, we watched this thing at least a hundred times together. Remember?" Zoe was stretched out on one bed, Seana on the other, propped by a ridiculous number of luxuriously soft pillows.

She smiled at Zoe, feeling a fountainhead of love shoot out the top of her head. "How could I forget?"

Later that evening, they walked to a park, stopping along the way for hot dogs. "Barth wouldn't approve of you eating that, would he?" Zoe asked as they sat munching while listening to crickets chirruping.

Seana went on guard but willed herself to sound casual. "Barth isn't neurotic, Zoe. He's just sensible about eating good foods, is all. He does occasionally enjoy a tasty hot dog."

Zoe raised her eyebrows then changed the subject. Seana felt hurt begin to fester inside her. A tiny burst, but one that rendered her tired and discouraged.

"Why can't you accept Barth?" Seana asked suddenly.

Zoe's countenance shut down. She shrugged.

"I don't understand. Why do you close up when I talk about him?"

Zoe began to look irritated. "Because you're constantly talking about how marvelous he is – trying to convince me that he's this Mr. Wonderful. Obviously that's the way you see him." She shook her head, brow furrowed. "I'm sorry, Mother, but there's something about him …."

Seana had held it in for months now. And it needed to be said. "Remember that first family gathering I brought Barth to, Zoe? He wore his heart on his sleeve that night at your house, trying to be nice. So trusting. And you treated him abominably."

"I talked to him," Zoe insisted in her overly calm way. "What did I do wrong? Huh?"

"I know you, Zoe. You were fishing, trying to catch him in a lie. And you got your friend, Connie, involved … asking him questions about a fictional Nova Scotia town, trying to trap him."

"He did lie."

"No, he did not lie." Seana caught herself as her voice began to rise in protest. "He simply said 'uh-huh' to shut down the third degree. He knew what you were doing. And so did I."

"Connie smelled a fish, too," Zoe continued as though Seana hadn't spoken. "Her husband lived near the town where Barth co-pastored that church." She snorted. "At least we guessed that was where he lived. He never verified the actual town."

Seana reined in her temper. "I've told you there was a scandal, Zoe. You already know Barth's wife, Betty, ran off with a local policeman, a church member."

"Why did he leave the church and eventually leave town?"

"Because he was devastated, Zoe. That's a hard thing to survive."

Zoe looked at her long and hard. "You believe every word he says, don't you?"

"Of course I do. Barth is the most ethical man I know. Doesn't his record as a man of the cloth speak to you at all?"

Zoe huffed softly. "Mom, his *record* speaks poorly, from where I sit. And I don't understand how my mother – the strongest, usually smartest woman I know – allowed this man from nowhere and with nothing to his name except for questionable clergy credentials, into her life and married him after just six months. With no pre-nup, dad blame it! You could have at least protected yourself in that respect. Daddy worked hard to leave you secure and –"

"And that won't change, honey."

Zoe sighed heavily and shrugged. "There's just something more here than meets the eye , Mother. I don't trust him."

Seana held her tongue. There *was* more but she wasn't about to place any more ammunition into Zoe's jaded charge.

"I just don't get it," Zoe added, her brow wrinkled. "How you can be so hysterically happy."

Seana smiled at that. No, Zoe wouldn't. "Don't judge every marriage by your unhappy one, honey. I respect –"

"This has nothing to do with my marital disaster. I'm sorry but so far I've not found much to like about Barth. He's evasive as a feral fox, and a control freak to boot. He talks non-stop, is a know-it-all, is intrusive, and he whistles and hums all the time, even in church – during a funeral even." She made a face that almost made Seana smile. She could see where Zoe was coming from. Only thing, Zoe was looking through eyes of disdain. She didn't see the real Barth.

The Barth who was good clear through, who softly whistled to songs he loved and wanted to make sure everyone he knew got the best of nutrition and care. The Barth who innocently walked into a unique Southern culture that made him appear awkward and bumbling. Like a cat in a tinkling crystal shop. But Seana didn't laugh because sadness settled inside her like lead. Mother and daughter grew quiet and, within minutes, headed back to the hotel.

They woke up to rain the next morning. They toured some antique shops and stopped for ice cream cones before deciding to head home.

Seana knew that Zoe felt the same as she did.

There was nothing more to be said. It was a silent, unsettled truce between mother and daughter. Seana reassured herself that it wasn't the end of the world. *She's my daughter and I won't alienate her. She means too much to me.*

chapter three

*"I know why families were created with all
their imperfections. They humanize you.
They are made to make you forget yourself
occasionally, so that the beautiful balance of
life is not destroyed"*
– Anais Nin

*T*he week began unusually pleasant. Had Seana had any
portent of things to come, she would have stayed in bed,
covered her head, and never emerged. But she remained bliss-
fully unaware of what fate had in store.

Winter was definitely over. March winds were kind. "The
groundhog didn't see his shadow, huh?" Barth came out on
the back deck to join Seana as she sipped coffee and dreamily
surveyed the farm's blossoming greenery.

"Nope." She smiled at him and stretched luxuriously as he
placed his own steaming cup beside hers on the patio table and
lowered himself into a matching lounge chair. "I smell spring."
She'd put on a sweater to ward off early morning chill, but
found that she really hadn't needed it.

"Say," she said, "I'm going to take that computer course at
Tech. Need refreshing. Also need it to help Tim and Sherry at

the office." She rolled her eyes. "I'm growing more clueless by the hour. Peyton and Ashley have to help me now with lots of the more technical computer stuff."

"When does it start?" Barth reached down to ruffle Brutus's neck.

"This week. Begins Thursday. I've already registered online."

A sharp whistle pierced the air and Brutus was up and off the deck in an eye's blink.

They both laughed as Brutus joined Billie Jean on her morning run.

"Billie Jean's doing great. She's sprinting like an Olympic runner." Barth's voice conveyed his awe of the scrappy female fighter.

"Yeh." Seana sighed contentedly. "She's something else. I've never seen so much courage in my entire life. Never a complaint."

"An overcomer." Barth slowly shook his head in awe. "And it's working, her faith and spirit. The cancer's in remission."

"Thank God. By the way, would you look at this rash on my face and neck, please? It's come back."

Barth leaned over and peered. "You're going to have to get that checked out," he insisted. "It's been going on for some time now."

"I know," Seana sounded mildly impatient. "It's not bothering me that much. Just makes me look slightly witchy. But, you're right. I'll call Dr. West today for an appointment."

"Can't be too careful, honey." He reached over to take her hand in his. "I want my girl to stay healthy."

"Wealthy and wise," Seana grinned at him when he looked puzzled. "The rest of the song."

"Must've missed that one," he murmured, turned her palm up and kissed her hand thoroughly, giving Seana delicious goose bumps.

Later that afternoon, she called and scheduled an appointment with her dermatologist. "Come on in tomorrow," the nurse told her. "Since you've been having this problem for so long, we need to see you right away."

Can't be too careful. Barth's words rang in her head and she smiled. She loved his caring.

Savored it.

❧ ❧

"Here's a prescription for some prednisone. This should knock it out." Dr. West wrote with his unique flourish and handed the prescription to Seana.

"So you're not sure what's causing the rash?" Seana tucked the paper in her purse.

"May be an allergy thing. Without tests, it's hard to tell. But no need in being hassled any longer. Let me know if you have any more problems."

Seana left with a lilt in her step. She took a dose of the medication with her lunch.

"Always safer to take meds on a full stomach," Barth said as they dined on one of his tasty veggie dishes, a squash and tomato concoction over brown rice, made superb by Barth's spice skills.

"I'll be glad to get this annoyance behind me," Seana grumbled, then smacked her lips on the food. "You outdid yourself, Barth. I usually don't even like this combination."

"Just fo-uh you, dahlin'," he drawled in Southernese that pushed Seana's tickle button.

"I know." She gurgled with laughter. "I bring out the best in you."

His countenance slid into serious, then warm and affectionate. "That you do, Seana, my love."

Seana's heart soared.

❧ ❧

Computer classes at Tech went well. Only thing, on the third day, when new software was introduced that Tim's real estate office was implementing, Seana began to feel strange and could not remember things the instructor said.

As the day wore on, she grew more and more disturbed. The words seemed to go in one ear and out the other. There was no pause inside her brain, not even for a second. She left the class distressed.

Panic washed through her like icy rapids.

What was happening to her?

&

Barth's mouth dropped open when Seana joined him at the dinner table that evening. Her face seemed to belong on another person. It seemed frozen into a mask of stunned remorse.

"Something's wrong, Barth," she muttered through tight lips. "Something horrible's happening to me."

Barth scooted around and took the bar stool next to her. He took her icy hands in his. "What do you think it is?" Her distress was viral. His pulse began to pound in his ears. This is ridiculous, he told himself. Stay calm and reassure Seana.

"I can't remember a thing the teacher said in class today."

Pull it together, Barth.

Barth sucked in a deep, raw breath and drew Seana into his arms. She was limp as a noodle. "Listen, Babe, you're okay," he murmured gently. "You hear me? You're *okay.*"

Her head moved slowly from side to side. "No, Barth. I'm not okay." The lackadaisical words pierced his heart and shot terror clean out his fingers and toes.

"Yes, you are." He heard the edge in his voice then backpedaled to gentle mode. "A good night's sleep is what you need. After that, you'll feel better. You'll see."

&

Barth slept restlessly, and every time he turned over, Seana's eyes were wide open, staring at the ceiling. "You need to relax, darling; there's nothing to fear," he reminded her each time. "Close your eyes and just – let your mind drift."

"I can't." That's all she said. Just "I can't."

That in itself scared the dickens out of him. Now he knew what that Southern term meant. He was living it. Still … he felt that this was only temporary.

Finally, around 3:30 a.m., he gently nudged Seana over on her side, into a fetal position, then he spooned against her back, wrapping her in his arms and warmth. The night had been dark and desolate. Endless.

At least he could give her solace.

Then, through the floor-to-ceiling window, he watched as daylight swallowed up the darkness and the mountain range grew clear and blue.

And he felt a spurt of hope.

That today, Seana would come back to him.

❧ ❧

But Seana did not come back. Was not, in fact, able to function. She was barely able to go to the bathroom and crawl back in bed. She refused to eat unless Barth spoon-fed her. Then she would turn her head away most of the time.

Barth called Tech and cancelled her lesson for that day, then the next, and finally all of them.

Sunday came and Seana didn't go to church, an unheard of thing as a rule. Barth asked Billie Jean to stay with Seana and he volunteered to teach Seana's kindergarten-age Sunday School class. Easy enough, he decided.

Joanie Knight volunteered to help him. "Sort of a teacher's aide." She grinned at him, and her periwinkle blue eyes, which matched her top-of-the-knees dress, twinkled as she watched the innocent-faced cherubs enter the classroom.

Barth began to relax. Heck, what could go wrong with such sweet students?

Gaining their attention, after five minutes of getting them all situated in tiny chairs, wasn't too bad. Curiosity won out. They'd not seen this gigantic male before in their little setting. They peered openly at him as he read the Sunday school story of the week, about David and the giant, Goliath.

Barth found himself getting carried away with the drama and began acting out the roles. Only thing, when he got to Goliath, he wasn't sure how to demonstrate the actual murder. One child, little red-haired Harry Woodall, was on his feet in a heartbeat. "I know," he pealed and ran to the corner toy box. There, he extracted a rubber sword. A long one. "Dis how Da-bid did it," he lisped, spraying spittle in all directions. He grabbed a feeble looking doll from the box and plopped it on the carpeted floor.

Barth watched, transfixed.

Like a professional golfer, Harry boy grasped the sword handle, shuffled his feet, harnessed energy to his arms, raised the sword, then punched it down with all his might, sending the doll's head flying across the floor, hitting Judy Smith's black patent leather shoe.

"Aaaaiihh," Judy wailed. "He hurt da baby!" Then the wails turned to earnest sobs, tears big as his thumb dropped off her flushed cheeks. Her dimpled hands shot up to swipe her wet face as she snubbed and renewed her sobs.

"No, no," Barth crooned rushing to her and dropping to his haunches. "He was only pretending."

The blue eyes opened, peered tragically at him. "No." Her blond head swung from side to side in denial, bouncing her curls about frantically. "Hawi *hurt* her. B-bad."

Her huge snuffling hiccup caught Barth's heart and tugged it mightily. "No, sweetheart. It's not alive. Like you."

"Aaaiiih." Wails recommenced as other little faces watched and reflected emotions from curiosity to the beginning of tears.

Harry Woodall had shrunk into a corner chair, guilt written across his freckled face as clearly as the scarlet letter A.

Barth peered helplessly at Joanie, who shrugged mightily, took a deep breath, squared her shoulders, and stood. "Come 'ere, sweetie. Let me show you something." She took the broken doll, put its head back in the hole and said, "Y' know, I might just have something that will fix this baby up like new by next Sunday. How about that?"

Judy's tears stopped. She nodded, looking hopeful. "You fix it?"

"Sure as shootin'." Joanie nodded big time. "She'll be good as new." Then she took the little girl on her lap, winked at Harry, and guided the attention back to the teacher.

Barth was able to finish the story, this time soft-pedaling the sword murder and majoring on the shepherd David's slingshot expertise.

Now, that got their attention.

Even little Judy's.

After class, Barth pulled Joanie aside. "Thanks. You saved my honor."

Joanie giggled. "Aww. All in a day's class."

"How're you going to fix the doll?"

Joanie stage-whispered. "I know where they have a dozen of those particular dolls. New, dontcha know?"

Barth's head rolled back in laughter. "You females."

"What?" Joanie peered at him, speculation glowing.

"You are such glorious, brilliant creations."

"And don't you forget it," Joanie trilled over her shoulder as she sashayed down the hall.

∾∾

Back at home, Barth found Seana curled up in a fetal position on the sofa, exactly where he'd left her. Her cell phone, lying on the coffee table near her, was loping away with its God Bless the USA melody. Seana stared blankly at the TV screen.

"Aren't you going to answer your phone?" Barth asked,

slightly annoyed. He knew she didn't feel well but couldn't understand this apathy.

Seana didn't reply. He snatched up her phone, flipped it open, and barked "Hello?"

A startled silence, then, "Barth, I'd like to speak to my mother." Zoe's request was cut in cedar.

"Of course." Barth held the phone out to Seana, whose gaze never wavered from the television screen. She shook her head.

A definite no.

"Ah, look, Zoe. Your mother's not feeling well and –"

"I know she's not." As in I'm not stupid. "She wasn't at church. Is she awake?" Zoe's tone was definitely up there with royally ticked.

"Yes, she's awake. But she doesn't want to talk to anyone right now." Barth knew it wasn't sitting well with his step-daughter. Couldn't blame her. He, too, was frustrated that Seana didn't seem to be trying at all to function.

"Well, I'll be right over. I want to know what's going on with her." The line went dead.

"Sure thing, Zoe," Barth muttered to the dead phone, staring at it before clicking it shut.

"Have you had your shower?" he asked Seana, knowing full well she had not because she still wore her nightgown and her hair was a mass of tangles.

"No." The eyes remained fixed on the screen, yet – Barth was certain she did not really see it. For the past two days, she'd insisted on finding a ball game on one of the sports channels. And she was not, as a rule, a really strong sports fan.

"Well, come on. I'll help you," he insisted, reaching to help her up.

"No."

Hands on hips, Barth sighed heavily, gauged his wife's dug-in mien, then tried again. "Seana, you have to bathe." He tugged at her until she finally let him help her onto her wobbly feet and to the shower.

There, he undressed her and guided her into the stall.

He turned the faucet on warm and watched water cascade down her body. She made no move to lather up. Nothing. Just stood planted there like the danged sycamore tree outside their window.

Exasperated, Barth stripped off his own clothes and got in with her. He began to vigorously lather her all over with a nylon scrubby. She frowned at times as if in pain or aggravated and something about her pierced his heart. Vulnerability shimmered over her like an electrical current.

He paused in his ministrations and stared at her, looking into her eyes.

They were vacant. "Dear God, honey. What's happened to you?" The words ended on a sob. He pulled her unresponsive body into his arms and held her as if she were fine crystal or a fragile egg, weeping as unrestrainedly as he'd ever done in his entire adult life.

When the sobs subsided, he gently dried her off and dressed her in sweats, simply because they were easier to manage. Then he combed the tangles from her chin length hair and silently thanked Joanie for the good cut and perm when the damp strands shaped up rather nicely. As soon as he finished, Seana turned from him and made her way back to the den where she curled up again on the sofa.

Barth shook his head, pulled on jeans and shirt, and went to the kitchen to decide what to do for lunch. The doorbell pealed. He closed the fridge and went to answer the door.

"Hi, Zoe," he said and stepped aside for a splendidly angry Zoe, who swept past him without a word of greeting. He shrugged and followed her into the den where she marched over to her mother.

"What do you mean, not taking my calls?" Zoe crossed her arms and peered down at her mother, waiting for an explanation. Silence stretched out and Zoe wilted before Barth's eyes.

"Sit down, Zoe," Barth said softly.

Zoe did, practically collapsing on the love seat across from Seana. "How long has she been like this?"

"A week. I thought it was temporary. But it's continued so I'm going to take her to the doctor tomorrow for a thorough examination." Barth sprawled in the easy chair, anticipating some degree of turbulence.

But he didn't bargain for Zoe's next statement.

"I know about your first wife, Barth. I know about how she died." Zoe's eyes and voice accused and convicted Barth on the spot.

"Oh?" Barth struggled for composure amid the onslaught. The worst thing was happening ... the thing he'd dreaded most. "Exactly what do you know?" He was proud that his voice at least sounded steady while his heart was flogging his ribs like a runaway bass drum.

"I know that she was murdered. And that you were arrested for it."

Shock began to morph into anger. "Then you should know that I was released for lack of evidence."

"Oh?" The lovely brow lifted. "How convenient for you." Zoe smiled then. Not a pretty sight, her sly one. "But I also know that no one else has been arrested. The case is unsolved. Cold."

"So you're going to assume that I did it, even without proof?" He shook his head, disappointed and disgusted.

Zoe stood. "Look. I'm only interested in the safety of my mother. You'd have a lot to gain if something happened to her." Anger crackled about her like static as she marched over to Barth's chair, leaned over, and in a deadly calm voice said, "I'm here to see that nothing happens to her. In fact, I'm going to ask that she get drug tests to see if you're trying to poison her."

Barth stood so abruptly that Zoe nearly lost her balance backing away. He narrowed his eyes and took a step forward before restraining himself. "Get out of my face, Zoe. *I love your mother.*" He gritted his teeth to stymie the tears burning behind his eyes. "That's something you toss aside like garbage. And I plan to take care of her, whether you like it or not."

Zoe smiled again but it didn't reach her eyes. "What have you done to her, Barth? A person doesn't just change overnight.

It's not mere coincidence that you're the one who prepares all her food and who shoves all sorts of additives and supplements at her. And *voila,* she turns into this – zombie."

Barth cut his eyes down at Seana, who seemed detached from their discourse. But he knew that she could hear and discern some things. At least he thought so. "We shouldn't talk like this around her," he said quietly.

Zoe cut a glance at her mother and her face gentled. "You're right. It's not her fault."

A flicker of hope sparked in Barth in that moment, that maybe Zoe would relent and at least do teamwork on her mother's behalf. Instead, she pivoted and marched to collect her purse, then slammed out the front door. Without so much as a backward glance. Or a fare-thee-well.

So much for Southern hospitality and charm.

He realized then that his legs were shaking and collapsed into the chair. Elbows on knees, he planted his face in hands.

He sat there for a long time, head spinning, emotions pummeled by Zoe's words and accusations. Until he felt a cramp in his neck. Only then did he lift his head and roll his shoulders. His eyes locked with Seana's. He felt a surge of guilt. How much did she actually hear and take in?

"Honey?" he ventured gently. "I love you."

She blinked. Then looked away.

And he knew. Somehow, he felt it in his soul of souls. She was not there behind those lovely eyes.

She's gone away inside herself.

Away from him.

అసా

Seana's sleeplessness increased in following days. Dr. Jackson prescribed Ambien, to be taken at bedtime. He also had a startling diagnosis.

"From our conversation and your meticulous notes on

Seana's behavior, I suspect this has to do with the predni-sone. Let's see how the Ambien works and have a follow-up in a week."

Seana did sleep but her depression and anxiety grew worse in following days. "Do you think you could refer Seana to the Carolina Center for Behavioral Health, Dr. Jackson?" Barth asked. He'd called him after a particularly bad episode during her high school class reunion. Her girlfriends, Joanie and Chelsea, had joined with Barth to strong-arm Seana into attending.

Seana agreed, with Joanie and Chelsea dressing and grooming her before the event. But when Seana arrived at the hotel assembly room, she'd found a sofa outside in the luxurious lounge and laid there for the entire time. At eight o'clock, Seana had insisted that Barth administer her medication and take her home to bed.

"She's getting obsessed with time, Dr. Jackson. Not at all like her."

"Hmm. I'll call and make an appointment with the center."

The next day at noon, Barth arrived at the behavioral center with Seana in tow. He was surprised to find Zoe already there, sitting in the waiting room, thumbing through a magazine. When he raised an eyebrow, she stood and came to meet them.

"I told you I wanted drug tests made on Mother. Wanna know what's happening."

"Be my guest," Barth responded mildly, too tired to muster up umbrage. He'd not slept well lately, worrying about Seana. He still hoped for an instant turnaround. Maybe this group of doctors would know what to do for her.

Dr. Castile was Seana's attending psychiatrist. She was assessed and admitted that day. For a week, Barth prayed that something could be done there that would bring Seana back. Meanwhile, meds were experimented with. Her hormone replacement therapy was changed. The Wellbutrin caused Seana's ears to ring. The Clopam had an iffy affect. Ativan seemed to work successfully. To Barth's dismay, the entire process was all trial and error.

Seana was released after a week, no better than when she was admitted.

Barth was devastated but was somehow able to function and do what had to be done. Only when he was alone did he give in to the angst and weep. Soon, that drained his strength. He had to rein in his emotions. So he decided he must look at his glass as half full rather than half empty.

Would he not rather have Seana alive, however flawed? There was always the chance that she would be cured. He must believe that.

He simply must.

And if she did not? He wouldn't even allow himself to go there.

One good thing did come from all the medical tests: Zoe now knew that Barth was not trying to do her mom in. He would have laughed at the absurdity of it all had the implications not been so macabre and vile.

No, he was grateful that Seana still lived and breathed.

He would fight to get her back. If it took the rest of his life.

❧ ❧

Four nights after Seana's release from the hospital, Barth was awakened by her moans. "Barth … help me."

He rolled over, instantly alert. "What's wrong, honey?"

"My arms." Her breath came in short spurts and she was clammy. "What's wrong with me, Barth?"

He gathered her in his arms. "Ah, honey. You're sick, but you're going to get well soon."

"Help me," she cried out in panic. "Please, help me." She was rubbing her arms.

"Are they hurting?" Barth began rubbing them, too. But she pushed his hand away.

"No. They buzz." She now sat up, rocking back and forth. "Help me."

"Come on," he pulled her from the bed and threw on her

housecoat and put on her slippers. After sliding into his jeans, shirt and shoes, he guided her to the car.

"Where we going?" she asked, resisting. She was beginning to have an aversion to going anywhere.

"To the emergency room. To get help." He settled her in the front passenger seat and got in. On the way, he called Dr. Castile and described her symptoms. "She feels like her skin is crawling," Barth told him. "And she's very, very anxious."

"Hmm, could be heart related with the arm symptoms. Get her here as soon as you can."

"We're on our way."

❧❧

Barth called Zoe and filled her in. Simply because he'd promised her he would keep her abreast of her mother's condition. Barth believed in doing the right thing. Regardless. That's as far as he would allow himself to go with the subject of Zoe.

She arrived right after they did, looking as thrown together as Barth and Seana, with her hair haphazardly pulled up in a ponytail holder, jeans and pullover and sneakers sans socks. With no makeup, Barth was struck by how childlike she appeared. How vulnerable.

But when he tentatively smiled and she did not respond, he reminded himself of what steely entrails lay beneath that delicate exterior. The two silently struck an uneasy truce as they waited for the tests and then the results, drinking terrible hospital coffee and watching mundane television in the waiting area.

"Do you want to call Tim or shall I?" Barth asked Zoe.

"I'll call him." She left the room to talk privately. This didn't bother Barth. Not much, anyway. He'd survived worse.

Zoe came sweeping back in, clicking her phone shut, and dropping it in her oversized leopard-skin purse. "I told him not to come. That I would keep him informed of Mom's status.

He and Sherry are up to their necks in work at the office."

"Good call," Barth murmured, impressed as always with Zoe's in-charge attitude.

Finally, by nightfall, the results came.

"Her heart is in good shape," Dr. Castile informed them.

"Thank God," Zoe breathed huskily.

"Yes, absolutely." Barth felt such immense relief he thought he would slither to the floor any moment. But he braced up for the rest of the results.

"Her blood pressure is in the 160/100 range. Her pulse is in the 90 to 110 area." He did not add any further comments and left.

"Her blood pressure is higher than usual," Barth said to Zoe. "It usually runs around 110/70 range. And her pulse is way up."

He spotted a nurse, called her over, and asked about it. The nurse assured him that he should not be concerned about it. But he couldn't help himself. This was way above her normal range. He felt antsy and helpless.

The doctor gave Seana an injection and, after another six hours, she calmed down and was able to be released.

Barth traipsed outside and drove the car to the exit door. Zoe stayed with her mother, who sat glumly in a wheelchair, vacant eyed and beyond weary looking. Barth's heart tugged as it always did when he saw emptiness on that beautiful face.

He and Zoe assisted Seana into the back seat where a cushion was slid under her head to make her more comfortable on the drive home. "'Night, Mama," Zoe whispered and leaned to kiss her cheek. "I love you."

Seana didn't reply.

"Good night, Zoe." Barth waved as he got into the driver's seat, feeling as bad for Zoe as he did for himself.

They both loved Seana. This was one bond that would always connect them.

Unfortunately.

Zoe didn't respond but he saw her in the rearview mirror, watching them until out of sight.

కుల

"Steroid psychosis." Zoe ran that around her tongue as she tidied up the dance studio for the upcoming evening. Peyton was helping her, singing softly as he worked, and Zoey was again impacted by the sheer wholesomeness of her son.

Too bad his dad hadn't appreciated him enough. Women and wine had, in the final analysis, meant more to Daddy than his own family. She shook loose from that vein of thought. Refused to allow Wilton's ghost to spoil an otherwise beautiful day.

Actually, she hid her negativity from Peyton, knowing it would wound him. He did, after all, love his daddy. Except for being a totally absent husband and parent, Wilton was a fantastic person. Life of the party. Always. That was the one thing she missed about him. His upbeat, fun-loving side. That's the side Peyton got during his increasingly rare visits. She wouldn't take that from him.

But to have that *whoopdy-do* Wilton, she'd had to put up with the rotten part, too. So to survive, she had, in the end, opted for divorce.

Peyton's soft singing along with the stereo's 101 Strings's rendition of "Night and Day" halted her in her tracks as she covertly watched him polishing mirrors to a high shine, seeing his guileless reflection as he stretched up and down to reach the floor-to-ceiling surfaces. She hadn't done too badly raising him alone.

And she'd always had her mom for backup. Her frown reappeared along with that little flutter around her heart that reacted to the thought of something happening to her mother, the one rock left in her life.

The diagnosis, steroid psychosis, from her mom's doctor, had sounded ominous. Mystifying. So she'd looked it up to see exactly what she was dealing with here. The web info verified a wide range of psychotic disturbances from mild depression to anxiety to violence.

At least she was certain that her mother wasn't being fed poison or hallucinatory drugs. Or was she? Zoey paused, dust cloth stilled atop the stereo speaker. She still couldn't get past the fact that Barth had been accused of his first wife's murder. The woman had been shot in the head at close range, in the parking lot of the middle school where she taught. She'd stayed late and there were no witnesses to the brutal crime. The police had found her in her car behind the wheel, her window rolled down. So it was someone she'd known well.

Barth, her ex-husband at the time, had been the prime suspect because he'd not wanted the divorce that freed Betty to marry the man she'd fallen for. The suspected motive was revenge. After the divorce, she'd married her paramour, a police officer in the Canadian province of Nova Scotia.

That much Zoe had gleaned when she got a policeman friend of Scott Burns to do a background check on Barth McGrath. He'd also discovered the murder arrest via his ample resources.

Scott Burns.

She smiled now, dusting away, as she thought of Scott. Hunky he was. And he would do anything in the world for her, though he steadfastly stated that he did not think Barth could be guilty of such a crime. Period. No further discussion. She truly liked him, but just couldn't begin to think about any sort of commitment after her ugly divorce and the long relationship with Corey Adams, who, in the end, could not leave his mother.

Zoe actually couldn't fault him too much for that. His mom was elderly and had health problems and depended on Corey. He was a great son. Just not husband material. She shook her long hair free from her shoulders, stopped, and pulled it up into a ponytail holder she carried in her jeans pocket for hair emergencies. There. That was better. Cooler. Grabbing the dust mop, she attacked the parquet floor with unfeigned vengeance.

Zoe still couldn't shake this – feeling. A subterranean certainty that there was more to Barth McGrath than meets the eye.

How could she trust a virtual stranger with the care of her mother?

She would have to keep close watch on the situation.

Her mother's life – not to mention sanity – might depend on it.

Bottom line: Zoe wanted her mother back.

∾∾

Two things happened in the following months. Seana's condition worsened. Barth kept a journal of her meds and schedule, down to what she ate and her behavior. He felt this would aid the doctors as to her progress or lack of. It would also help them adjust meds according to her needs.

It also gave him something positive to do. It helped, in a small way, to ward off some of the helplessness that wracked him in the midnight hours.

The other thing that happened was that Pastor Keith asked Barth to assume the ministry of music at their church. Frank Lutz had retired to Florida after a twenty-year stint there, leaving them without a music leader.

Barth was reluctant at first but his friend had urged him to consider it. "You'd be perfect, Barth. You have the heart for it, not to mention the talent. Honestly?" He'd laid his hand on Barth's shoulder as they stood in his office that Sunday, nearly a year after Seana's diagnosis. "You need this. There are many of Seana's friends who will be glad to sit with her, rotate the duty, while you minister at church."

"I don't know, Keith." Barth slowly shook his head. "Seana requires 24/7 care. It's not easy."

"Exactly why you need a break." He patted his shoulder and smiled. "Let me know."

"Take the position," Billie Jean insisted later that evening as they sat at the kitchen bar. Barth refilled her decaf coffee. "You know I'm here any time you need me."

"I know." Barth frowned as he refolded his long frame onto the stool. "I just hate to leave her."

"Barth, how much good you gonna do her if you drain out? Huh? You can, you know. And you can't get anything outta a dried-up turnip. So look at it like this, you're staying well in order to help her heal."

Barth looked at her long and hard. Then his eyes began to smile before it reached his lips. "You might just be right, Billie Jean."

"Doggone tootin'." Billie Jean's shoulders lifted and she puffed out her flat bosom. "Just look at me. All those vitamin supplements and holistic treatments you've found for me are working wonders. I'm cancer free, Barth. And I'm not even gonna add 'for now.' I'm gonna be well. Totally."

Barth, by now, was beaming. "That's the spirit."

"And so is Seana." Billie Jean's burst of coppery curls bounced as she nodded resolutely.

Chin set, she slid from the stool and marched into the den where Seana lay curled up on the sofa, her eyes vacantly watching television's ball game of the day. She'd already, at exactly twelve noon, eaten her pimento cheese sandwich with a glass of water, her ironclad menu by now. Nothing more. Nothing less.

Seana wouldn't eat just any pimento cheese, either. No sirree. It had to be Joanie Knight's homemade version. Barth had tried to slip other brands past her only to have her shove it away with a petulant "I don't want this."

He would apologetically call Joanie and ask her, again, to tweak and mollify Seana's craving. Thank God, Barth would silently breathe, Joanie was faithful; she dropped a fresh weekly supply by the house each Monday.

Today Billie Jean dragged over an ottoman and planted herself on it, within mere inches of Seana. Barth watched her get in Seana's face and held his breath. Seana did not like such intrusiveness, but how would she ever get better without human interaction?

"Look, Seana," Billie Jean leaned forward, dug elbows into knees, and clasped her hands together. "I want you to listen. I know you can hear me. I want you to know this one thing.

Look into my eyes. Seana? Look at me! Yeh. Like that. Read my lips. You. Are. Going. To. Get. Better."

Seana didn't respond. Neither Barth nor Billie Jean expected her to. But in Barth's heart of hearts, he knew that on some level such loving, caring feedback would take root deep in Seana's soul.

Such faith would make a big difference.

"Thanks, Billie Jean. I needed that." Tears filled his eyes and he removed his glasses to wipe them away. "And thanks, too, for showing me that I must continue living while Seana is in this – hibernation. I need to be in top form when she emerges."

Billie Jean gave him a high five. "The magic word. *When*."

Barth laughed and looked over at Seana, curled up on the sofa just as she had been for the past year. The sight of her, wounded, slowly bleeding life and sanity, was imprinted into his brain for all eternity. But he wasn't whipped.

"You know what comes from a cocoon, don't you, Billie Jean?" He shook his head, tears again pooling along his lower lids. "A daggum butterfly. And yeah, Seana, I know you're hearing my Southernese. Heck, honey, somebody has to take up the slack for your silence."

❧ ❧

After the initial onset of the psychosis, Barth never left Seana completely by herself. She could stay alone for short periods and knew to call him if she needed him. Her cell phone lay conveniently within reach at all times, charged and ready to use. But at the same time, she would sometimes panic when alone or in the dark.

As months passed, Seana's deviance from her former self grew more pronounced. Whereas before, she'd watched TV news religiously, she now hated it. Barth described *hate* as when she seemed to bristle, her face turned stormy, and she would turn completely away from the object of her distaste. This proved to be bothersome, that she did nothing to hide her aversion.

Barth trudged on, doing the best he could to avoid catastrophe.

chapter four

"Here I am,
and there I am
Dancing on the glass."
– Sarah Kane

*S*eana was, if nothing else, contrary.

On some murky level, she knew it. But she didn't care. Her emptiness allowed no regret or culpability to penetrate the cocoon wrapping her. Heck, it permitted no emotions at all. Only weapon she had to turn away invasive irritation was her voice. By George, she could say "no." And as with a two year old's blank mental canvas, Seana used the word often and loudly.

She sat in the doctors's office, an outsider, listening to Barth's discourse with the current physician – one of a menagerie littering her dark journey – from the time of her diagnosis. She'd long ago lost track of who was who. Hardly recognized any of them.

"Tell me some of the most notable changes since her diagnosis." Dr. Wallace wheeled his chair around to a computer.

"She barely tolerates coffee anymore. She always loved it. Only half a cup a day now. Loved sweets. Now hates them.

Her gag reflex was slightly above normal. Now she gags for no discernable cause. She was always cool natured, but now she freezes most of the time."

"Okay." The doctor typed into his computer as they talked. "Go on."

"Umm. Let's see … Seana's appetite was always good. Now she has to force herself to eat most of the time. She used to diet occasionally, but now she's lost over twenty-five pounds. Another thing, she used to love low, soft lights in the den. Now she wants the lights very, very bright there."

"What about pastime activities? Social things?"

Barth laughed tightly and shook his head. "She was a very social being before, outgoing, fun-loving. Now she hates to be around people. Fun? I don't really know anything she truly enjoys, Dr. Wallace. Once upon a time she watched news and discussed it. No more. Only thing she still will watch on television is a ball game. I turn it to the Atlanta Braves games because they were her favorite team at one time, but now, though she watches, she's no longer interested in who's playing." He shrugged listlessly.

Seana watched the clock. How long were they going to be here? They'd already been here for an hour and four minutes and thirty-five seconds.

The voices droned on, aggravating her.

Barth continued. "Every morning after I force her to shower, know what she says to me, doc? She asks me, 'Barth, do you have enough to do at the church office to keep you busy today so you won't bother me?' That's how I get sent off."

Barth and the doctor laughed uproariously as though it was funny. It wasn't funny to Seana because she *did* want Barth to stay away from her. Wanted everybody to stay the heck away from her. Barth didn't know that when he sent her to shower and stood guard at the bathroom door to listen until she turned on the water, that she only pretended to shower. She would step back into the stall's corner so the water did not touch her.

Sometimes he would sniff and say, "Seana, you need a bath. You're beginning to smell." And he would strip himself off and get in the shower with her and soap her up all over with the loofa sponge, then rinse her down before briskly toweling her dry.

Oh how she hated for him to do that.

"She has this one shirt she loves," Barth said. "She wears it all the time. It's yellow with green stripes. I have to take it off her most of the time to launder it."

Seana heard that. The striped shirt was loose and comfortable, along with the stretchy black slacks, which were the only ones that fit her anymore. The clock now said three twenty-six. They'd been here an hour and twenty-six minutes and ... fifteen seconds.

"Can you think of any other significant changes, Mr. McGrath?" Dr. Wallace looked up from his computer screen.

"Yes. Perhaps the most significant of all. She loved her children and grandchildren with a passion. The iconic Nana, Seana was. Now they make her nervous. It hurts them, though they're both troopers and cover it well."

"Sex?" The doctor asked.

"Oh, before, Seana had a healthy libido. Now, she has no libido."

"None?"

"Absolutely none. It's like making love to an inflatable mannequin. No response."

"Must be difficult for you." The statement was sympathetic.

A long sigh. "Yes. It is."

Seana crossed her arms. When was this going to end?

The doctor stood and so did Barth. They shook hands. "Let's just hope better times are coming."

Finally, Seana thought standing abruptly.

Better times? The words fizzled as quickly as they appeared.

One late afternoon while Seana was alone – Barth was at his church office – the front doorbell pealed. Occasionally, he now would leave her alone for a couple of hours at a time. Most of the time, Billie Jean was downstairs and could be quickly summoned via Seana's ever present cell phone.

The doorbell pealed again.

Brutus, from his floor pillow positioned near the sofa, rwooofed.

Seana rolled onto her back and stared tersely at the ceiling. Why? She wondered. Why did people bother her?

The loud peals continued for what seemed an eternity. Brutus barked and trotted over to the door, sniffing. Seana jerked upright, slid into her robe, and stalked to the door. Cautiously, she opened it.

Sadie Tate and Fred and Elsie Johnson stood smiling from ear to ear, laden with a beautiful bouquet of red roses and a huge goodies basket filled with a colorful, fragrant assortment from Fred's Grocery Store.

"Hello, Seana," Sadie gushed and shifting the roses to one side, stepped forward to give Seana a hug, customary in the past. Today, however, Seana stepped back, frowning, deflecting the embrace.

Annoyed, she waited for them to reveal their mission.

Something like pity brushed Sadie's sharp little features before the smile reappeared, only heightening Seana's impatience. "We came to see how you're doing. The church sent these flowers to cheer you up."

"Yeh." Fred nodded at the big basket of fares in his arms. "Here's some goodies, too. We all miss you, Seana, and want to see you well again."

Hurry, she thought. *Hurry and leave.* Seana reached for the basket, roughly deposited it on the floor, turned and snatched the flowers from Sadie, whose startled expression did not register with Seana.

"Thanks," she muttered – simply because she knew she was supposed to – and slammed the door in their faces. She turned and leaned her back against the door, heart pounding away with apprehension. Why didn't they leave her alone?

She tossed the flowers on the bar then returned to curl up beneath the blanket on the sofa, pulling and tucking her warm, snug cocoon back securely around her. Brutus sighed and nestled back down to nap. After Seana had first fallen ill, he'd laid his head on the sofa while his tawny eyes begged for her affection, which he was so accustomed to. But after awhile, he became resigned to just lounging near her.

Later, she heard Barth come in and Brutus's paws clicking toward him for a greeting.

She heard Barth's gentle "hi there, buddy," as he vigorously ruffled neck fur.

"Seana? Why did you throw the flowers on the bar? Couldn't you have managed to stretch yourself a bit and put them in water? The vase is sitting right here on the counter. Didn't Sadie offer to fix them for you?"

"No."

He came to stand before her, puzzled, as he looked over his shoulder at the goodie basket still planted next to the front door. Then he peered into her face as she kept her eyes fastened to the Atlanta Braves game now playing on TV.

"Seana? Did you invite them in?"

"No."

"Why?"

"I didn't want to."

"Dear God," he said, pivoting away and striding to collect the roses. "I should have warned them when they told me they were coming."

She heard him running water into the crystal vase and arranging the flowers. Then she heard him carry the basket to the counter and rummage through the food, exclaiming over the consideration of the church folks. "I hope they understand by now," he muttered.

Eyes now fixed on the large wall clock she'd insisted on having, Seana heard him begin to prepare dinner. She smelled the chicken stir-fry he put together and meticulously seasoned.

Hawk-like, Seana watched the clock's second hand move. One minute till six.

Dishes rattled as Barth pulled them out and ice tinkled into a glass. The loaf bread package crackled.

Thirty seconds till six.

Water being poured into an empty glass. Bowl sliding from fridge.

Fifteen seconds till six.

Fridge door slamming shut.

Five seconds till six. Four. Three. Two. One.

Six o'clock.

Seana sat upright, rolled off the couch and padded over to the kitchen. Barth held out her plate.

She moved back to her sofa perch, sat her plain un-iced water on the coffee table, and began to eat her halved pimento cheese sandwich.

Barth brought his food over to join her. He shook his head as he deposited his own iced water on the table next to Seana's. "Sure hate that you weren't hospitable to those kind church folks, honey," he murmured. "I'll have to apologize to them."

He looked at the screen, his eyes grief stricken. "Seems I'm doing a lot of that lately." Then his eyes met Seana's as she chewed her gooey pimento cheese sandwich.

His smile was instant and complete. Accepting. Understanding.

A tiny – minute – something inside her flickered. Then in the next instant was gone.

She returned her gaze to the TV screen and the baseball game.

❧

The one venture Seana agreed to was to Joanie's Homecombing Queen's Beauty Parlor. Once a week, she compliantly allowed Barth to drive her there, leave her for a silent hour, and then pick her up after Joanie performed miracles on her hair.

Though it utterly agitated Seana, Joanie managed to slide a firm shoulder hug in as she seated Seana in the styling chair and tilted her back for a warm, sudsy shampoo. It wasn't too bad, Seana decided each time.

Joanie cut her hair a bit shorter than usual because by the time Seana wallowed on the sofa all week, her hair looked like a bird's nest. That didn't bother Seana at all. Nothing bothered her anymore. Except noise and people.

"At least I get to see it looking pretty for a few minutes," Seana overheard Barth tell Joanie one day as he picked her up. Joanie gave him a sympathetic smile and patted him on the shoulder as he collected Seana.

On the way home, he drove by the Mater and Onion Buffet, overriding Seana's demands to go home. "I'm hungry," he told her. "And tired. I want to relax a few minutes and enjoy some good home-cooked food. You can enjoy it, too, if you choose." He sucked in a drag of air and rolled his eyes heavenward, shaking his head. "If not, then you can sit with me while I do."

Seana was not pleased as he steered her inside and greeted the Wests, the Cherokee proprietors, while Seana ignored them. As usual, Joseph West – called Chief by the locals – seated them in their little private corner nook.

Jet, the Filipino keyboard artist, immediately began playing one of Seana's favorites, *Girl From Ipanema*, with its syncopated Latino beat. Seana frowned at the noise and turned away as much as possible. Brett's heart dropped to his toes, like it always did when she behaved so. But in an instant, his heart went out to her and he reached and took her hand to gently kiss it.

Seana's scowl deepened as she wrested her fingers free.

Chief West appeared again to take their drink order. The Friday evening trade was heavy so he personally catered to the McGraths because they were old friends and he understood that Seana was not herself.

"Water. Without ice," Seana muttered, not meeting his pleasant, expectant gaze.

"Same, with ice," Barth said, giving Chief an apologetic roll of eyes.

Chief shrugged, smiled, and waved it away with a flick of bronze fingers as he left to collect their order.

"Do you want me to fix your plate?" Barth asked, to save time. This was a usual battle of wills. "Or do you want to go to the buffet yourself?"

"No."

"No, you don't want me to fix your plate, or no, you don't want to go to the buffet?"

"I don't want to go."

"Shall I fix you chicken or ... Oh, come on, Seana. Go with me and I'll help you."

He tugged her to her resisting feet and nudged her to the lovely buffet that was fit for royalty.

It took Barth twenty minutes of haggling and cajoling Seana to try different foods that she'd once adored. To her, the array of choices looked sickening. Disgusting. She finally conceded to try a piece of ham, mashed potatoes, and peas and carrots, though the latter gave her serious pause and guardedness.

He seated her and then went to fill his own plate. When he returned and began to eat, Seana said, "I can't eat this."

Barth visibly reined in his impatience. "What's wrong with the ham, Seana? Huh?"

"I don't like it. I don't like these peas and carrots either." They looked and smelled vile.

"You haven't even tasted them, Seana. Go on, try a bite."

He watched her pick up her fork and take a bite. She slowly began to chew, her face already wrinkling into a torturous mask of misery. Then she gagged.

Once. Twice.

"Oh ... no, Seana. Spit it out into your napkin. Here." He held out a napkin for her to spit out the offensive substance. She wiped her mouth savagely and took a gulp of the tepid water.

"How about some chicken? You've always loved fried chicken." He kept pushing things at her when she wished he'd simply leave her alone. She could eat a pimento cheese sand-wich when she got home.

"I don't want to eat," she insisted.

"You have to eat something." He dashed to the buffet and collected a golden fried chicken leg, Seana's favorite part in the past.

He presented the plate to her with a flourish and reseat-ed himself beside her. "M'lady, I hope you enjoy this delicious fare. I intend to." He crunched into his own crisp drumstick and smacked his lips. "Mmm. This is delicious."

Seana eyed hers like it was a pit viper ready to strike

"No." Her refusal was succinct. Final.

"Honey," Barth said softly. "I'd give a king's ransom to have you do something familiar." He sighed heavily. "Some-thing, *Seana.*"

The heartfelt words bounced off her like drops of water off a hot griddle.

She saw Barth watching her and grew more irritated by the moment. Finally, her peripheral vision revealed that he re-laxed and began to eat his own food.

Good. Now he would leave her the heck alone.

❧

"Seana, Ashley is counting on you to be at Happy Feet Studio tonight. She and Peyton are doing a clogging dance special."

"No." Seana frowned. *Go away.*

"Ah, honey. Please." Barth pulled the ottoman up close to the sofa where she reclined and reached to take her hand. It was like handing him a cold fish, but Seana was sure he would persist, darn it.

She was right.

"There are some things that are extremely important in young folks's lives. This is one in Ashley's life that you simply must honor. As far as that goes, it's important to Peyton, too."

"No." She slid her hand from his and tugged her ever present blanket higher to ward off the omnipresent chill.

"Anybody home?" called Billie Jean from the stairwell.

"Come on up," yelled Barth, his loud volume reaping an extremely irritated scowl from Seana.

"Wha's happening?" Billie Jean slid into the nearest easy chair.

"I'm trying to get Seana to go to Happy Feet's party tonight. Peyton and Ashley are doing a bang-up clog performance and want their grandmother to be there and celebrate them."

"Hey!" Billie Jean swooped in on Seana, earning an even deeper scowl from her. "There's no reason you cannot roll yourself off that casket-sofa there and be there for this momentous event in your perfect granddaughter's life, Seana."

"No."

"I do not want to hear that word in this dialogue, Cuz. You sound like a sulky, rebellious toddler, doncha know? Not like you at all, Seana."

Seana stared at her, something inside her rising – just a smidgeon. Then it evaporated.

Please, she thought, turning her eyes back to the television screen, go away.

એ જી

Billie Jean moseyed over to the kitchen stove and served herself some stir-fry chicken over brown rice. "Mmm," she smacked her lips on the first taste. "You outdid yourself here, Barth."

She ate at the bar and Barth joined her for decaf coffee. Recently, Billie Jean's former coolness toward him had slowly thawed. Their mutual love for Seana was, Barth was certain, the catalyst. And, too, they had searched the web for holistic cancer fighters to battle Billie Jean's bone cancer.

So far, so good.

"She's getting skinny as one of Chelsea's Glad Rags mannequins, Barth," Billie Jean muttered. "Have you weighed her lately?"

Barth ran his hand over his face and dragged in a ragged breath. "Ninety-eight pounds last time I put her on the scales."

Billie Jean's mouth dropped open. "Heavens to murgatroyd, Barth. What we gonna do?"

He shook his head, feeling that saying it out loud had brought it home too vividly. "It's been near on three years now and no improvement. In fact, she's worse."

Billie Jean reached to take his hand in hers, a rare display of affection. "She's gonna get through this in one piece, Barth. And I can tell you from experience that she's gonna get well."

She thrust out her chin. "Huh! Look at me. I was at death's door, wudn't I? I am cancer free now. Can't get any more miraculous than that. And it's all because folks like you and the rest of the church family joined me in believing it would happen. I believed it and it did happen. Seana will get her miracle, too."

Barth gave her a weary smile. "Thanks, Billie Jean. You're just what the doctor ordered today. I just hope I can get Seana to the dance studio in the next hour."

"Huh." Billie Jean got to her feet to help tidy the kitchen. "Leave it to me. I'll get her peeled off that blasted sofa."

✺

And true to her word, Billie Jean did, indeed, get Seana dressed and into the car. Stiff and resistant as she was, Barth was pleased that they were on their way to Happy Feet Dance Studio for tonight's special performance.

Refreshments were soft drinks – Zoe opted for family friendly atmosphere at all times – and finger foods, compliments of Fred's Grocery's Deli Department – a recent, much-needed, and enormously welcomed addition to the little town.

Barth settled Seana at a corner table, distanced from the customary busy-ness of the dancing crowd. Even so, he watched her pretty brow wrinkle with annoyance. Billie Jean had done a credible job of pulling Seana together, making her presentable in snatching away the worn, faded, striped shirt and insisting she wear a clean, casual pullover and ever-present black slacks. Seana adamantly refused to wear anything closely fitted. The blue pullover hung on her thin frame, but the color pulled out the azure in her diverted eyes.

Tonight, in her affliction, Seana projected a brusque or bruised beauty. And despite Barth's having seen the worst, unappealing sides to her, to him she gave off an earthy yet ethereal sensuality.

And memories swooped in of him holding her in his arms, dancing … her vibrant, smiling face turned up to his in complete devotion.

God in heaven, how he yearned for her return.

Suddenly, sitting there watching her, Barth felt something hit him in his solar plexus. The impact was stunning, like a freight train slamming him. Tears gathered suddenly, burning behind his eyes, pushing, pushing against the knot in his throat, one the size of California. He gulped back a sob. That fast. He turned in his chair to face the wall for long moments, fighting the grief that welled up like Mt. Saint Helens.

"Barth?" Zoe startled him, speaking from behind him. She circled and was watching him curiously. "You okay?"

"Mm, yeh," Barth snuffled and smiled a wide, wide smile. "Just hay fever."

Zoe watched him a moment longer, obviously not convinced. "Did you have much trouble getting her here?" She jerked her head at her mother.

Barth chuckled huskily at that, took off his glasses, and wiped his wet face. "Billie Jean saved the day."

Zoe actually smiled. "How?"

"Told her that if she didn't get off her arse and get in the car she was gonna take her clocks away from her."

Zoe burst into laughter. "No."

Barth laughed, too. "Yup. Sure did. It worked. This time. With a bit of added haggling and force, anyway."

Zoe shook her head and sat down beside him a moment. She'd long ago compromised her misgivings to team up with Barth in the care of her mother. Barth nursed no notions that she'd completely accepted him at face value. There were still times that he caught her watching him with cynicism oozing from those cool blue depths.

He pushed that thought away.

Tonight, they celebrated together the fact of Seana's being here. The family had gotten through three Christmases by having the celebration at Seana's house. They had, collectively, coaxed her to put away her blanket, to dress, and unwrap her presents with the family looking on.

She would open each gift and mutter "thanks" because Barth and Billie Jean had preached its necessity during the preceding hours. Then she'd toss the item aside and go to the next. That she did not *ooh* and *ahh* was ignored. By now, the family accepted that Seana had nothing to give.

Zilch. Nada.

"This is special, Barth." Zoe recaptured his attention tonight, then sighed, looking at her mother's set profile, the scowl deeply grooved into lovely features that never smiled anymore. "She's made an effort, however prodded, to come and celebrate the kids. And ...." Her voice choked off and she took a few moments to collect herself. "I'm sorry. I just miss her so much."

"I know. So do I." Barth reached over and patted her hand, quickly withdrawing it for fear of reprisal. He never knew with Zoe.

But for the moment, he would enjoy the warmth of shared bonds.

"Oh. Gotta run." Zoe sprang to her feet. "It's time for Ashley and Peyton to do their thing." She dashed off to the microphone to announce the number. Barth scooted his chair closer to get Seana's attention.

"Your two grandchildren are about to entertain, honey." He reached to take her hand, always surprised to find it icy cold. Dr. Wallace had informed him that it was one of a host of physical symptoms that pointed to the chemical change in her.

"I want to go home," Seana said tightly, her frown lines deepening. Barth thought, not for the first time, that he sure hoped her face didn't freeze: those grooves seemed to etch deeper with each passing day.

"No, Seana." He looked at her, beginning to feel real irritation. "You can sit here and watch those kids entertain you. It won't kill you, for crying out loud."

In the next heartbeat, Billie Jean swooped in and dragged a chair up to the other side of Seana. "Yeh. Don't you so much as look like you want to leave, ol' girl, or you'll have me to deal with."

Seana didn't even look her way. Acted as though she'd not heard the warning.

Barth sighed as Peyton and Ashley positioned themselves in the spotlight and hoedown music blasted from all directions. Seana might not have heard Billie Jean's edict, he realized. At least not with a full understanding of the words's potential impact.

He understood that her emotional vacuity deleted important nuances of communication. Most of the time now, it didn't bother him too much. He pushed the current standoff from his mind, determined to enjoy the kids's efforts.

Peyton and Ashley thrust themselves into the complicated, hypnotically stimulating choreography of the clog performance, and Barth thought how much they'd changed in the past three years. Now fourteen, Ashley was becoming quite the little beauty, but that didn't in any way thwart her inner loveliness, a sweetness that splashed over on anyone passing by, just like Seana's. In fact, Ashley looked more like Seana every day with her wheat-streaked hair and blue, blue eyes and fine, aristocratic features.

Peyton, nearly nineteen and growing more darkly handsome each day, was about to embark on another level of academia. He was seeking Barth's counsel while weighing his college choices nowadays. Tonight, the two teens were knocking themselves out for Seana's benefit.

Barth felt it in his bones, their desperate grasping for some tiny glimpse of their Nana behind that closed face. Oh, they reverenced her, even in her constant rejection of their presence. They understood that she was in another land where they could not follow. And like everyone else, prayed fervently for her safe return to their familiar shore.

"I love you, Nana," Ashley always murmured and insisted on kissing Seana's cheek, even when she knew Nana would draw back as if struck and wipe away the kiss. Then the girl would sit quietly in the den, non-intrusive and kind, just soaking up her Nana's presence.

Peyton was just as loving and kind. And attentive. More and more lately he would come to the house and hang out with Barth, chatting about things guys talked about, sports, news, the dance business, education possibilities, and, in their case, the shared interest in music and literature.

Barth smiled now, watching his two grandchildren shining like bright, spinning, spiraling comets through the sky. Yep. They were his grandkids, too. His chest seemed to expand a bit and he chuckled. Seana cut him a sharp, annoying glance.

"When can I go home?" she asked, impatience vibrating from her.

Billie Jean leaned over. "Not until after you tell these two kids how much you've enjoyed their special performance. Soon as you do that, we'll drive you home."

Seana didn't like it one bit, but she apparently got it, that Billie Jean meant business. Barth sighed tiredly, glad for the feisty cousin taking up the slack in times like this. He got so tired of fighting sometimes that he nearly despaired.

The instant the music ended and the place erupted into applause, Seana sprang to her feet and headed for the exit. "Oh no you don't." Billie Jean snared her arm and spun her around. "Not until you tell Ashley and Peyton that you enjoyed their dance routine. I'm going to take a picture of you with them."

Barth assisted Billie Jean in steering Seana to where the two performers lingered, receiving accolades from friends for a job well done. In the past three years, Ashley had perfected her technique and now could hold her own in any choreography.

"Tell them 'I enjoyed it,'" Billie Jean coached Seana as they approached.

"Nana!" Ashley pealed, beaming like a lighthouse beacon. "I'm sooo glad you came. I still can't dance as good as you, you know." Despite Seana's stiffness, the girl seized her in a mighty hug and passed her on to Peyton, who was a bit more cautious as he wrapped a long arm around Seana's rigid shoulders for a side hug. He quickly released her, ignoring her frown of discomfort.

Awkwardness settled in as folks moved about and music from the stereo system belched out "Dancing Cheek to Cheek" for the fox-trot lovers.

Billie Jean and Barth both surreptitiously nudged Seana in the back.

For once, Seana heeded. "I enjoyed it," she muttered tersely, cutting her gaze away to glare into space.

"One more thing," Billie Jean whipped out her phone and turned on the camera. "Stand beside your Nana, kids. And smile."

They scooted to comply. Seana stood planted between them, like a rigid, straight pine.

"Smile, Seana," Billie Jean ordered.

When hell freezes over, Barth thought, then felt distinctly disloyal.

Seana's face never relinquished its grim mien. But the picture wasn't too bad, they all agreed.

"Thanks again, Nana," both Ashley and Peyton spoke at once, truly grateful for the smidgeon of praise. A crumb, but in this case, Barth knew for a fact, it was like the widow's mite to those two.

Zoe came over and smiled at Barth and Billie Jean. "Thanks," she said softly. Then to Seana, "Love you, Mama."

"I want to go home," snapped Seana and spun toward the door.

Barth, Zoe, and Billie Jean looked at each other, shrugged, then burst into laughter. As Barth and Billie Jean followed

Seana's frantic stride out the glass door, they high-fived each other. Thank God, Barth thought. Seana didn't break their hearts.

❧ ❧

Barth had earlier dropped Seana off at Joanie's Homecombing Queen Salon for her weekly appointment. Then he went to his church office for the next hour to review his music selections for the week. Due to his home commitments, Pastor Keith only asked the choir to perform for the Sunday morning service. That required less rehearsal time that took Barth from home.

He checked the hymn lineup and mentally went through the special arrangement of an Andrae Crouch song, "My Tribute." The melody and words flowed through his brain … *"How can I say thanks for the things you have done for me? Things so undeserved …"* and for the first time ever, completely bypassed his heart.

He stopped mid song, closed his eyes in frustration, and sat back in the executive desk chair, hands clasped across his midriff. Looking out the window into a golden, sun-washed day, he reflected on his uncharacteristic barren response to his music-soul connection.

Had he so tamped down his emotions in order to survive Seana's constant dismissal of him that they had withered away? He dragged in a deep, cleansing breath and willed his frustration to ride out on its release. For long moments he sat there, absorbing the tranquility of the setting.

Barth's office offered a quiet sanctuary for his battered spirit. His gaze moved upward, beyond the buttermilk, frothy clouds back-dropped by azure infinity. *Please? Help me,* he prayed. Nothing profound happened in that moment, but he was able to put away his music paraphernalia and go pick up Seana.

He was able to smile and speak to Sadie Tate who sat in

the pink waiting room chair at Joanie's salon, texting on her Smartphone.

"Barth," Joanie called from the back. "Come here; I want to show you something."

Curious, Barth approached the styling station. Joanie turned Seana around and whispered, "Look behind her ears."

Joanie gently pulled the hair back behind one ear. Barth nearly gasped at the red, crusty skin. Crud.

"Just thought you'd want to know," Joanie whispered. "She still giving you a time about bathing?"

"Yes," he muttered, feeling his face begin to burn. Barth wanted to slide through the floor. Embarrassment didn't begin to define what he felt. "I'm sorry, Joanie. I'll be sure this doesn't happen again."

Joanie gave him a sympathetic smile and patted his arm. "Don't worry about it. I understand. I was just afraid it would become infected over time."

Barth managed somehow to get Seana out the door and into the car before exploding. "You've not been washing behind your ears, Seana. Can you imagine how embarrassing it is to have that pointed out to me? In public?" Of course Joanie had kept it quiet so Sadie didn't hear, but it still galled him.

Seana didn't respond. Not even with a blink of her eye. That made him even madder. "Well, from now on, your ears will be clean before you leave the house. I'll see to it."

And Barth kept his word. Not only did he scrub behind her ears for several days to insure the buildup was gone, but he checked them regularly to make sure she kept them that way.

Seana? He knew by now that as long as Seana could hibernate in her blasted cocoon, curled into a fetal knot on the sofa, she was content.

On second thought, he *hoped* that she was content.

He had no way of knowing.

That was the hardest thing to deal with.

∾

Zoe marched with the choir into the loft that Sunday morning. She noticed that Billie Jean wasn't at church. She was on Seana-sitting duty today, no doubt. Zoe loved music, any way or shape. So, despite Barth assuming the music ministry, requiring her to suffer his presence even more, she remained a faithful choir member.

Behind her, tall and uniquely male in his own white robe with navy-blue yoke, towered Scott Burns. Somehow, he managed to sit directly behind her, within touching distance. She stifled a smile as she inhaled his spicy Halston Cologne. She'd recognize that fragrance anywhere.

Today, it tweaked something inside her, something distinctly feminine. She pushed it away.

From her alto, third-tier section she was able to watch the congregation during the hymns and preliminaries. Chelsea Brown, dressed to the teeth in her Glad Rags Shop finery, winked at her and gave a fluttered-fingers wave as she moved her well-endowed self to a seat in the sanctuary, alluring hips swinging without any effort and looking entirely too good to be middle aged. Her black bob never seemed to muss, Zoe noted with a grin. And those Cleopatra eyes. Ahh. On Chelsea, not overdone. Simply appealing.

Zoe loved Chelsea, one of her mother's lifelong friends, like Joanie who sat beside her in the alto section. Peyton seated himself at the piano for the special Andrae Crouch arrangement. He would also play the offertory hymn, next on the program, a style mixture of traditional and his own improvisations. Today it was "Rejoice Ye Pure in Heart," a majestic song of praise.

Zoe's heart swelled with something more than pride as he added his master's touch to the keyboard. It was that, too, pride, of course, but something beyond. Something pure and maternal and unconditional. Something blood related and forever. She swallowed back a knot in her throat as he ended the piece on a grandiose crescendo.

Barth, looking a bit pale today in his robe, stood and adjusted his music podium as he faced the choir. He nodded at Peyton, who slid into the soft arpeggios as fluidly as a harpist's ripple over strings. Zoe noted Barth's wan appearance. And the dark circles beneath his eyes. But she also noted his press toward excellence as his baton swung down and the choir came in on cue.

Barth's mouth moved in unison with theirs while he strode back and forth before them as the song ebbed and flowed, his energy and exultation pumping out his hands as their cadence drove and harnessed the music into magnificence. When they came to the chorus, Zoe heard Scott's mellow baritone behind her rise with emotion, raising the hair on her arms. *"To God … be the glory … to God … be the glory … to God be the glory … for the things He hath done. With his blood he has saved me … with his po-wer, He has raised me … to Go-o-o-od be the glory … for the things He hath done."*

Zoe watched in awe as Barth began to weep, silently, never missing a beat. She felt her own throat begin to close, so touching was his response to the powerful praise song. He began to smile even as tears coursed down his cheeks. Dimples appeared as he began singing again with the choir. It was the first time Zoe had really noticed them. The dimples. Her mother had talked endlessly about them in the beginning ….

And somehow she knew that this was spiritually momentous for Barth.

Lord knew the man needed something, what with the load he carried while caring for her mother.

Her singing halted in that second. Listen to me, she thought. But there he stood, like the Apostle Paul, that 200-watt smile of his that stole her mother's heart beaming through the tears.

She blinked back tears and finished the number with the choir. In the moment of silence just before the congregation stood to their feet and applause erupted, she heard a snuffle behind her. She looked over her shoulder. Scott's face was tear stained, too. Yet – he looked so ... manly. Her smile burst out of its own volition. .

For a heartbeat, he looked a bit startled. Then he smiled back and what she saw in his eyes shot through her like a silken Taser, flooding her with a peculiar warmth. She quickly turned her attention to the front.

Whew. What a jolt.

This is silly, she thought as they remained standing for Pastor Keith's reading of the day's scripture.

Stupid. That's what it is. She sniffed.

After all, it's only Scott, for crying out loud.

☙ ❧

Another trip to the doctor.

"They still suspect your HRT might be playing a part in your illness," Barth told Seana. He shrugged. "May as well rule it out or be enlightened."

Seana suffered the supervised shower and ear check before she and Barth traveled to see yet another doctor, this time an OB-GYN endocrinologist at Memorial Hospital Medical Center.

"We're going to test you for possible endocrine problems, Mrs. McGrath," Dr. Price told her.

Her mind could not wrap around that. So she watched the clock. Magazines she'd once devoured no longer held any appeal. The tests didn't take but a couple of hours, and they were able to leave. Seana was relieved to get back to her sofa and blanket.

And her pimento cheese sandwich for lunch.

Within the week, Barth told her, "The tests revealed nothing wrong. Dr. Price put you back on Estratest. You've taken it for years so we know you won't react unfavorably to it."

"He also said that you should be getting up and moving around. He suggested you do simple household chores, like washing dishes and dusting. And reading your Bible."

Seana curled over, turning away from Barth, facing the back of the sofa. That was her reply.

She heard Barth sigh deeply and slough out of the den. Presently she heard the back door shut and the sound of him descending the deck steps. She felt a frisson of fear. She was beginning to hate being alone. Yet she hated crowds. They terrified her.

Why did she have to feel this way?

Why? She rolled back over and divided her attention between the wall clock and the television ball game. Her med time was coming up in forty-two minutes. Barth only measured out her ration of meds for the day now and locked the rest up. So even if he wasn't back, she could take them herself. He watched her like a hawk because she had gotten mixed up a couple of times and taken them early, throwing the whole thing off kilter.

Feeling restless because med time was near and the aloneness was getting to her, she got up and walked around inside the house a few laps. She'd done this off and on for the past two years when fear and apprehension built up.

She was still walking when Barth came back in. "Getting cold out there," he said. "Winter's setting in. Hey! Where are you, Seana?" he called out, a note of worry in his voice.

"Walking," she called, now getting winded. She tired easily.

"Say," Barth's eyes lit up behind those thick lenses when she completed the circle through the upper level quarters and returned to the den. "That's great, honey. You need to move more."

Seana avoided his outstretched arms and returned to the sofa. She pulled the blanket up to her chin and settled down to watch the clock.

∞∞

Joanie met Barth in the vestibule that Sunday morning. "Barth, thanks for getting me off the hook." She rolled her contacts-enhanced turquoise eyes. "I'm no teacher by any stretch of imagination or prodding. So I appreciate you filling in to teach Chelsea's first and second grade Sunday school class today. But I *can* help till Jesus returns."

"What's wrong with Chelsea?" Barth asked, still wondering how he ended up subbing for the usually robust woman.

"Stomach flu. Bad bug. In fact her regular substitute teacher, Elsie, has it, too." She made a face. "I can take over about ten minutes before class ends so you can leave early to get into your choir robe before the main service."

Barth frowned. "You've got to get into your choir robe, too."

Joanie smiled but shook her head. "I'll have to play hooky today, Barth. If one of us is sacrificed for the cause, it'll have to be me. You can do with one less alto this one time."

He gave a reluctant nod. Later, after a chaotic trip through Jonah's experience of ending up in the whale's belly and being spat out, they corralled the kids to individual work tables to entertain themselves with colorful paper, kindergarten scissors, and a bottle of carefully monitored glue.

The two of them spent time rotating between different students, helping them create something faintly recognizable. Barth managed to fit his long frame into impossibly small chairs, knees nearly to chin, and was feeling immensely pleased with himself when an ear-splitting scream froze him.

"Aaiiiah!"

He knocked over the dwarf-sized chair and pivoted to see second grader Harry Woodall standing next to Judy Smith, holding up what appeared to be straw. Joanie reached them before Barth. Judy began to cry in earnest.

"Harry did it!" She sobbed, pointing at the straw.

Déjà vu. Barth felt like Looney Tunes had dropped from the sky.

Harry cringed as Joanie reached to touch the pale straw. "Oh my Lord," she moaned and cast Barth a look of utter desolation.

His heart skipped a beat. "What?" He really, really didn't want to know.

"This," Joanie brought it close to his face, "is hair. *Judy's* hair."

That's when Barth saw them. The scissors. In Harry's other hand, with silken strands still sprouting from them.

"Where did ..." He peered closely at the small girl's head, hoping against hope that it wouldn't be discernable. He walked around the chair and then he saw it. Her beautiful long blond hair had a gap center back, a jagged, ugly chasm that stopped at least four inches from the bottom of the remaining hair.

"*Uhnnn,*" he groaned, peering helplessly at Joanie, then around at the other witnesses who, by now, had gone back to their own artistic endeavors. "What in heavens' name are we gonna do?" He paced across the room and back, as distressed as he'd ever been in his life.

Joanie looked at the hair for long moments, then took Judy's small chin in her fingers and turned her head this way and that, studying her closely. Then she smiled.

Barth scowled. How on Earth could she smile at a time like this? "What?"

"I've been trying to get her mama to let me cut her hair for a long time. She just recently said she was leaning that way, you know?" She raised her brows, then wiggled them. "I'd say that now is the perfect time to bring up the subject again, doncha know?"

She pulled a ponytail holder from her purse, wedged it between her teeth. Then she gathered the girl's long hair up into a ponytail and tethered it in the back. "Voila. No sign of the damage. This will get her through the morning service, until I can talk to Colleen about a free haircut, courtesy of Homecombing Queen, Joanie."

Barth's head rolled back in relief and he closed his eyes for a moment.

"Get going," Joanie prodded him, looking at her watch. "You need to jump into your robe and do your thing."

Barth started out the door, then turned back. "May there be many stars in your crown in the by-and-by, Joanie Knight."

He heard her laughter as he dashed to the choir room.

و وۍ

"Barth told me that we should drive on over to the Mater and Onion Buffet and meet him." Billie Jean prodded Seana from the sofa. Her efforts reaped faster results because her strident demands catapulted Seana into agitation, which rolled her to her feet in a bid to escape.

Billie Jean grinned, pleased with her accomplishment as Seana curled from the sofa and slid into her slippers. She'd already dressed. Such as it was. Even iconically casual Billie Jean grimaced at the results.

"Do you have to wear that ever-lovin' striped shirt all the time, Seana?"

Seana didn't answer. Simply marched staunchly to the door.

"Didn't you forget something?" Billie Jean stood planted, hands on hips.

Seana turned and scowled at her.

"Your hair. It looks like a danged haystack. And not a pretty one either. Come on."

"Joanie would have nightmares if she saw this," she muttered as she marched her to the bedroom, sat her down before the mirror, and patiently, gently used a wire hair pick to smooth and place it in a more civilized arrangement. "There. It'll pass."

The drive there was pleasant for Billie Jean. She didn't mind staying with Seana on Sunday mornings. Sometimes she alternated with Tim's wife, Sherry. A sweetie pie was Seana's daughter-in-law. And then there was teenaged Ashley, who seemed to actually enjoy sitting with her grandmother and root for the current ball team, even when Seana showed no interest whatsoever.

Only time Seana spoke during the drive was to repeatedly say, "You're taking me too far from home. Let's go back."

"No way José. We're meeting Barth at the restaurant."

"I want to go home."

"Huh-uh."

Once there, Billie Jean took charge. "Hi, Chief West," she greeted the proprietor warmly and shepherded Seana to their corner spot. The Sunday crowd, fresh from church, was thick and jovial, apparently feeling buoyed by having done the right thing, Billie Jean thought, amused as she looked around, waving at folks she knew.

She glanced at her cell phone timepiece, figuring their church crowd would be filtering in any time now. She looked up and spotted Barth making his way toward them.

"Hi, Billie Jean," he smiled, showing his dimples, and Billie Jean thought how lucky Seana was to have snared him. 'Course, she figured Barth was just as lucky. At least he had been, in the beginning.

"Come on, Seana," he coaxed. "Let's go fix your plate."

"No."

Feeling extremely sympathetic after having spent her morning with the recalcitrant woman, Billie Jean stood. "I'll fix Seana's food this time, Barth. You go get yours and relax. And that's an order."

Barth smiled gratefully and did just that.

Billie Jean gave Seana a dollop of this and that, small amounts of all the foods she'd once liked. On another plate she forked up a chicken leg, sliced ham, and pot roast. She deposited it before Seana, who visibly recoiled from it.

Leaving her, Billie Jean went to fix her own plate. Barth was already seated by the time she returned with loaded plate. Her appetite, today, was ferocious. A far cry from when she'd been diagnosed with incurable bone cancer near on four years ago.

Barth said the blessing and they dined while Seana, arms folded, examined her food as though she wanted to throw it at her worst enemy.

"Seana, there has to be something on those two plates that

you can force yourself to taste," Billie Jean said evenly. "But if you don't you can go hungry till the cows come home."

Barth shot her a stunned look, then sighed, relaxed, and returned to his own food. Billie Jean knew that her no-nonsense approach still threw him off at times but she knew a side to Seana that Barth did not. She'd known Seana from babyhood up and somehow sensed what Seana needed on this particular level. Maybe it was a female thing. She didn't know. She just operated on instinct.

And fortunately, most of the time, it worked.

Joanie came over and spoke to Seana and left unacknowledged. So did Sadie Tate. So did the Johnsons. So did son Tim and his family. But Billie Jean knew that each one of them understood and simply wanted to connect with her, even if one-sided.

Barth went to get dessert. Billie Jean caught Seana's eye just then. Billie Jean winked and grinned at her.

"You'll be back, Seana," she murmured.

"Yes, she will," Barth slid into the booth with his healthy fruit bowl, smiling. "And thanks, Billie Jean. I really needed to hear that."

&

"Mind if I join you two?" Scott Burns stood poised, loaded plate in hand, smiling uncertainly at Zoe. She and Peyton were among the church crowd dining at the Mater and Onion Buffet today. She'd already spoken to her mother, been ignored, and had walked away feeling like crap. She still felt the impact that her mother's appearance had made on her.

Seana appeared to be in the throes of Alzheimer's. Totally not there at times.

Zoe had absorbed the shock and turned away. Then she'd migrated to a lone table rather than mingling at a larger table to chat with friends. She'd opted to sit alone, just she and Peyton because she didn't really feel like talking.

"Sure, Scott," she said dismally, gesturing to the empty chair. He hesitated, then took the seat.

Peyton returned with his food, grinning from ear to ear. "Hey, coach," he said, setting his plate down and extending his hand for a hearty handshake. The two males settled in, seated across from each other, and launched into a vigorous exchange centered on Paradise Springs High news. Peyton had graduated that spring and was hungry for updates.

"Decided on a college yet?" Scott inquired, then bit into a drumstick while his focus stayed intensely tethered to Peyton. And Zoe felt relieved that the laser gaze didn't bull's-eye her. Rather, he seemed truly interested in Peyton's future. It struck a tiny chord inside her. Zoe watched him, amazed at how masculine his movements were. How unselfconscious and ... self-assured he was when talking with Peyton.

She was glad he didn't zero in on her like he usually did. At those times something inside her thrashed about in protest. She went to the bar and chose delectable choices, today favoring the pot roast. It was like her mom used to make, years ago before her dad had passed away. Nostalgia hit her like a scud missile and she pushed it away somewhat viciously.

Her wonderful father had been everything to Zoe in those early years. So she understood Peyton's hunger for a father figure in his life. Oh yeh, she saw the look on his face when he was around strong male figures, felt his reaching out. Losing her dad had been one of the lowest points of her life. But even then, there'd still been her mother, one hundred and ten percent there for her and Tim.

That had lasted until Barth McGrath's appearance.

Everything had changed. And now? Nothing was left of her ... security.

She had no one to lean on.

She harshly dolloped out mashed potatoes beside her pot roast. Hah! The powers that be had chosen not to send her a man strong enough to take her on. Zoe knew that she was a force to be reckoned with. Couldn't help it. She was wired that way. And men – strong men – steered clear of Amazon women like her. She only attracted the weaker ones.

So she tended to regard men who came on to her with a huge dose of cynicism.

On that dismal note, Zoe listlessly selected green beans and yams. When she returned to the table, Scott and Peyton were imbedded in a lively discussion on the state of the current economy, of all things. She noted that Scott didn't even acknowledge her return. Neither did Peyton, but for Scott to ignore her was a new … adventure? She didn't quite know how she felt about it at that precise moment.

Oh well. She sighed and dug in to her sumptuous feast.

Zoe half-tuned in to the guys's discourse, surprised that Peyton was concerned about the economy. When had her little boy gotten so – so worrisome? Duh. She took a deep breath and blew it out. She'd been hoofing it alone since Peyton was four years old, making a living. By the time her ex had changed jobs every three or four months and finally gotten on disability – Lord only knew how he managed that – she'd given up.

She decided then and there that she'd rather wade through crocodile-infested rapids than depend on her ex, Wilton Adams – the deadbeat – to raise their son. Outwardly, she'd put on a good face for Peyton. Though she'd had to often bite her tongue, she'd never said an unkind word against his father. She'd always been generous with visitation privileges.

A lot of good that had done Peyton. His father had moved several hours away, to the low country and rarely ever showed up to visit. His failure to visit was always because of sudden ailments or life or death situations he simply could not avoid. So many times she'd seen Peyton's little face fall and his body wilt with disappointment when the apologetic phone calls came. Later on, his dad didn't even bother to explain; he simply didn't show. Wilton had royally abdicated the "daddy" role.

Zoe grimaced that her son had been exposed to too much struggle, too soon.

Zoe had seen her son, drip by drip, lose a child's trust in his father.

Such a loss. And Zoe had deluded herself that Peyton had not seen her struggles to make ends meet in the early days of the dance studio business. She'd used every artistic gene in her arsenal to shape it into a family-friendly, lucrative diversion for the little town. Her discount introductory coupons and half price family deals, along with other brainstormed specials, had drawn folks into the wholesome, fun atmosphere. But even so, with the economy shifting, she was steadily losing business.

After all, dance lessons were definitely the first things to go when trimming a household budget.

Today, hearing her son venting frustration about soaring costs and families's struggles to survive cut into her heart. He'd grown up somewhere along the way. Without a daddy.

Oh, she knew he missed that vital connection in his life. She'd thought Corey Evans had been the man who could fill that void. He and Peyton had connected from the very beginning. Peyton had trailed him like a puppy dog, emulating him and hanging onto his every word. Corey had been a wonderful man.

But five years later, he'd still not been willing to commit to marriage. His reasons were good ones, but Peyton's devastation – when she'd broken off with Corey – still tore at her heart.

Today, she wondered why life was so complicated. Why did her disappointments inevitably become her son's? Not fair.

On their way out, Barth and Billie Jean waved bye, with her mother tromping ahead of them, anxious to get home.

She glanced at her watch. "Hate to break up this world's problems-solving chitchat, but we'd better get going, Peyton."

Peyton looked disappointed, but Scott grinned, barely sparing her a glance. "Sure thing."

"Enjoyed it, buddy." He shook Peyton's hand and patted

him heartily on the shoulder as they made their way to the cash register.

Before Zoe knew what had happened, Scott snatched the bill from Peyton's hand. "My treat," he said.

"Oh no." Zoe reached to retrieve it only to have her hand brush Scott as he turned his back and paid the bill. She glowered at the space between his shoulder blades and then at Peyton, who shrugged and raised his eyebrows above twinkling eyes.

As they walked out, Scott held the door for Zoe. "You shouldn't have done that," she sniped.

"Oh?" Scott replied breezily. "Says who?"

"Says me."

"With all due respect, you don't always get your way, Zoe." His words were soft yet firm. Her gaze traveled from his strong, clean jaw over his nicely sculpted nose to eyes twinkling with a hint of humor.

Zoe expected to feel mutinous. Instead, his bossiness was eerily satisfying.

"Whatever," she snapped, stomping out ahead of him, hearing his soft laughter trailing her. And she didn't miss her son's speculative gaze bounding back and forth between them.

Darn.

chapter five

"Safe isn't living ....
Safe is a cocoon that shuts out the world."
– Seana McGrath

*S*teroid psychosis was what they called it. The name meant little to her. She just heard it batted around when Barth had company. She never had company because she turned her back and slid into her snuggly isolation.

Seana allowed Barth to tuck her into bed after giving her the 2 mg Ativan and 10 mg Ambien. She would have been grateful for the gesture if only she could *feel* gratitude. As it was, she felt nothing. It was like being heavily numbed with Lidocaine. Not a dreamy, silky float. No. She was like a drained, dried-out gourd.

Worse still, she didn't care that she didn't feel. She didn't care about anything. The clock was the closest thing to a friend she now had. Or wanted. Tonight, she had watched the bedside clock until exactly ten o'clock. Not one second sooner nor a breath afterward. It had to be dead on. Something inside Seana demanded precision.

Most of the time.

Sometimes she wavered because she didn't *know* she

demanded precision. It was like her insides were mechanical and at times the timing would alter a bit. But the next day, the precision would have kicked back in. Then, too, sometimes her symptoms would intensify and she would automatically reach for her meds, that is, until Barth locked them up. "For your safety," he insisted.

Actually, she went to bed at eight sharp. Then waited until ten on the dot to summon Barth. "It's time for my medicine," she would say. And he would come to her bed and administer the meds. Then he would read some scripture and have prayer, even as Seana turned her face to the wall.

Sleep would soon overtake her because of the Ambien pill. Barth always explained this to her when she'd grow panicky, worrying that the insomnia would return to attack her. She hated the dark and the feelings it stirred inside her.

She hated the nothingness. Lots and lots of things she hated nowadays.

But the meds kept her from feeling as panicky. She just had to make sure she took them exactly at the appointed time. Those times were eight a.m, twelve noon, six p.m, one half hour before bedtime (her 150 mg Serzone), and ten p.m. Barth explained that the Serzone would help her not be as depressed. She didn't care as long as she could sleep and take everything exactly when she was supposed to.

Even then, because the doctors – she'd seen three separate psychiatrists by now – had changed her meds so often, she continually had to readjust to them.

Tonight, she stared at the window, seeing the full moon hanging low over the mountains. It stirred nothing inside her. Barth lay sleeping beside her. She could hear his deep, even breathing. It didn't bother her too much, the sound. Not like other noises that grated on her nerves lately, like the television, when not on ball games. For some reason, the games didn't bother her. People talking bothered her. So she didn't want them around.

Her eyes began to grow heavy. She remembered seeing Zoe today when she came by to visit. Her daughter's voice, talking,

talking, talking got on Seana's nerves. So did Billie Jean's prattle. Barth seemed to know to keep his voice down, but sometimes he forgot when someone else dropped by. Seana hated to see company come. Why didn't they stay away?

The nothingness inside her hummed at times. It was a bizarre monotone, not unlike the Tibetan monks's drone. It blocked out all other impressions.

She closed her eyes, turned over to face the wall, and curled herself tightly into a fetal knot.

Waves of slumber washed over her, lulling ... then pulling her under.

∼♥∾

Barth scrambled Seana's two eggs, his eye on the kitchen clock. He placed her plate across from his at exactly seven thirty. Sure enough, he heard her feet hit the bedroom floor. She padded barefoot into the kitchen and went immediately to the stove where water boiled for her decaf coffee. He sat and watched her measure instant grains into a coffee cup and fill it one-half full.

No more. No less. He would have found some dark humor in it had it not all seemed so sad to him just then. Her love for perked coffee had left with her. Like so many other things.

Endless losses.

She sat on the stool opposite him and slowly ate her eggs and sipped her coffee. Silent. When finished, like an apparition, she slid from the stool and went straight to the sofa and curled up facing the TV. She flipped on the sports channel.

"Would you turn on the overhead lights, Barth?" she asked.

Barth sighed and went to flip on the lights. Seana liked every light in the den blazing day and night. He cleaned away the dishes, packed them in the dishwasher, and wiped down the counters. He then made their bed and picked up dirty clothes.

"Seana?" he called. "I need to wash that shirt you're wearing."

He got no reply. He gritted his teeth, feeling aggravated

at having to go through the same song and dance every day of his life. She'd not moved. "Please take off that shirt, Seana. I'm doing a load of clothes."

She rolled upright, stripped off the shirt, and put the one on he held out to her. "Actually you need to take a shower first. You know?" He started out of the room, then resolutely turned back and gestured. "Come on. Shower time."

No response.

He tugged her to her feet and ushered her to the shower. "I'm going to watch this time, Seana. I want you to wet yourself down then soap up before I leave."

Scowling furiously, Seana complied. Only when she was fully lathered did Barth leave, closing the door softly behind him.

He heard her call out, "Are you going to be busy at the church office all day?"

"Yes," Barth said. Half truth. Only part. But this is what she wanted to hear.

"Good," he heard her mutter as she got out of the shower stall. "You won't be bothering me."

"Hi, Zoe! Joanie!" Billie Jean called out to Joanie's back shampoo area. "How's it going, you two?"

"Great! Any better I'd be flying, any worse I'd be dying," Joanie called to her while scrubbing Zoe's dark mane. "How're you doin', Billie Jean? Haven't heard an update lately."

Billie Jean sauntered to the back and slid into a vacant styling chair. "Barth recently found out about this bone cancer alternative treatment called Cesium Chloride."

"Huh. Never heard of that one." Joanie began vigorously rinsing Zoe's hair.

"Me either. But I read about it and it's one of the very, very few alternative treatments actually strong enough to deal with bone cancer." She nodded. "Yep. Barth dug this one out and contacted the vendor who oversees the treatment. It's too potent to not have expert support and guidance. Barth's real careful about that kind of thing, dontcha know?"

"He's a smart guy," Joanie agreed, towel-drying Zoe's long hair and guiding her to her work station. Billie Jean trailed behind them and plopped into another nearby styling chair.

"Whatcha getting today, Zoe?" Billie Jean asked.

"Just a trim."

"Don't know how you manage that long hair like you do." Billie Jean shook her head, watching curiously as Joanie combed out the hair and sectioned it off to cut.

"Her hair's very manageable, is why," Joanie commented as she began to separate, pin up, and comb down small segments to snip. "Has lots of body."

"Huh. Mine's like a Cripple Creek bushy pine." Billie Jean laughed at her own reflection.

"It's nice curls," Joanie insisted. "Just need to keep it shaped is all."

"That's what I'm here for."

"How's Mom doing today?" Zoe asked.

"Hey. She's having a fairly good day. By that I mean she's keeping quiet and watching the Braves."

Billie Jean saw Zoe's features fall. "No improvement at all," Zoe said flatly.

"Well … I wouldn't say that." How she wished she could encourage Zoe. But truth be known, Seana was getting worse. "She's holding her own," she partly lied.

"I'm sorry, Billie Jean," Zoe's eyes softened. "I haven't called lately to touch bases with you on your own health problems. So, the new treatment is helping you? What was its name again?"

"Cesium Chloride."

She frowned. "Are you sure it's safe? I mean, if it's so potent, wouldn't there be risks?"

"Huh. Barth and I checked it out completely. But I'd have gone on Barth's recommendation alone. Thing is, treating bone cancer is a long, drawn-out process. Have to have patience because it takes the bones so long to heal. Yep. I'd trust Barth with my life."

"That's a mouth full," Zoe said blandly. "What if the treatment isn't —"

"Look," Billie Jean leaned forward, elbows planted on knees, her dug-in stance. "Zoe, I'm not about to do anything stupid. Cesium Chloride's cure rate is high. It's been at the forefront of alternative treatments for over three decades. That's a long testing period. And as I said, the recommended vendor, Larry of Essense of Life, has the needed expertise to oversee my treatment." She shrugged and relaxed back into the chair. "Barth encouraged me to try it. It can't hurt to take extra precautions, doncha know?"

Billie Jean watched Zoe's eyes flatten. "You're very trusting. Think that's wise?"

"Zoe!" Joanie scolded. "Billie Jean doesn't need to hear this. She has to think positive thoughts, have faith and confidence."

"You're right," Zoe conceded, visibly flustered at the reprimand. As Joanie began to use a gigantic hairbrush to blow her hair, she sighed deeply. "I'm sorry, honey. I'm just not as trusting as most folks are. It's not the treatment I don't trust, actually. I —" She clamped her lips together and gave a tight smile. "Just blow it off, will you, Billie Jean? I'm sure everything's gonna work out fine with the treatment. In fact, I know it will."

"Sure thing." Billie Jean got up and strolled to the front window, more than a little perplexed. She peered out into the sunny, wintry day. And she wondered why Barth's name still evoked such anger in Zoe.

✌✎

"I think you need a break from all this, Barth," Zoe said. She'd dropped by after she left Joanie's salon. She'd felt a rush of guilt after talking with Billie Jean. Yep. She had. Major self-reproach issues. Because, regardless of her suspicions about Barth's pre-Paradise Springs days, Barth had done a splendid job of caring for her mother.

That was an indisputable fact. Oh how she'd tried to find fault with him but God help her, she'd not dug up one morsel of anything pointing an accusing finger at his ethics or character.

In spite of her efforts and subtle – and also not so subtle – incriminations, he'd remained unswervingly devoted to Seana's care.

A daggum better job than she could have done. One day with her mother's cantankerousness would have had her scrambling into a cave and pulling it in behind her. Peyton was much more patient. Zoe wished again that she had a sweeter, milder nature.

Barth motioned for her to bring her coffee from the bar into the den, where Seana lay curled up on the sofa with the incessant ball game racket in the background. "Turn it down, please, Seana," he asked politely.

Amazingly, she complied. Sometimes she surprised Zoe. But Zoe quickly realized that if she was waiting for her mother to suddenly be *there* to really see and hear her daughter, Zoe was in for a brutal crash landing.

So, she took a deep, calming breath and gazed into Barth's soft brown eyes. They struck her as trusting. Kind. She saw not a flicker of guile behind those thick lenses, which nudged something like guilt loose inside her. "What do you mean, Zoe?" he asked, curious.

She burrowed deeper into the easy chair and crossed her stylish stiletto booted legs. "I mean that you've handled Mom too long by yourself. I'm ashamed that I haven't stepped forward sooner."

Barth shrugged and smiled awkwardly. "I don't mind caring for Seana."

"I know you don't," she said quickly. Then she wet her lips nervously. This was something she needed to do. It wouldn't be easy, but it was the right thing to do, so she hurried on before she changed her mind. "But you've had her 24/7 for the past four years. I see your fatigue, Barth." She looked down at her hands folded tensely in her lap. "And I feel embarrassed to have allowed it. So I want to start relieving you on weekends. I'll take her for at least two weekends out of the month and I believe Tim and Sherry will be willing to take her the other two. That should help you get some – relief. Some down time, just for yourself."

Barth peered intently at her, as though he hadn't heard her right. "Wow," he said softly. "I wasn't expecting that." Then he looked apologetic and held out an entreating hand. "Oh, please don't feel offended. I didn't mean that like it sounded."

Zoe couldn't suppress a grin. "No offense taken. I haven't been the nicest to you."

Barth shrugged limply and shook his head, looking awkward, uncertain. "I'm sorry, Zoe. Of course, I appreciate your offer but –"

"No buts." She stood decisively, collected her purse, and slid into a long leather coat that matched her black boots and gloves. "We'll begin next weekend. Okay?" Her direct gaze defied any objection.

"If you're sure, Zoe." Barth shrugged again, looking somewhat stunned. "I don't know what to say. Except – that's very generous of you."

Zoe laughed then, a loud boisterous burst of sound. "Generous? Maybe *insane*." She shook her dark head while her pointer finger drew air circles near her temple. "I'll no doubt later regret it but –"

Barth's laughter joined hers. "Just call when you have your fill. Between Billie Jean and me, we can relieve you guys."

"Huh." Zoe shot over her shoulder as she left. "Keep your phone charged. I might take you up on that."

❧❧

The next Saturday morning came quickly. Too quickly, Zoe decided when she went to pick up her mother. Fortunately, Peyton went along to help. He was excited. Zoe felt terrible that she did not look forward to this exclusive time with her mother.

But then – her mother wasn't exactly the kind of guest one celebrated these days. Zoe rolled her eyes at *that* thought, feeling truly despicable.

Seana already had her little overnight bag packed. Zoe's brow furrowed when she examined its contents. That blasted striped shirt lay right on top, like blinking yellow and green neon, and underneath it were the near tattered stretchy black slacks. All clean, thanks to Barth. Her regard for Barth was rising by the moment.

Only reason her mother wasn't wearing the overnighter contents was because she was still in pajamas. Loose, stretchy ones at that. Seana could not abide anything that fit, to Zoe's consternation. She knew that – with Peyton having to help out at the dance studio that night – she would have to take her mother to Happy Feet Dance Studio with her for the Saturday night party. She simply had to find her something decent to wear.

"Just a minute, Mom," she said as Seana headed back to the sofa. "I'll be right with you."

She backtracked to the bedroom and scrounged in the closet and dresser drawers until she found a red knit outfit that had seen better days. It had fit Seana beautifully in former days. Maybe, she eyed it skeptically, just maybe it would magically fit and transform her mother into a presentable human being for one night. She hated seeing her mother dressed so – shabbily. Did she dare to hope?

Sure she could. She shoved the items into the bag and headed for the den, where she had to coax Seana from the sofa again. "I don't want to go," her mother insisted.

"Sorry about that. But I must insist." Zoe began to tug her to her feet and into the mules she wore around the house.

"Come on, Nana," Peyton coaxed gently, sliding his long arm around her frail shoulders, and somehow she seemed to hear something in his voice that lulled her momentarily, at least until they accomplished seating her in the car's back seat.

Brow wrinkled, Barth stood in the doorway, watching them leave. He waved and blew Seana kisses as they drove off.

Seana ignored his wave and blown kisses.

Zoe felt an unexpected stab of pity for him.

In the rearview mirror, she spotted Barth watching them until they were out of sight.

❧

"But Mom, I thought you loved pimento cheese sandwiches." Zoe felt like pulling her hair out by its roots and it was only eleven o'clock a.m. She'd gotten through settling her onto a new sofa. The new surroundings raised Seana's wariness. Zoe'd had to buy a danged wall clock for her mom to watch. Oh, Barth and Billie Jean had educated her all week long.

Now, she was thankful.

"That's not my pimento cheese," Seana grumped and tightly folded her arms across her bony chest. She had eventually dug in to Zoe's sofa and now only sat up in anticipation of her lunch.

A lunch she now refused.

"Then why didn't we bring yours?" Zoe asked, exasperated.

Seana didn't respond. Instead she absently watched the ball game on the television screen.

"I know what's wrong, Mom," Peyton said from a nearby overstuffed easy chair, where he hooked an ankle over his knee and watched the action. "Joanie makes her this huge bowl of pimento cheese every week. That's what she eats all the time. Not this store-bought kind."

"Huh." Zoe slid into a matching chair and took a long, ragged breath, already weary with the tug of war. Just then the doorbell pealed. She rushed to the door, thankful for a moment's reprieve from the dismal drama that was now hers.

Barth stood on her porch, a pained, apologetic look on his face.

"Hi." Barth gave her a lopsided grin. "I forgot to give you this. Sorry, Zoe, with so much to remember to send, I simply overlooked it."

He held out the big Tupperware container of pimento cheese.

"Thank the good Lord," she breathed passionately, seizing the bowl. "You are the hero of the day."

His dimples flashed as he turned to go. "I figured as much."

అ్౮

That evening, Zoe haggled her way through forcing her mother to dress in the red knit two piece outfit. She'd even thought to throw in a red pair of Seana's dozens of sharp casual shoes. The low-heeled shoes fit, though by her mother's pained reaction, you'd have thought Zoe was performing Chinese torture just sliding them on.

The red skirt and sweater, ah, that was another adventure entirely. By the time Zoe had struggled to pull them on her, Seana was squirming like a worm in a red, hot BBQ pit. "Too tight," she groaned, pulling with all her might at the stretchy material.

"Mom!" Zoe shrieked. "It's hanging on you like a tent! Stop. Stop stretching it. You're gonna ruin it for sure."

Which did nothing to ease Seana's hysteria. Zoe realized that the phobia was real. She watched helplessly as her mother fell more and more victim to despair and agony while experiencing the "fitted" garments.

When her mother nearly collapsed with fatigue from resisting and wrestling the clothing, Zoe peered at Peyton, who appeared just as traumatized as she felt. "Mom?"

Zoe recognized his appeal for mercy. For his Nana. Zoe caved. "Okay, Mom. C'mon." She led her to the bedroom and disrobed her. The only other outfit was the dreaded yellow-and-green-striped shirt. It would have to do.

Seana calmed as Zoe helped tug on the familiar garments. Zoe had, on impulse, brought along her mom's regular black slippers that she wore when she went out to eat. "Okay, Mama," she said softly, picking the disheveled hair out and placing it carefully into a semblance of order. "You look fine."

"Doesn't she?" Zoe asked Peyton as they came through the den to collect coats and scarves. At his questioning look, she repeated. "Mom looks fine, doesn't she?" Lordy but she needed a little emotional reinforcement at that precise moment.

Peyton looked his Nana over from head to toe, then grinned. Zoe noticed it was genuine and warm. "Yeh, Nana. You look beautiful."

And suddenly, Zoe saw her mother as Peyton saw her. She *was* beautiful. Not classically like she once was. But, by cracky, she was lovely. Suddenly, Zoe wasn't embarrassed by the tacky clothes. The woman in them was her *mother*.

And she was proud of that fact.

❧

Zoe was surprised to see Barth already at Happy Feet Dance Studio, sitting outside in his car when they arrived. "What're you doing here?" she asked curiously as she unlocked the entrance door and turned on the lights. "I thought you'd be chilling out when you had a chance."

"Oh, I don't know." Barth shrugged, hands shoved in his slacks's pockets. "Just lonesome, I guess. Miss my girl." His eyes rested on Seana, and Zoe could see unmistakable adoration behind those darned lenses. Why didn't he get contacts?

Other dance folks began filtering in within minutes, and Peyton manned the stereo system, cranking up a lively icebreaker tune, a California Hustle rhythm that got the activity in full swing.

Barth sat with Seana, whose crossed arms and fierce frown kept most faint hearted at bay. Chelsea, decked out in some of her more glitzy Glad Rags finery for this occasion, approached. "Hi, Seana," she said, not expecting any response. "Wish you'd try a little harder to be friendly." She shrugged and sighed her disappointment. "I sure do miss your beautiful smile."

"Me, too," Barth murmured, smiling sadly at Chelsea.

"Hey, good looking, how about dancing this one with me? It's a bit more sedate."

Barth looked uncertainly at Seana, who ignored the two of them with a vengeance. "I don't know –"

"Oh, she should be okay for three minutes, don't you think?" She, too, looked uncertain by now.

"Go on, you two." Billie Jean appeared, dressed up for once in a navy-blue, classy jumpsuit, with curls piled stylishly atop her head. And Zoe noted her thinness. Not gaunt. Just fashionably slender.

When Barth hesitated, Billie Jean insisted. "I'll sit with Seana. Go on, Barth, you always enjoyed the line dancing."

So Barth and Chelsea joined in the Electric Slide line dance already in progress on the expansive floor. Zoe watched them surreptitiously as she moved through the four wall line dance, set to Marcia Griffith's song, *Electric Boogie*. The steps, created by the famous choreographer, Ric Silver, could be done to any 4/4 song, but this particular Griffith version was one of the group's favorites.

Peyton danced to Zoe's right, as boneless and smooth as an eel in water. To his right was Scott Burns, every bit as graceful as Peyton, truth be known, in his cream slacks and black silk shirt. She'd not known until now that sports could shape a man into a buffed Fred Astaire. The man had even invested in some black dance slippers. She rolled her eyes in the opposite direction and blew away the rush of warmth she was beginning to feel when he was nearby.

Yeh. She could feel the vibes.

Darn it all.

Zoe had enough problems without adding relationship woes to them. She'd been there, done that. She dropped out on the lengthy number, ready to fly away to safer territory. She looked for her mother in the place she'd left her.

The chair was empty.

And Barth was still line dancing up a storm with Chelsea, laughing and not only keeping up but nailing each brush, clap, and pivot. She began searching the entire room, each nook and cranny. No Mom.

Then she spotted Billie Jean standing at the far office door, grinning and dancing in place, watching the entertainment that comes from synchronized teamwork in line dancing. She rushed over.

"Have you seen Mom?" Zoe struggled to reign in her fears.

"Sure." Billie Jean jerked her head back toward the inner office. "She's in there."

Zoe brushed past her and into her private quarters. There on her sofa lay Seana, curled into a tight ball, watching a wall clock. Zoe silently clicked off a few choice phrases between clenched teeth. "Mom, couldn't you spend just one hour doing something – alive?"

"I don't want to go in there," was the recalcitrant reply. "I'm tired."

"Mama, you *stay* tired if lying on a sofa is any indication. Please … get up and come back to the party. You used to not only enjoy watching, you enjoyed kicking up your heels, too. Never a better line dancer than you and …" Her voice choked off as she watched the dull eyes stare unseeing at her. They looked right through her.

Heaven help her but she missed her mother. The loss struck her like a sharp spear.

Then, the fizzle went out of her. Poof. Defeat smacked her broadside.

For this round.

"Okay. I'll turn on this TV."

"The ball game."

"Yeh, I know. There, the Braves." She sighed and brushed

her hands together. "Just lie here and I'll come get you when the party's over. Okay?"

"Okay."

"Want me to help guard her?" Billie Jean asked when Zoe passed her on her way back to the dance area.

"Sure. Thanks." Zoe stopped and gave her a hug, feeling a deep affection for her selfless cousin. Funny. She slowly shook her raven head of rhinestone-tethered hair. She'd been oozing sentimental feelings lately that she'd not felt in many, many years. Not since she was a child, actually.

When her dad was alive and the family was all together, safe … secure.

Zoe passed the proficient dancers whose exuberance smote her in some profound way that highlighted her loneliness. Loneliness? Her? Zoe, who could out-party, out-dance, out-BS the world?

Loneliness? Crap!

She was astounded when tears began to burn behind her eyes and grief pushed up … up. Next thing she knew her cheeks felt wet, even as she forced her lips into a tight smile. She reached the stereo cabinet area and snatched a Kleenex to dab away the dampness.

"What's wrong, Zoe?"

She looked up into Scott Burns's face and saw such concern that the tears began to flow more freely. "Nothing. Just hay fever."

"In February?" The words were soft. Non-judgmental. And they were her undoing.

"Let's step outside," she muttered and snatched her cape on the way out. "I'm sorry." She snuffled and shrugged. "Just a lot going on, you know?"

"Yeh." His gaze seemed to x-ray and see into her very soul, which only made the tears reappear.

Zoe tried in vain to stem the flow with the shredding Kleenex. Scott whipped out a clean, starched handkerchief and pressed it into her hand. "Here."

"I – I'm so embarrassed. Blubbering like an idiot." She blew her nose and looked balefully at Scott. "I'll take this and launder it for you. That was crappy."

He chuckled. "Not at all. But you can take it with you so I'll have an excuse to come by and pick it up."

Zoe cut her teary eyes at him in comic reprimand. "I didn't take you for a manipulator."

"Oh." His finger gently brushed a tear from her cheek and then began to trace her bottom lip. "I might surprise you."

Zoe felt his gentle touch all the way out her fingers and toes. She narrowed her gaze on his strong, even features and focused on eyes the color of metallic silver, almost blue but not quite. More a gray. They were steady, direct, and consuming beneath his butch-cropped brown hair.

Zoe dragged in a deep, ragged breath and looked away, willing her skittering pulse to settle down. "I'm feeling better," she said briskly. "I'd better go check on Mom and then get the next line dance started."

He nodded slowly. Confidence shone like a halo around him, creeping her out.

Lordy.

Zoe, 'ol girl, get yourself out of this.

Survival kicked in.

She pivoted and strode purposefully back inside, and when Billie Jean gave her a thumbs up on Seana's whereabouts, she cranked up Tim McGraw's "I Love It" and thrust herself into the line dance formation and danced as if her very life depended on it.

That vibe hit her. Full force. Her breath nearly left her as she looked around.

Scott now danced step for step, elbow to elbow with her, smiling down at her like the Devil himself.

❧

Peyton and Zoe managed to get Seana to the exit. It was

ten-thirty. She'd taken her medicine on time, and now she was getting groggy. Barth lingered and helped them get her into the car's back seat. "I'll follow you," he said.

Zoe shook her head. "There's no –"

"I insist."

She threw her hands in the air. "Okay. Okay! But you're not getting any rest, Barth. That's the whole idea of my keeping Mom, you know?"

Silently, Barth got in his car and drove off. Zoe felt like a shrew having chastised him like that. She closed her eyes tightly and took a couple of deep breaths, then climbed into her car.

"Mom? Why did you act that way with Barth?" Peyton asked softly.

"Because I'm a class A–"

"Don't say that, Mom." He reached over to touch her tense arm. "I just hate to see you try to – fix everything that you can't fix. You know?"

"No," Zoe said, blinking back tears. "I don't know. Tell me."

"Well, Barth's just trying to help us get used to working with Nana. Just a temporary thing, you know? She's not always easy to handle, and he's trying to spare us too much hassle. Anyway." He shrugged. "That's what I think."

Zoe was silent for long moments as they drove home, watching landmarks along the way: Chelsea's Glad Rags Dress Shop, and directly across, Joanie's Homecombing Queen's Hair Styling Salon, Fred's Grocery and Delicatessen, their brick church on the corner.

"What about me? What do you think I chewed him out about?" Suddenly, she wanted to know. Because honestly? She couldn't for the life of her figure out who she was anymore.

"I think you were just trying to help Barth."

"But I didn't do it very nicely, did I?"

"Well ... not really. But I think he understands."

Zoe huffed a dry laugh. "How can he when even I don't understand?" They reached the historical section of the little town.

Soon, their white, two-story dwelling, a duplex actually, appeared in her headlights, and as always, she felt an enormous rush of gratitude to her parents. This property had been bequeathed to her at her father's death. The adjoining, roomy apartment was an added blessing. The rent went a long way in supplementing her salary. Right now, it was empty, just when she needed that extra income.

Barth's car came to a smooth rest behind hers. He quickly helped Peyton guide Seana inside and upstairs to the nice guest bedroom, where he assisted her into her floppy pajamas and tucked her in.

Zoe was drinking a cup of coffee when he came down into her cozy, classic kitchen. "Coffee?" she asked.

"Thanks, but I think I'll go turn in. I think she'll be okay now. The meds are kicking in. If you need me, just call." He headed for the door.

"Barth?"

He turned and looked questioningly at her, hand on doorknob. "Yes?"

"Don't worry about her. I can take care of her."

He smiled and Zoe saw the extreme weariness in his face. "I know."

"Go get some rest."

"Thanks."

She watched him leave, and despite her still rampant misgivings, she felt sorry for the man.

But pity did not equate trust.

She'd gotten Scott to push his police buddy to do another check on the murder case in Canada. Still no arrest.

That didn't set well with her.

❧❧

The next week, something profound happened.

There was little omen. No headlines when it happened.

One morning, Seana woke up with a clear mind. "I feel better," she told Barth upon awakening.

Cautiously, Barth watched her get up and go to the kitchen and begin to prepare her breakfast. An omelet. Excitement began to rise. But he kept pushing it down, watching. This wasn't supposed to happen.

He called their current physician and described what was happening.

Dr. Caston told him, "It's temporary, Mr. McGrath. It won't last. Just enjoy it while you can. And whatever you do, continue her on her meds."

Heart plunging, Barth rang off and returned to watch Seana go about doing normal things, even smiling at him when she caught him following her around.

As the day wore on, he decided to do what the doctor said. Enjoy this time. He wouldn't let himself go beyond that.

"What's today?" Seana asked at one point.

"Saturday."

"I want to go to church tomorrow," she stated as she dried off from her shower.

"That's great, honey," he hugged her and was eternally grateful she didn't shrink from him. But still, she pulled out the darned old green- and yellow-striped shirt and black slacks.

Barth decided to surprise her.

So he paid a visit to Glad Rags Dress Shop.

"Chelsea, I want to buy some church clothes for Seana. She's actually wanting to attend services." Barth knew his pride was splashing over but he didn't care. He went on to explain the temporary improvement.

"Really?" Chelsea clasped her many gold-ringed fingers together with glee. "Oh, Barth! I'm so tickled." She hugged him and then dashed off to pull some pretty outfits off the hangers. She was careful that her choices not be too fitted, for fear Seana might backslide into her recalcitrance.

Barth didn't seem to harbor such fears. By now, he'd convinced himself that this was the answer to all his prayers. God wouldn't tease him like this, would he? He didn't know but it was all he could do to stand still while Chelsea packaged the clothing. After he retrieved them, he stopped at the door, dashed back, and kissed Chelsea's blushing cheek. His exit was quicksilvery.

He burst into Joanie's salon and startled her by tossing the packages down and grabbing her for a bear hug. "These clothes are for Seana. She's going to church tomorrow. And miracle of miracles, she *wants* to."

Joanie, between customers, slapped both hands to cheeks and fought back tears, slowly shaking her head in disbelief. Barth snatched up the packages he'd dropped and dashed out the door.

He'd called Zoe this morning when Seana had awakened acting differently. Like she was more *there*. Zoe and Peyton were there at their door minutes later. The visit was tearful and exceedingly affectionate.

Zoe had even hugged Barth, such was her exuberance to have her mother back. Peyton, well, he softly, tentatively played Seana's piano favorites for a short period of time. Barth could tell that they all tread softly for fear they might loose the terrible affliction upon Seana once more. The next morning, Seana dressed herself in one of the lovely outfits from Chelsea's shop. She seemed pleased with the way the blue knit dress fit. She was as willowy as a fashion model, which wasn't too bad, Barth quickly decided. Her face ... well, her face with *her* behind those eyes, was so beautiful he could hardly hold back the tears.

But he did as he proudly escorted her to her regular seat – her preference today – three pews back from the front. Billie Jean sat with her on one side, and Ashley, grinning like roadkill, flanked the other. She scooted over for her parents to join them.

Excitement over Seana's presence rippled over the gathering. Necks craned and whispers rode the air, even during the three hymns and preliminaries. They only lulled when Barth arose from his high-backed pulpit chair, opposite the platform from Pastor Keith's, and moved to the center podium facing the choir. There he opened his music.

Accompanied by Peyton at the piano, Barth conducted the choir in a fitting Bill Gaither arrangement of "He Touched Me." In the choir, Zoe sang with tears flowing, as did Chelsea and Joanie, sister altos. Behind Zoe, in the fourth baritone section, grocer Fred Johnston and Scott Burns, too, were seen reaching up to swipe moisture from their faces. At the end of the number, when contemplative silence settled, loud snuffling erupted throughout the congregation.

Pastor Keith looked somewhat red-eyed when he arose from his pulpit chair to address the congregation. "Welcome back, Seana. We have a great God," he said, his voice cracking. He vigorously cleared his throat and visibly bucked up.

"Now let us open our Bibles and read together today's text."

⁂

"What a great week," Barth slid his arms around Seana as she piddled around in her kitchen. He went at it very gently, assessing her, still testing the waters. He could tell that even though she claimed to feel better, she was still fragile. Most of her gestures were slow, hesitant.

She opened the cabinets, exploring subtle changes that had simply evolved from someone else being in charge. She was still quiet, almost pensive. Not her former exuberant self yet.

Yet.

His mind froze there.

Still ....

"I love you, sweetheart," he murmured, nuzzling her clean hair. Yes, she'd begun tending more to her hygiene. She smelled clean. What a miracle.

Seana turned in his arms and embraced him. "I love you, too, Barth. I'm sorry for all –"

"No." He pressed a fingertip to her lips. "None of that. You've been sick. You couldn't help it."

She gazed into his eyes, a muddle of expressions flickering

in the blue depths. Swirling. Not settling on any one thing in particular.

"Trust me." He kissed her then, and she sank against him. Surrendered. Soft and pliable. Her mouth responding to his. Barth froze for a second, then deepened the kiss.

Was he in Heaven?

When she took his hand and allowed him to tug her to the bedroom, he *knew* he was in Heaven.

He rolled his eyes heavenward.

Please, Lord. Don't let me wake up.

❧ ❧

Ashley's sixteenth birthday was a joyful family occasion. She was their Thanksgiving child, born one day before the holiday so it was easy to track. Seana wanted to cook a special dinner party, but the family refused to allow it.

"Mom, you don't need to do all that work," take-charge Zoe had insisted the week before as they ate at the Mater and Onion's Sunday Buffet.

"Billie Jean, Sherry, and I will take care of the food. Too, Fred's Deli is a wonderful source of fare for birthday parties, doncha know?"

"That's right, Seana," Billie Jean spoke around a mouth full of crispy fried chicken. "You just get your strength back."

Seana sighed and shrugged. "Okay." She bit into a drumstick and thought how it wasn't so bad after all. She could taste the nuances of buttermilk, wheat, a touch of salt, pepper, garlic, and rosemary, Chief West's special concoction.

"Not bad," she declared and wondered why the simple act of eating a drumstick sent everyone at the table into ecstasy. Lots of what she did was drawing those sappy reactions nowadays.

She enjoyed the affection but the attention –

Seana still didn't embrace intrusiveness. Didn't know why. She just didn't. But Barth reassured her she was on the mend.

She trusted Barth's judgment. He also insisted she remain on her meds.

The doctors's reactions were less than enthusiastic. She knew that Barth soft-pedaled most of their comments past her. Why didn't they celebrate her progress? It puzzled her.

"Seana?" Pastor Keith spoke to her from across the table. He and Louanne had joined them today after service. They tended to rotate their table visitation amongst members so as not to contribute to any predisposition toward jealousy.

"Seana?" he repeated.

Seana blinked. She'd drifted off somewhere. "Huh?"

"I hope you can convince Zoe to help chaperone the upcoming Round-Up Youth Weekend."

Seana nodded. "She's bossy."

"I heard that, Mama!" Zoe wailed from the other end of the long table. Today the joined tables seated twelve.

"You didn't hear me!" Seana snapped and reaped an explosion of laughter.

"I hear everything," Zoe called back, her eyes twinkling.

"She's not lying," Peyton joined in, rolling his eyes at her.

"How about it, Zoe?" Pastor ventured. "You'll make an excellent chaperone for the Round-Up event. Why not give it a go?"

"Aw, she'll do it," Seana muttered and took another bite of her fried chicken.

Zoe gazed at her mother, her eyes growing moist, making Seana feel that keen "being analyzed" sensation again. For some reason, her daughter was getting all teared up. Go figure.

≈୨ ৎ≈

"Okay," Zoe said and shrugged, trying to tether her emotions into submission. Her mother's lucidity and mere presence awed and choked her up. "Oh, am I the only one being corralled for this?"

"Nope," Scott Burns spoke up from the seat beside her. "I'm already lassoed."

Zoe's face fell. "Oh." The word came out flat.

Darn it! Why hadn't she asked earlier? She was trapped.

Scott burst into laughter then murmured quietly for Zoe's ears alone, "Oh? Define that for me, please? 'Oh, I'm surprised' Or 'Oh, as in ouch?'"

Zoe's mouth twisted into a grimaced smile. "Y' know, Scott. I really don't know. But I promised and I always keep my promises. So what does it matter?" She speared a Brussels sprout from her plate, popped it in her mouth, and viciously chewed it.

Scott watched with amusement and slid Peyton a sly wink.

Zoe saw it all. He thought she didn't but she did. She also saw Peyton's subtle thumbs up.

Zoe had her work cut out for her deflecting this blatant conspiracy.

And deflect it she must. Because she knew something that they didn't. She was bad news. Men liked her at first but as time passed, the interest waned. Any experience she'd had with the opposite sex had ended up the same way.

They walked.

She, Zoe, could not hold a man's love.

Nope. She'd not set herself up for that particular heartbreak.

Never again.

"Let's go, Peyton," she said, standing and gathering her purse and coat. This time, she snatched the check from the table before Scott had the chance to sabotage it.

Seana dressed in a turquoise velour jumpsuit, one of her new outfits, for Ashley's party thrown at the dance studio. Of course, it was more intimate, with only family and a few close friends attending. It was loose enough that she felt comfortable. She finished her makeup and touched up her hair, newly done by Joanie just that morning.

"I'll have the prettiest girl there," Barth pronounced as he drove them there.

"You're not so bad, yourself," she said, looking at passing wintry Paradise Springs's landscapes.

Barth chuckled. "Say that again."

She swiveled her neck and looked at him. "Why?"

"Because it's been so long since I've heard you say that kind of thing."

Seana sighed and looked again at the evolving scenery, and beyond at the blue mountain range. It was cold up here in the foothills today. Mornings displayed frost-crusted grass and leaves. "I know it's been bad."

"Ahh, honey." Barth immediately backtracked. "No, no. I didn't mean it that way. Please don't take it as criticism. Please?" He peered at her, obviously upset with himself and needing forgiveness.

"I'm not angry," she said. "It's okay. I know it's been tough."

Barth reached to take her hand, thankful she didn't snatch it away. "No tougher than for you, darling. Let's not look back, huh?"

She smiled at him and squeezed his hand. "Okay."

She was amazed to see tears shimmer behind his glasses. "It's like a dream, Seana," he murmured huskily. "A beautiful, impossible dream."

Seana unexpectedly pressed a kiss into his palm. "Not impossible. I'm here."

❦

The party was lovely and fun and magical. Especially for Zoe. Because she had her mother back. But something still hung heavily and darkly above her head. Low enough to smother her at times. Perhaps it was because her mother's case had seemed so hopeless for so long. And Barth had shared with her the doctor's dismal prognosis.

Zoe struggled to keep her expectations realistic. She had to.

But this smothery feeling went beyond her mother's precarious situation.

Perhaps it was because Scott Burns showed up tonight with a gaily wrapped gift for the birthday girl. Peyton rushed to Zoe and quietly confessed to having invited Scott.

"Mom, he's my friend. We hang out together a lot and he genuinely loves our entire family. I hope you don't mind." His appeal was so heart tugging that she found herself smiling and hugging him. What a great guy, her son. She didn't dare try to turn him into a male clone of his odious mom.

The world could handle only one of her, thank you very much.

"Of course not, Peyton. I'm fine with it," she lied.

Then she'd busied herself to tune out the butterflies that flapped away inside her every time Scott ventured near. As if reading her mind, he'd seemed to steer clear of her so far.

"Hey, Aunt Zoe," Ashley called from her place of honor at the head of a special table set up for her and her chosen ones. Nana, of course, got to sit next to her and was catered to for the entire event. "How about putting on that KC and The Sunshine Band number for a line dance?"

"No," Peyton called, headed for the stereo. "'Boot Scootin' Boogie's' better!"

Ashley slapped hands on hips, stuck out her chin, and boldly enunciated, "Hey, Peyton! It's *my birthday* and I get to do what I want. Right?" Peyton grinned and winked at her, revealing he'd just been yanking her chain. "Yeh, Ashley. It's your party." He slid the CD into the system and, from the sideline, Zoe laughed at the cousins's little mind games.

"Let's all join in, okay?" Ashley summoned as she arose from her chair.

"Not me." Seana held up a hand.

"That's okay, Nana; you're excused." Ashley swooped down, gave her an exuberant kiss on her cheek and rushed to join the entire party on the dance floor as *That's The Way (I Like It)* blasted from the speakers.

Pride gushed through Zoe as she surveyed the entire family along with Chelsea, Joanie, and Scott moving smoothly and efficiently through the catchy choreography.

Choreography and dance steps she'd taught them.

Zoe easily and bonelessly navigated heel tap, cross and tap, heel tap, one-fourth pivot with slap heel, tap and repeat. Just then she felt the warm rush of air from Scott's movements beside her. They stirred that blasted thing inside her that reacted to those insane vibes that he gave off.

Whew. Powerful they were. One-fourth pivot with slap heel … she now faced his back. His broad shoulders tapered down into narrow hips, long legs and … one-fourth pivot with slap heel. *Good.* He was no longer in her line of vision.

Tap and turn, clap … Zoe didn't know how it happened but it was during the one-fourth pivot that her ankle turned. The mishap catapulted her to the hard floor. It could have been cement, so hard was its impact against her hip. It was there that the pain centered.

The festivities instantly turned to somber concern as she writhed in agony. The music continued as Peyton's white face loomed above her.

"You okay, Mom?" he croaked. She saw Scott's arm slide around his shoulder as he lowered himself to peer into her eyes, his strong features frozen with concern.

She tried to say words to reassure her son but her head, hip, and back screamed with pain like she'd never before experienced. Her words jelled as her teeth clattered and her entire body spasmed with chills. Cold sweat beaded on her face as she moaned incoherent sounds. Dimly, she heard someone calling 911.

Pain … Someone said, "She's gone into shock."

Then all the world turned black.

శ్రీ

Barth took Seana home, downplaying the accident. "Scott and Peyton have it all under control," he told her as he watched her dress for bed. She'd taken her meds as soon as they got home, not too far off schedule. For the time being, Seana had relaxed somewhat from her clock vigilance.

"Do you think she'll be okay?" Seana asked, her features tired, emptied.

"I do, honey," he said reassuringly. "Scott promised to call as soon as they knew anything. He's called in a doctor who works with the football team at Paradise Springs High. He says he's the best. So, don't worry, sweetheart."

Seana nodded and hung her discarded clothes in the closet. "Thanks," she murmured.

"For what?" He slid out of his own clothes and climbed into bed. He opted not to wear pajamas. Too warm-blooded. Seana once told him that he was a natural heater, with all the warmth he gave off during sleep. She'd enjoyed snuggling up to him on cold nights, she said.

He smiled tonight as she slid in beside him, dressed in her usual flannel pajamas and a pair of thick socks to keep her feet warm. She sighed and curled up with her back to him. He spooned against her and had just begun to doze when his cell phone's latest tune, "Moonlight Sonata," startled him awake. He grappled in the dark for it, not wanting to disturb Seana from her deep sleep.

"Yes?"

"Scott here. Doctor Quinn just got through examining Zoe. He found an egg-sized knot on her cranium where she hit her head in the fall. She's also strained her hip flexus muscle, which is a pretty painful injury. So both – the head lick and the hip injury contributed to her blacking out. But thank God, she's stabilized now and moving slowly if painfully."

"Are they going to admit her?"

"No. Doc says she's able to go home, and he's prescribed an amazing kit we use for football injuries that put the guys back on their feet in record time. I know how Zoe needs to be mobile for her line of work, so since I'm familiar with the process, I told Peyton I'd bunk down there with him at their place and see to helping her heal."

"That's mighty generous of you, Scott."

"Glad to help. You get some sleep now, Barth. Everything's under control. Tell Seana Zoe'll be good as new soon. G'night, man."

"G'night, Scott." Barth quietly rang off and returned the phone to the bedside table.

Seana breathed deeply beside him, the evenness revealing her sound state of slumber. He said a prayer of thanks that Zoe was okay. He didn't have to alarm Seana.

Thank God. Somehow, he knew. She was still fragile.

Barth curled up to her back and soon slept.

❧ ❧

"But I don't need help," Zoe protested. "Go home. Peyton can take care of me. He's a smart kid and can —"

"Mom." Peyton held out his hands in entreaty. "I don't know the first thing about the therapy and stuff Scott does. He's trained to do it, doncha know?"

"That's right. I was going to be a physical therapist before I decided to coach, so no arguing."

Zoe, woozy from meds given at the hospital, peered blearily at him from her bed, where he and Peyton had gently placed her after she'd managed to pull off her clothes and pull on a comfortable gown. She'd had to force Scott from the room to do that after he'd insisted that she needed help. So to save face for lying, she'd even refused Peyton's help.

The effort had drawn more cold sweat and nausea, but she'd managed to drag the gown over her head and shoulders. Then gritting her teeth, she'd slid it down to her waist and tucked it down underneath the covers without moving her hips too teeth jarringly much.

And she wondered again how she'd managed to screw

things up so tonight? She'd been doing okay, if not superbly, what with the money woes that seemed to pop up daily. The empty apartment of her duplex posed a serious matter of budget deficit. Plus the drop off of dance enrollments.

Now, this.

"Mom?" Peyton tapped on her door. "Okay to come in?"

"All clear," she croaked.

Peyton's face poked through the doorway, then Scott's, both settling into relief when they saw her surviving the harrowing bedtime preparation efforts.

"You okay?" Peyton pulled up a chair and took her hand, his elbows resting next to her.

She looked at him and smiled groggily. "I'm fine, son."

"I can sleep on the sofa outside your door," he offered.

"You don't have to do that. I've got enough painkiller in me to knock out a football team." Her words slurred. "You get some rest."

"Scott's gonna bunk with me, so –"

She was shaking her head back and forth. "There's no need for Scott to stay. I don't –"

"Listen." Scott lowered gently onto her bedside, leaning over her, eye to eye. "I'm going to stay. It's perfectly respectable, Zoe. Tonight, I'm sleeping on the den sofa because it's closest to your room. That way, I can hear you if you need help and Peyton can get some rest. Peyton will sleep in his room because he knows I'm here for you. I'm qualified to take care of your injuries."

"But –"

"No buts, Zoe. This is what's best for you." He stood, reached to flick off her bedside lamp, and strode to the door. He turned just before he closed it behind him. "Get some rest." His deep voice resonated masculine strength.

The thought stuck in her brain for a moment, then floated off.

"I'll check on you during the night to make sure you're okay, but you won't even know it. So relax."

The door gently clicked shut behind him.

Zoe peered at it, trying to work up some umbrage. The door blurred as she tried again to be angry. Then she forgot what was she was supposed to be mad about.

She sighed and surrendered to the soothing, lulling white waves that pulled, pulled … tugged at her. Slowly, like candles in the night flickering out, everything subsided, ceased to exist … as the last wave pulled her under.

❧❧

"But – where's Peyton? He can help me to the bathroom," Zoe staunchly insisted the next morning as Scott patiently tried to assist her to her feet.

"He's gone to the church to go over Sunday's music with Barth. Remember?" Scott bent again to lift Zoe's arm over his and proceed to ever so gently tug her to her feet.

On the way up, however, sharp pain shot and ricocheted through her upper hip, lower back, thigh front, and in the groin where it joins the pelvis.

"Uhnnn," she groaned and sipped air fiercely through clenched teeth and tight lips.

"Okay?" Scott asked.

Blinking back dizziness, Zoe nodded.

Scott took most of her weight as they made their way to her bathroom, a mere ten feet away, but to Zoe, at that precise moment, it seemed ten miles of littered boulders. Sweat beaded on her forehead. She felt its cold clamminess as Scott eased her down into a small chair at the dressing table.

The elegant bathroom was one of her treasured luxuries in this hundred-plus-year-old historical dwelling. Her father had refurbished and modernized it when he'd decided to bequeath it to her long before his death.

Scott hovered, peering anxiously into her face, which was deathly pale. She knew because she'd glimpsed it in the mirror when they'd entered, before Scott carefully turned her into the softly padded chair. This little nook had once served as a place for conversation and such during her marriage.

Long ago and far away. She sighed weakly.

"Zoe," Scott softly ventured, "I can help –"

"Oh no you don't!" Zoe shook her head and grimaced when it began to spin. "No, Scott. I'm not so addled that I can't take care of this. Now go away like a nice boy."

Scott hesitated, peering into her face.

"Shoo," she managed to hiss warningly.

He watched her worriedly as he backed out of the room, quietly closing the door behind him. She knew he stood just outside the door because his footsteps stopped there.

Darn! What now?

She struggled to work her gown up and her panties down, teeth clenched the entire time, especially when she had to struggle to her feet and slide the undergarment off. Slowly, she lowered herself back down into sitting position but the muscles all sharply protested and she cried out, "Aaiii."

The door sprang open. Scott rushed to her. "This is nonsense, Zoe," he scolded none too gently. "Do you think I haven't seen anybody pee before?"

"Get out," Zoe husked weakly.

"Get over it," Scott's voice was firm. "Just consider me a doctor."

"No."

"I'm not going anywhere till you do what you have to. So get going."

Weakness and pain reduced Zoe to a quivering, addled mess, so she automatically relieved herself as Scott held her wobbly head and shoulders against him.

He pulled off toilet tissue and handed it to her.

"Thanks," she whispered, and since she'd already compromised herself to shredded mortification, she finished the task as he waited. Then he repeated the gentle shift of her weight to him and assisted her back to bed, where he placed her with infinite care and precision. She was amazed that he'd taken the stress off the blasted simmering flexus muscle.

From the pillow, she looked up at him in befuddlement. "How did you do that?"

He lowered himself onto the side of her bed and smiled. The steely gray eyes warmed her and began to thaw her from the icy shock of pain. "I know all about this injury. I've had it myself and know where the pain pressure points are that set it off."

Zoe noted that he was not bragging. Rather, he entered her world to generously gift her with his expertise. But an alarm went off. It was more than expertise that he offered

"Scott." She wet her lips and saw his gaze go there then return to study her now wary features. She knew he saw it, but his gaze never wavered. "I can't be – look, I appreciate you for what you're doing. I really do."

A touch of amusement sparked in Scott's eyes. "But?"

"But, I can't get involved with anybody. Not in a romantic way, at least."

"Have I asked you to?" He smiled then. An openly male, knowing one.

Zoe had the decency to be embarrassed. "I know," she muttered, her gaze sliding to the window where, beyond, tree limbs wore an unseasonable coat of November frost. It could be a cozy scene in her warm bedchamber with this handsome, truly decent male tending to her like she was the danged Queen of Sheba.

But.

She cut her gaze back to him and caught just a glimpse of – hunger? In the next instant it was gone. Perhaps she'd imagined it because he looked as self-possessed as any dignitary she'd ever met.

"Look, Zoe. If you want to be just friends, that's fine with me. Right now, the important thing is to get you up and on your feet. Fast." He hesitated then but seemed to gather determination and said, "Another thing. I want to rent your duplex apartment."

The air whooshed out of her. She peered at him to see if he was serious. "No way, Scott!"

He raised his eyebrows and cut her a severe look of disbelief. "The way I see it is this: you need someone paying rent to make ends meet a little more – comfortably. I need a nice apartment like this. The one I'm living in downtown is crappy. This is a much better place. And ..." He shrugged and looked so logical Zoe wanted to slap him. "And I can be here to help you through this time. You desperately need to work through this therapy."

"No."

"I can guarantee that you'll be on your feet within – two to three weeks."

"No way."

He grinned again, that confidence oozing from his dad blasted hide. "Lease me the apartment so I can be here to help you, and you won't lose any more rent."

"You really think you can get me on my feet and going in two to three weeks?" she asked slowly, hopefully.

"Positive. Now if you'll hang in there with me and do exactly what I tell you to, I'll get you there. And just friendship. I promise. Deal?"

For a long moment Zoe experienced a sharp pang of disappointment that he'd given in so easily. But wasn't that what she wanted? Just friendship?

Zoe looked at his extended hand. Big hand. Beautiful square fingers.

She blinked and reached for it. "Deal."

≪♀≫

What really astonished Zoe was that Scott was true to his word. No hanky-panky attempts were forthcoming. He'd moved into the apartment, with Peyton's help, within forty-eight hours. The initial treatment had been, of course, anti-inflammatory meds along with the RICE technique (Rest, Ice, Compress, Elevate). By the third day, however, things sped up.

"You need to lightly use those muscles, Zoe. Don't overdo it, but a little stretching and strengthening will help reduce swelling and also ensures that new muscle forms properly and scar tissue is broken down and removed."

By now, sitting and moving about slowly and carefully, Zoe raised an eyebrow. "How'd you get so smart, Burns?"

He laughed, sending off something inside Zoe that she pushed away. That darned flapping of butterflies had to go. "Zoe, I grew up on football and soccer fields, baseball lots and everything in between that involved a ball. Of course, injuries are an integral component of contact sports. So I've seen it all. And then when I studied to be a physical therapist, it all came together."

"Why did you end up coaching?"

He shrugged. "I couldn't stay away from the action. As simple as that."

Zoe frowned. "But – you ended up coaching rather than going into professional sports."

"That's because I love the interaction with people. Rather than being one team player, I can train entire teams and maybe, just maybe, influence lives along the way. Does that make sense?" He sat in an easy chair in her bedroom suite, his long, powerful legs crossed at the ankles, buffed arms crossed over his flat abdomen. His face, in animation, slid into olive-complected, fierce-eyed intensity

Untamed glimpses bled through

Why did he have to be so danged masculine?

Zoe blinked and had to jog her memory as to what he'd asked. "Uh, yes. That makes perfect sense, Scott. It really does." She shifted carefully in the matching leather chair that faced Scott's, her bare feet resting on the chair's ottoman.

Zoe loved this comfortable conversational arrangement of heavy dark furniture with splashes of eclectic colors that fit her offbeat taste.

It was *her*, from the brightly colored Indian cushions to the funky souvenir yard sale and antique barn "finds."

Many had tried to squash Zoe into a standard mold, including her parents, but she'd never fit any of them. She felt blessed that her parents loved and accepted her as she was. But – men did not. She'd do well to remember that when her hormones went loping ahead of sound reasoning.

"Hey!" Peyton called as he slammed in the front door and deposited his coat into the foyer closet.

"Hey yourself!" Scott uncrossed his ankles and slid fluidly from lounging to sitting, elbows on knees. "Back here!"

Peyton was all smiles when as he collapsed onto the burgundy-hued leather love seat. The heavy furniture was one of Zoe's few concessions to traditional. The smells and textures reminded her so much of her father's study at home. How she still missed him.

"How'd the music session go?" Zoe asked and shifted again so as to keep moving just a little. Scott said that would help, even when sitting. He'd taught her how to move so as not to stir up the vicious muscle contractions.

"Great. I love the choir's special arrangement."

"Yeh." Scott grinned and gave a thumbs-up. "Can't beat Andrae's music."

"Which one?" Zoe asked.

"'Jesus Is the Answer.' A real groovy arrangement. Syncopation and soul beat."

"Ohhh," Zoe groaned. "I'm gonna have to miss. Not fair."

"No you don't," Scott countered. "You can walk now, and you can stand for brief periods. You have to be careful of course, but ..." He shrugged and spread his hands. "You can do it."

Zoe pulled in a deep breath and exhaled. Was it possible? She'd sure love to get out of these walls for a spell after being laid up, a very foreign experience for her. Amazon superwoman, her ex had teasingly called her. How she hated his take on her. Thanksgiving was next week. Lordy, she couldn't be an invalid during the holidays.

Not to mention she would owe dance lessons that students now missed, what with her being out of commission. *Aargh,* she hated it. Peyton had taken up some of the slack, but he couldn't do it all by himself. She had to quickly get back into the flow of things.

She nodded decisively. "Yeh. You're right. Peyton, how about going over that song to refresh me on it? Can't get up there with egg on my face, messing up all over the place, now can I?"

She carefully navigated her recovering bulk to the den and resettled there in a comfortable overstuffed chair. There, Peyton struck up the music and began singing tenor to Scott's baritone and Zoe's alto. Immediately, Scott switched to lead and the result was – well, it was beautiful.

Zoe couldn't help but grin as she belted out a lusty alto.

∽

Thanksgiving dinner at Zoe's was noisy and festive.

Tim and Sherry had provided the turkey and dressing, while teen Ashley did homemade cranberry sauce. Zoe had coached and worked while sitting at her bar as she and Peyton prepared other traditional dishes to fit the spread. Even Scott pitched in and helped.

They'd all felt it wise not to allow Seana to prematurely jump in to handle holiday preparations, fearing dire consequences.

Seana, Barth noticed, shrank a bit from the boisterous cousin-bantering and male-ribbing racket. Even the women's softer chatter failed to engage her.

Barth held his breath until she finally began to listen to Ashley's soft voice catching her up a bit on what was happening. Ashley was sensitive to her Nana's reactions and somehow knew not to tarry at her side for long.

Space was the word now. Give Nana plenty of it.

The food was wonderful and plentiful, but Barth noticed Seana's expression of – what? Disapproval? Disappointment?

Trepidation hovered.

"What are you thinking?" he asked, ready to face it head on.

Seana looked at him. "I was thinking that I want to cook for the family at Christmas. I want to do it all, like I used to." Her features settled into a melancholy mien.

"But honey – do you think that's wise? You've not been well and it'll be major."

"I can do it," Seana insisted, a stubborn set to her chin. "I want to."

Barth nodded, something inside him flailing in protest. But – how could he say no to something Seana wanted so desperately to do for her family?

In the end, he could not. He'd just flow with it.

What was the worst that could happen?

~᳖৵

Christmas loomed. Seana got out her old recipe stash of traditional holiday favorites. Many were from her late mother's collection as well as from her aunt Kate's, Billie Jean's late mother.

Billie Jean came in while she was pouring over the assortment of choices. "Can I help?" Billie Jean asked, sliding onto a bar stool opposite Seana, watching her curiously. Seana saw the guardedness in their scrutiny. Like Seanna was some daggum lab bug.

"No."

"Hey, there's that dessert Mama used to make when we all got together at Grandma's for Christmas. Party Strawberries, made from coconut, condensed milk, and strawberry Jello. Mmm. Remember?"

"I remember." Seana shifted through some more pages that she had, years ago, recorded in a journal made just for recipes.

"Yeh," Billie Jean sighed. "I really miss those days with family. So many are gone now. Grandma and Grandpa. All our parents. Sheez! Makes me feel sad at times."

Seana didn't reply. She simply didn't think that far any more. She knew that she had stepped one foot out of the fog. She didn't know how. But she felt the thing circling her.

Stalking.

Suddenly restless, she stood and shuffled her choices together and put them in a drawer. Then she slid the recipe journal back onto its proper shelf. She went to the den and turned on the day's ball game and sat down.

Billie Jean joined her. "Who's playing?"

Seana shrugged and drew her bare feet up under her. Why didn't Billie Jean leave?

"Shouldn't you be leaving?" Seana heard herself ask.

"Huh?" Billie Jean looked at her. Then frowned and scratched her head. "You know, I really should." She stood and strode out of the den. "See you later, Seana."

Seana heard her footsteps tromping downstairs.

She breathed a sigh of relief. She was alone again. Now she needed to plan her menu for Christmas. She would have to make her cakes in the next couple of days. And then the fudge. Zoe loved it. Actually, they all did.

The turkey. She went to the freezer, got it out, and put it in the bottom of the fridge to thaw. Dressing she could make ahead and freeze until Christmas Eve. She took out that recipe and began to measure ingredients and stir together.

Two hours later, Barth came in from choir practice. "What?" He looked around the kitchen at all the clutter of pans and batter-crusted bowls.

"I'm cooking. Don't worry, I'll clean it up," she snapped as she squirted dish detergent into the sink and furiously slapped a pan into it and began to scrub.

Barth moved behind her and laid a hand on her shoulder. "Honey? I wasn't criticizing. I'll help."

"No. I'll do it myself." Seana proceeded to attack the dirty pans and counters as though it was all out war. And it was at that moment. Seana knew that she had to do it. It would prove something.

She just didn't know what.

"Honey? Please don't push yourself so."

Seana peered at him, determination rumbling in her like a volcano. "I'm going to do it all by myself."

Barth spouted out a rush of air and threw up his hands. "Okay."

She looked at the kitchen clock on the stove. Ten till ten. "It's time for my medicine. Where is it?"

"On top of the fridge. In the cookie jar."

Barth hid the meds now so she wouldn't take them too early and so he could supervise the dosage. She had taken more than the prescribed dosage at times. He'd stopped locking them up because she now wanted to stay by herself. That meant that she could call him, if he was away, and he could tell her where to look.

Seana took her meds and dressed in her flannel floppy gown. Then slid into bed. Barth spooned up to her back. She had an itch to push him away. But she didn't because she was growing woozy from the combination of Ambien and Xanax.

The thing hovering above her swirled black and angry.

Go away. She squeezed her eyes shut but that didn't diminish the other thing in her brain that was messing with her wiring.

She would not allow it control again. *Stop it!*

Her eyes sprang open and pierced the darkness.

Go away!

❧❧

Seana had risen early today. She'd set the alarm for six. The turkey was ready for the oven.

"Merry Christmas." Barth had halted her to kiss her cheek as she rushed about lining up her cooking tasks as a drill sergeant would his troops. Her two family-favorite cakes, carrot and chocolate, posed beautifully upon crystal cake pedestals, displayed through clear domes. Pies, both pumpkin and sweet potato, nestled together on one counter.

Now hours later, she bit her lip, frowning. Then she rushed to the fridge to take out perfectly squared fudge chunks to place beside the other sweets. Earlier in the afternoon, roasting turkey had mingled with aromas of cornbread dressing and sweet potato soufflé baking in two giant ovens. That had been a necessity in Seana's earlier years, when she did the lion's share of the family's holiday cooking. The double oven had been a miracle worker. She looked at the clock on the stove. Three-ten.

The family would begin arriving any minute, and today, she looked around at all she'd accomplished. One entire counter sprouted delectable desserts, even the Party Strawberries Billie Jean so loved. Another showcased the golden-brown turkey, gravy, mashed potatoes, veggies, and every imaginable trimming.

Seana would have felt a sense of pride if that darned *thing* would stop circling overhead like a reconnaissance plane. Or a black vulture. She rubbed her arms and scowled at the sense of darkness that invaded her brain and kept messing with it. It had stopped for a while. At least had lapsed. She'd hoped – prayed – it would stay gone.

The doorbell pealed. They all poured in, laughing and bubbling with cheer.

"Merry Christmas!" called Peyton and Ashley. They rushed to hug her and she felt a smothery resistance rise up inside her. She managed to endure it because they quickly moved to greet others in the family.

"Merry Christmas, Mom." Zoe hugged her and kissed her cheek. Then she slowly turned and surveyed the food. "Dear Lord, Mama. What a spread!"

She turned, hands pressed together in glee. "You outdid yourself." Then her gaze zoomed in on Seana's face. The smile faded. "You okay, Mama?" she asked quietly.

It irritated Seana. "I'm okay," she snapped and walked away.

"Wow!" Ashley twirled round and round like a ballerina. "Everything looks great, Nana. Can't wait to taste your cooking again!"

Barth came up behind Seana as she stood rigidly at the window, staring unseeing at the mountain range. "It's time to eat," she said loudly, and she felt Barth move away, relieved not to engage.

Barth prayed as they sat around the long dining room table holding hands. Then, because of the volume of dishes, the family formed a buffet line and filled their Christmas china plates and returned to the table.

"Here, Mama," Zoe said firmly. "You sit down. We'll take care of everything else."

Billie Jean joined in pouring iced tea and doing all the things required in noisy Southern family holiday gatherings. Seana was relieved to sit down and go into neutral. Zoe produced a filled plate before her.

Then they were all laughing and talking at once. Seana's ears began to hurt. She ate a few bites and then when she could stand it no longer, left and lay down in the den to watch the clock.

The racket grew quieter after she left the table.

It seemed forever before they joined her in the den and began to give out gifts. When Barth nudged her, she sat up to receive her own with as much politeness as she could muster. Managed to open them, endure the expectant smiles, and mutter "thank you" for each present.

And when the girls all had cleaned the table and put away the food, Seana figured they would all leave.

That didn't happen.

Tired beyond exhaustion, Seana slid down on the sofa, inclining completely, wishing them away, watching the clock. It was six-twenty. Didn't they have any place else to go, for goodness sake? It was Christmas. Couldn't they find other things to do other than bother her?

She saw Barth watching her with a certain worried expression he got at times. She clamped her teeth together and ground them. Six-thirty.

Seana tossed over to face the sofa's back and pulled the blanket up to her neck to ward off the chill and shut out the intrusion. She closed her eyes. But the noise continued for an interminable time.

"Bye, Mama," Zoe whispered and kissed her cheek. "You worked too hard. Please rest."

Each of them said their goodbyes to her. She suffered each one silently.

Finally, the last of them left. And Barth said, "I'm going to the study to read awhile. You need anything?"

"No."

When she heard his study door close quietly, she felt like an elephant lifted from her.

Thank God. Alone at last.

❧☙

Seana's relapse was complete.

"I could have predicted this would happen," said Dr. Castor, irritating Barth to no end. He simply could not accept that this ailment was permanent.

No way.

"Shoot," Billie Jean huffed one evening as Seana curled up on the sofa, her eyes more empty than ever. "She's gonna come outta it, I tell you." She took a slurp of her decaf and poured a bit more cream in it. "Look at what I've come through. I'm well and whole."

Her cheery upbeatness roused Barth out of his angst somewhat. He went to pour more coffee and resettled across the bar from Billie Jean, whom he'd come to admire more and more as time passed. Her initial mistrust of him was long gone, replaced by an incredible camaraderie.

As usual, she seemed to read his mind. "I really missed out, not having a brother. And here God drops you in my life. How neat is that, huh?"

"Pretty neat." Barth smiled then and felt himself relaxing. "And now I've got a sister I never had."

They sat there in peaceful silence for long moments, an

easy, comfortable one during which they sipped their coffee, lost in their own thoughts.

"Thanks, Billie Jean. It helps to be reminded of the goodness in life. Of providential gifts. And yes, I do believe Seana will eventually be healed completely."

Barth later would recall these remarks and wish he'd known what lay ahead. He'd have run for the hills.

chapter six

"Sometimes you need to run away
just to see who will follow you."
– Unknown

Barth continued making meticulous charts of Seana's meds and activities, such as they were. Somewhere along the way, during her third year, Seana had begun walking on a treadmill at intervals. Barth figured it was a positive way to run off her anxieties.

Whatever drove her, he was glad she was finally moving, albeit somewhat sporadically at times. Other's she seemed obsessed with the activity. In some areas, he could set his watch by her, at others, he could not pigeonhole her.

The anxieties had increased. She was afraid to be alone, yet terrified to be in crowds – or even a small group. Then occasionally, she wanted solitude. It was a constant shifting of tides.

"She continues to lose weight," he told Zoe when she dropped by one wintry day in February. "She's lost a total of twenty-five pounds." He slowly shook his head, perplexed. "I've done everything I can to get her to eat but –" He shrugged dismally. "Let me pour you some coffee to warm you up."

"Thanks." Zoe deposited her purse and wool cape on a bar

stool and slid onto another. She cupped the hot, aromatic mug in her hands and sipped. "One thing I noticed that's changed, though, is that she now will eat a hot dog at Petee's Drive-In. And she sometimes has to postpone her eating time in order to do that." She shrugged. "Not much. But it's something. At least I get her out of the house for a little while."

Petee's, a short order drive-in restaurant, was on the outskirts of Paradise Springs, and sometimes Zoe would pick up her mom to get her out of the house for few minutes. It helped Barth to have those short intervals of relief.

Barth's nerves had been doing a number on him lately, with Seana's even deeper plunge into psychosis. Now, he tried to not second-guess Zoe's mood of the moment. He felt inept when trying to read female vibes. Especially from one as unpredictable as Zoe.

"How's Peyton doing at Converse College? Does he like it?" He was glad his voice came out pleasant and relaxed.

"Oh, he loves it. I'm so thankful to Scott. He helped him apply for a music scholarship. And even more that Peyton got it hands down. The music department there is impressed with him."

Barth smiled. "What's not to love and admire about Peyton? He's going to do well there. And he can drive back and forth, can't he?"

Zoe sighed. "That's the beautiful part. He can be a day student and still help me at the dance studio." She shrugged and Barth thought he saw moisture gather in her eyes.

"If only Mom ...." Her words trailed off and she seemed to go off into her mind.

And he wondered if her trust in him had grown. At times, he thought it had. Like now, when she let down her hair and really became transparent.

Like family.

In that moment, Zoe visibly squared her shoulders and turned to peer at her mother, who lay on the sofa, TV set on a ball game. Barth could see her brow furrow and her eyes grow troubled. "She seems to be getting worse," she muttered quietly.

Barth didn't say anything. Didn't want Seana to overhear negative words if at all possible. "The doctor said he'd expected this to happen," he murmured dismally.

"What nonsense!" Zoe's nostrils flared and her eyes iced over as she nursed her coffee cup. "It's just strange, is all. She seemed to be getting well and then, *boom,* she gets sick all over again. Like ...." Her voice trailed off and she stared into space, in deep thought.

Barth frowned at her biting tone. It sounded distinctly accusatory. "Like what, Zoe?" he cautiously ventured. What the heck? Zoe would say it eventually. Might as well get it over with.

The blue eyes pierced him. "Like – something made her fall ill again. What's the culprit this time, Barth?"

Barth stared at her, mouth open. Then he took off his glasses, whipped out a handkerchief, and wiped them clean. He replaced them and peered closely at her. Yep, she was ticked. But why? Was he hearing more than what she was saying? He certainly hoped so. But something brewed in that brilliant mind of hers. He could hear it in her voice and feel it stirring the air about them.

He sighed deeply and slowly shook his head. "The doctor is constantly changing her meds because nothing seems to be working." He shrugged listlessly. "I don't know what's happening, either. I wish I did."

Zoe stood abruptly. "I'm going to call him." She moved to snatch her cape up and slide into it. "I'm going to get to the bottom of this if it's the last thing I do." She slid her purse strap over her shoulder and marched to the door.

Barth watched her in disbelief. "Zoe –"

Zoe spun at the door and glared at him. "I mean it, Barth. She's my mother. And I love her."

The door slammed.

Barth's reply, to his own ears, seemed faraway. Surreal.

"She's my wife. And I love her, too."

સ્જીજી

"That's ridiculous, Zoe!" Scott peered at her, incredulity stamped all over his rugged features. "You can't believe Barth would do anything to endanger Seana."

Zoe paced across her den and back, halting to confront his lounging hunky bulk, at once all jock in his school jersey, jeans, and white cross-country running shoes and yet – somehow suave.

Darn his hide.

Before she could speak, his mouth quirked, then spread into a delighted grin. "Look at you. You're walking normally. No stiffness … your hips are all smooth and loose." His hands did sign language that did not fool Zoe for one second.

"That was – off color." She cut her eyes at him accusingly, then away, arms tightly crossed.

His brows rose in fake umbrage. "*Was not*! It was simply implying how wonderfully you are made and how – gracefully you move." He leaned back, crossed his legs, and smiled disarmingly at her.

Zoe watched him for long moments, realizing she was in over her head here. He'd been nothing but nice while doctoring her back to health in the past few weeks. He'd provided excellent care for her joints and muscles with that magical Severe Injury Treatment Kit of his, the one the football team swore by. The nine-day protocol of wraps, patches, and topical formulas had effectively restored strength, flexibility, and function to her hip flexor. And he'd patiently mentored her during follow-up stretching and flexing exercises at the studio.

A powerful emotion swept over her and she pivoted on her heel and marched to the chair farthest from him and sank into it. "What?" he asked, spreading his arms. "You're not going to fuss anymore? Can't believe you're giving in that easily."

"Not giving in. Just tired." She groaned and realized it was true.

He suddenly leaned forward, elbows planted on knees. "You know why I've teased and prodded you so these last few days, don't you?"

Zoe nodded reluctantly. "Yeh."

"Why?"

"Because you wanted to keep me fired up."

His eyes widened and he laughed loudly. "Hey! That's right. I wouldn't have exactly put it in those precise words but –" He reared back and guffawed again.

Zoe fought the urge to laugh but couldn't quite force her features into a scowl. "Why wouldn't you have said it like that?" Curiosity got the best of her.

"Whoooee, you'd have slapped my face, that's why." His chuckle was so contagious she couldn't help herself when she felt her traitorous lips tilt up at the corners, then open in laughter.

"I know what you meant," Scott said, still smiling, his eyes twinkling. "And you're one hundred ten percent right. I wanted to keep you pushing ahead and a little irritation sometimes helps."

Zoe rolled her eyes at him. "A little? Scott, you've got porcupine genes."

He looked at her, his smile fading. "Zoe, you've got to stop this paranoia about Barth."

Her good humor flattened. "Don't tell me what I can or cannot think, Scott."

"Zoe, you know – on some level – that these suspicions are just that. Suspicions. I'm just saying that you –"

Zoe stood abruptly. "I think it's time you leave, Scott. I'm going to shower and turn in early."

If Scott was shocked at her abruptness, he didn't show it. He arose smoothly, smiled, and turned to go. Then, seeming to reconsider, stepped back to her and dipped to kiss her cheek. He did it so quickly that she didn't have time to react.

This time, he did leave, quietly closing the door behind him.

Zoe stood there long moments, hand to cheek, wondering why he'd crossed that line. Why now? Why after these past few weeks of almost impersonal contact when the opportunity for intimacy had afforded itself, time after time?

And now, reflecting, she admitted that at times she'd felt disappointment that she was so – so *resistible*.

She had to snap out of this. Zoe pivoted and launched herself into bed preparations, deciding to become honest and actually take a quick shower before sliding into a silky teddy.

Once in bed, lying in the dark, she went over the past weeks and realized that though the injury had been bad in one way, in another the recuperation had allowed her time to decompress. Instead of a daily to-do list, she'd been forced to chill out. Scott had insisted she not worry about money problems or dance lessons. Or anything, truth be known. It had worked, because, at times, she'd felt absolutely cosseted.

Actually, Peyton had been coaching Scott in dance instruction. Scott was a quick study, according to Peyton, and had already taught several lessons while she was off her feet. She could use another teacher at the studio. Even part-time help would lighten her load considerably.

And Scott's leasing her duplex had eased her money worries even more. He'd insisted on paying the normal deposit and first month's rent in advance, even when she protested. After all, he was helping her.

Zoe didn't know how to take this entire knight-in-shining-armor stuff.

She'd never been exposed to it in her entire adult life.

Not since her dad.

"Zoe, you've got to stop this paranoia thing about Barth."

Her eyes popped open and she stared at the moonlight-dappled ceiling. She felt herself frowning. He was already telling her how she should feel … and act.

Somehow, that stung more than anything he could have done. He didn't walk in her shoes. He hadn't experienced betrayal by one who was supposed to love and honor … till death do us part.

Suddenly tears welled. She recalled Joanie's remarks the day before at Homecombing Queen Beauty Salon. "You and

Scott getting along well, I see." Joanie beamed at her in the mirror as she trimmed Zoe's hair.

"Oh, I'm not –"

"Pshaaw. Can't fool me, sweetie. I half raised you, remember? Scott's a nice fellow." Then her lips V'd into a kittenish grin. "And have you noticed what a hunk he is?"

Zoe had sighed. "Yeh. I have noticed that."

And in that moment she had to acknowledge the classic symptoms.

Infatuation.

Not love, she still insisted tonight as she glared into the silvery moonlit emptiness of her room. Oh she was experiencing the stupid light-headedness, rapid heartbeat, and quickened breathing at the mere thought of him.

Her emotions vacillated from tears to laughter in a moment's time. Anything emotional could set her off lately. But she'd been able to blame her sensitivity on the injury and inflammation.

Until now.

In that moment, she recalled something else Joanie had said to her yesterday. "Zoe, you deserve to love and be loved. Don't hold back, honey." She'd reached down to hug Zoe then, a quick but warm gesture from one who was like a second mother, and it had brought tears to Zoe's eyes.

Tonight, those words struck to the heart of Zoe's hesitation. "You deserve to … be loved."

Do I? Why can't I allow it to happen?

Then she thought about Peyton, who already idolized Scott. He'd not had a father's love since he was a toddler. He'd been dreadfully hurt by her five-year relationship with Cory Evans, one that abruptly ended when Zoe had called it quits after realizing it was a dead-end, noncommittal affair for Cory.

Not since his grandfather died had Peyton had any stable, significant male figure in his life.

Other than Barth.

She squeezed her eyes shut and quickly doused that line of thinking.

Being in love, to Zoe, was like going through an incurable illness. A slow, painful process with a predictably bad outcome.

She'd told Joanie as much yesterday during their heart to heart. "He'll leave, Joanie. They always do. Why would Scott want to stay?"

Joanie had laughed out loud. "Just listen to you," she said quietly so as not to be overheard. "You're beautiful and smart and witty. Peyton's a dream of a son for any man." She rolled her contact-enhanced ambers at Zoe. "Duh. I don't add too good, but even for me, it's a winning combination."

Zoe was shaking her head and Joanie gently poked her in the shoulder. "Look at you, already counting yourself out before you give it a chance."

Zoe dragged in a deep cleansing breath and exhaled. "These things, with me, have a life of their own. They never work out and I hate to see Peyton hurt again."

"Look honey, don't heap all men into one lump and label them jerks. My mama told me that the cream will always rise to the top. That applies to the male species, too."

"I'll take that into consideration," Zoe said and gave her a grudging smile. "Scott and I have already agreed that we're simply friends. Nothing more."

"Can I give you a little motherly advice?" Joanie asked.

Zoe braced herself but muttered, "Sure."

"Live in the now. Stop and smell the roses. Seize the moment – and all that flowery counsel, Zoe. Simple." Another big smile and hug and Zoe was on her feet and leaving.

Tonight, she realized she would love to do that. Seize the moment. Thing was she didn't know how to anymore. Scott didn't know it, but he was stepping into a vacancy she'd felt for years. He'd grown increasingly comfortable in her company, to the point that he'd performed on her some doggone intimate tasks with aplomb and innocuous warmth. He brought with him strength and joy and that inexpressibly male joviality to her home.

It was something she could not duplicate.

She yawned mightily as slumber lapped and tugged at her. The last thought she had was of Scott dipping to kiss her cheek.

ری૭

Seana's plunge seemed ongoing in her crazy world. The "inside herself" was now endless. Today when the doorbell rang while she was alone, the noise clanged in her eardrums, seeming to bounce against out-of- tune cymbals, then vibrate through her every pore.

She rolled over on the sofa and tugged the blanket over and around her head, trying to snuff out the racket. But whoever it was persisted until she tossed off the cover and stomped to the door, not even pausing to put on a robe.

She flung open the front door, fury furrowing her brow and flaring her nostrils.

"Mama." Zoe strode past her, sizzling with her own brand of rage. "If you're going to barricade the house, at least have the decency to answer the doorbell without an Act of Congress."

She spun and glared at her mother. "Holy Toledo. You look awful. Why does your hair look like a haystack? I know Joanie sends you out of her place with every hair in place. Do you style it with an egg beater? And that gown could fit a sumo wrestler!"

Seana brushed past her and slid onto the sofa, turning her back, and swaddling herself into the blanket like an infant. Why couldn't she go away? Didn't she know how intrusive she was being?

Zoe stomped her way over and leaned over her. "That's right, mommie dearest, run away. That's all you do anymore."

"Go away."

ری૭

"What?" Zoe's voice rose to pitch level when she heard the muffled words filter through the blanket cocooning her mother.

Zoe knew she was being cruel but she couldn't find her mouth's shutoff valve. The words kept gushing out of their own volition, like a blasted sewer spill. On one level she felt horrible and vile.

On another, she felt the euphoria of release.

The events of recent months raced through her mind like a crop duster jet spewing venom. "What's happened to you, Mama?" Her voice broke and she collapsed into the easy chair facing her mother's cocoon.

Cocoon. That's what it was. And she'd better get used to it because it seemed that's where Seana would eternally hibernate.

The anger began to fizzle and slowly morphed into pain.

"Mama? Can you really not help it?" Her voice came out wispy as she melted against the soft leather, flaccid as overdone pasta. "Are you that far inside yourself? Can you not be reached anymore?"

Zoe shrugged limply. "I guess not. So I'll just talk to you like you're here. At least it'll make me feel better." She propped her feet on the leather ottoman.

"You see, Mama. I miss you." Her voice broke again, but she reined in her emotions, determined to have a good mother/daughter talk even if it was one-sided.

"And guess what? I'm attracted to Scott. Yeh." A dry laugh burst from her as she rolled her eyes. "Who woulda ever thunk it?"

She stared at her mother's back, desperation rising. *Maybe, just maybe, she comprehends what I'm saying.*

Melancholy viciously stabbed her.

Maybe not.

Something primal floundered in Zoe's bosom. Something strong and invincibly *her*.

I'll pretend she does anyway, dadjimmit.

"Now don't get all romantic on me, Mama. I know you. It's not love." She huffed another dry laugh. "I'm not that stupid. You saw all the man-crap in my life, so you know. I just can't hold on to –"

The dam burst. Zoe dissolved into tears and then sobs so great they drew her into a knot, knees to chest as she rocked back and forth like a toddler. She heaved and gulped in air and wailed like a little child lost in a black forest at midnight.

When she finally ran out of breath and strength, she lay back like a dead thing, melded to the chair like something laid out to dry. Only she was already dried out. Her emotions now lay in a heap at her feet, stomped and battered beyond recognition.

But something timeless pulled Zoe to her bare feet and to her mother's side. She sank to her knees and softly buried her head against her mother's still, warm bulk. There, she surrendered to the need eating her alive. The need for a mother's love and nurturing. And even though her mother was not there emotionally, she was alive.

For that she thanked God.

Amazingly, more tears appeared, and she wondered, crazily, how a wrung dry sponge could produce more moisture. Tears puddled, then spilled over. For what, she could not say for certain. But she knew they represented emotions. That's what separated humans from animals. Tears, a uniquely human expression.

That realization connected her to the Divine. It awed her.

Tears certainly represented grief, for all things lost. But they went beyond that here. Gratefulness? For certain. As long as her mother lived, there was hope for her restoration.

What Zoe didn't want to admit, but here it was, staring her in the face.

Need.

She'd played this Amazon-woman role for so long, not requiring anybody or anything to get her through life, that this recent lapse had tossed her into a loopy insecurity.

She sat on the floor, back to sofa, and wiped her tears away, then squared her shoulders. Zoe didn't like the sense of inadequacy that pummeled her into this heap of wilted waste.

Nossir. She didn't like it at all.

Need was so not *her.*

She could not have survived all that she had if she'd ever for one moment surrendered to it. She'd relied on two men and they had each, in the end, abandoned her.

Now, her mother had done the same.

She pulled herself to her feet and took a deep, steadying breath. Oh, she knew Seana couldn't help it. That was another thing that needled her.

Zoe paced to the window to survey her mother's estate. "You know, Mom, you didn't have a seriously sick day in your life until Barth came along."

She gave a bark of a laugh. "The hero from nowhere."

She shrugged. "But he did come from somewhere, I discovered. Not a good discovery, by the way. Your Mr. Wonderful was a murder suspect, no less. And though he'd been released for lack of sufficient evidence, the murder remains unsolved until this very day." She rubbed her arms to ward off a chill.

Zoe walked over to collect her purse. "For all his charm and seeming great virtue, Barth McGrath still is hiding something." She patted her mother's shrouded shoulder. "And I aim to find out what it is."

Zoe's long-legged stride took her to the door, where she turned. "Oh, by the way, I enjoyed our mother daughter talk."

The door clicked soundly behind her.

∽⪦⪧∽

Barth closed his eyes.

Heartsick from what he'd just heard, he sat still as death on the stairs next to the den. He'd earlier driven his Toyota pickup to the back of the farm to trim some dead tree branches and load them into the pickup bed to haul off.

So Zoe had no idea he was around when she vented to her mother. But he'd seen her car and came in the downstairs entrance to drop off to Billie Jean a printed update on bone cancer treatment. Halfway up the open staircase, he'd heard Zoe sobbing out her angst and he'd frozen, just below floor level view. The vitriol had shaken him, causing him to sink down and sit it out, not wanting an explosive confrontation just then.

Not ever.

So Zoe had not shed her suspicions, as he'd hoped.

Prayed for.

He sucked in a deep steadying breath and went to check on Seana. He gently pulled the blanket down and saw that her eyes were open. She didn't look at him.

"Seana?"

"Is she gone?"

He experienced the same little shock every time she rejected her loved ones. It was so unlike the Seana he'd married. "Yes, she's gone."

"Good." She turned over, flicked on the television, and scrolled to the ball game.

He crossed to the easy chair and wearily sank down, hooking an ankle over his knee, steepling his fingers. "Seana, did you hear what Zoe said to you?"

"Yes."

"Does it bother you?"

"No."

That bothered Barth more than anything. That – short-circuited emotional system of hers. That non-feeling. It was like she was a blank screen.

Almost.

What did appear on the screen was angry and selfish and defiant.

It was not Seana.

Hopelessness, one that had hovered for weeks now, attacked him anew, gnawing at him mercilessly as he sat there, watching his wife stare unseeing at the moving players on the screen, not caring a hoot who was playing, winning, or losing.

They could have been animated outer space figures for all she cared. The less intimate to her, the better.

Fact was, Seana didn't give a fig about anything or anybody any more.

That was the hardest thing for him to swallow. The nightmare that he'd fought for so long was, day by day, becoming a glaring reality to reckon with.

"It's time for my medicine," Seana pronounced flatly, interrupting his rumination.

Barth gave her the meds and proceeded to prepare his warmed-over, stir-fry dinner and her pimento cheese sandwich. Suddenly, as he slapped the two coated bread slices together, an urge seized him to hurl them to the floor and stomp on them.

The impulse was instant and violent. He set his teeth together and resisted as he cut the sandwich in two and Seana joined him at the bar. The meal was, as always, silent. But tonight Barth felt the awful nothingness settle upon him like a damp, icy avalanche slowly heaping atop him, weighing him down, burying him.

He felt smothered and stopped eating just as Seana arose and returned to lie on the sofa.

"Brutus," Barth called as he made his way out the door to the back deck. He heard Brutus's paws clicking, trailing him across the deck and down the back steps. March weather was offering glimpses of spring but still held a cool edge near nightfall.

Tonight it felt good. The brisk touch was just right to tingle his skin and pleasantly fill his lungs. Brutus paused along the way to mark his territory as they circled the back perimeter of the farm. Now Barth viewed the spectacular way the property presented itself. The two-level house's wood and brick façade spanned the terraced landscape and, with it, curved as if to embrace the blue mountainous range that rose straight up from a vast forestland that spread as far as the eye could see.

Barth began to jog and heard Brutus loping along beside him. And like lightning Zoe's words came back to haunt him.

"Barth is hiding something. And I aim to find out what it is."
Would she? Find out, that is. After all his careful evasion?

He began to run, his feet kicking up tufts as he gained speed with Brutus panting at his side.

But Barth knew: he could not outrun his secret past.

᪤᪤

Billie Jean helped keep Seana's house in apple pie order. Of course, Barth was meticulous in everything he did so she really only had to do deep surface cleaning, like mopping and scrubbing bathrooms. She allotted her cleaning times to when Barth was at the church office.

She told him it was to keep him from being underfoot and make it easier for her. But Billie Jean had a deeper reason. Barth needed protection and nurturing.

The man was running himself into the ground. Plain and simple.

Joanie and Chelsea agreed. The three met at Fred's Deli each Wednesday evening following choir practice. From the church, it was a short walk down the street to his place. He had added booths in a cheerful little corner nook and piped soft music as folks stopped there to snack.

Tonight, Billie Jean mixed her little healthy veggie salad. "Barth's looking mighty tired these days, you know?"

Joanie sliced in half her ham and cheese on rye. "He does. I feel sorry for 'im."

"Yeh." Chelsea sipped her coffee because she was on another diet. "Even music fails to lift him anymore. Not enough, anyway."

The other two munched for a while, musing. Finally Billie Jean spoke, "Seana's really slipped deep into this psychosis … with a vengeance. She's so honkin' mean sometimes, I can't understand how Barth survives."

"Makes one wonder why these things are allowed to happen," Joanie said, blotting her lips, then pulling on an iced diet cola, ignoring Billie Jean's censorious glances.

"Yeh," Chelsea reached over to snag a chip from Joanie's plate and crunched into it. "Seana's the best of the best. It's creepy how this thing just took over her."

"Whoa," Billie Jean's palm shot out. "None of that *'taking over'* talk. That sounds like she's not coming back. Like – some other force is in charge. Not so, honey bun. *He's* in charge." She pointed upward. "And she is coming back." She took a bite of salad and munched contentedly.

Joanie and Chelsea looked at each other and raised their brows.

"I know what you're thinking," Billie Jean said, as calm as could be. "But you're dead wrong. Nothing is impossible, my friend. I'm a great example of that."

"You're right." Joanie grinned, displaying Dolly Parton dimples. "I keep forgetting how far you've come, Billie Jean."

"Yeh. Barth is constantly looking for anything that will help you," Chelsea joined in. "He's such a great guy. A little quirky at times but smart as a whip."

"My hero," Billie Jean stated proudly.

"Is there anything we can do to help with Seana's care?" Chelsea asked. "I have Wednesdays and Sundays off and every evening."

Joanie added, "Well, I have Thursdays off and half the day on Saturdays. I can always help when needed."

Billie Jean grinned. "Thanks, guys. You know, that's why friends come in batches, doncha? Because when one gets tired and bogged down, the others rally and fill in. Right now, Barth and I have it covered. But you can be sure that if and when that time comes, I'll be sending out the posse for you two."

Then she added, "We need to keep on believin' and hang together, girls."

She smacked her hand palm down on the Formica table-top. Joanie's covered hers and Chelsea's slapped on last. Together they chanted, "All for one and one for all."

And the fact that their *woo-hoos* drew a few irritated glances did nothing to dampen their sharpened camaraderie.

◦◦

"Seana, please, won't you go with me?" Barth was dressed and ready to go to a party honoring Pastor Keith and Louann's ten-year anniversary at Redemption Community Church. A big deal.

The entire church family would be there.

"No. And I don't want you to go." Seana's petulance over this superseded anything of the past. Barth had pleaded all day, trying every way he could to coerce her into going. She staunchly refused to cooperate.

Finally, frustrated, Barth set out alone. The parking lot was nearly full when he arrived at the church. Just as he pulled into the parking lot, his cell phone rang. "Hello?"

"I took all the sleeping pills in the bottle."

Barth froze. "What did you say, Seana?" Perhaps he misunderstood, but a squalling alarm set off inside him. "Did you say you took all the Temazepam pills in the bottle?"

"Yes." His mind began clicking off the number of pills that were left in the prescription.

Too many.

"Hang up, Seana. I'll call EMS."

She rang off. Barth's fingers were trembling so violently he could hardly dial 911. As he drove he gave them his address. The ambulance arrived at his house at the same time he did and had Seana in the ambulance within minutes. Barth followed the screaming siren all the way to Paradise Springs Hospital, where they whisked Seana into ICU and began treatment.

Barth was frantic. Guilt pounded him into pulp. *How could I have let this happen? I've not been vigilant enough.*

He'd let down lately and didn't always lock up the meds. Seana had seemed responsible enough in recent months. She'd wanted to stay alone more, and he felt, in a weird way, that was progress.

While waiting for the doctor to finish the emergency

treatment, Barth sank onto a waiting room chair, elbows on knees, face buried in hands. He felt as low as he'd ever felt in his life.

So he did the only thing he could.

He prayed.

෨෮

Seana did not want to drink the liquid charcoal they gave her in the ER. But they insisted, so she forced it down. She'd not wanted to come to the hospital, either, when the ambulance had arrived at her house. But they'd made her climb on the rolling cot and put her in the back of the EMS unit and, siren a'screaming, rushed her to the hospital.

Barth was here but not with her. She'd heard him tell the doctor that she'd taken a bottle of sleeping pills. So the vile black liquid she'd just swallowed was supposed to take care of that, either by making her vomit or forcing the pills out the other way.

The doctor on duty tonight came in and talked to her for a little while. "Why did you take the pills, Seana?"

She shrugged. "I don't know why I did it."

Later, she could hear him just outside her room, talking to Barth.

"I'm going to admit her to the Carolina Center for Behavioral Health."

Barth said something she couldn't quite make out.

"Yes," the doctor said decisively. "I think this suicide attempt warrants it. She definitely needs psychological treatment."

Barth came in and stood next to her bed, looking like an old man suddenly. She turned her face away. "You're going to be admitted to –"

"I heard."

A deep, ragged, indrawn breath. Then, "okaaay."

After emptying her stomach of the deadly contents, the

team of doctors referred Seana to the Carolina Center for Behavioral Health, where she remained for the next fifteen days.

❦

Something happened to Seana at the CCBH facility. Perhaps it was the new setting. Or a radically different agenda each day. Whatever it was, she felt, to some degree, once removed from the thing that held her captive.

Not enough to celebrate. Or to even acknowledge. But she realized right away that she did not like her roommate. Certainly not a new thing. And she didn't like to go to group sessions but she somehow knew that to earn the right to go home, she must comply.

And go she did but she never talked during those meetings. She just sat there and listened to everyone else vent.

"Would you like to share your experience here with us, Ms. McGrath?" Miss Fox, the therapist, would ask.

Seana shrugged. "Not really."

The therapist then moved on to the next patient. So Seana learned to get by with simply being there, not necessarily joining in. Secretly, she was afraid of some of the patients.

Her room was pleasant enough. Spartan-like but comfortable. The other patient sharing the room was strange. So Seana pretended she was asleep that night. When another patient came into the room and made plans with her roommate to go to another room to play cards, Seana never let on she was awake and heard.

Seana was certain this was against hospital policy, at least in her unit.

As her meds took over, Seana surrendered to sleep. The next day, she quietly, surreptitiously approached a supervisor. "I need to talk to you," she whispered to the nurse.

"Okay. Come into my office."

There, behind the safety of closed doors, Seana divulged

the episode, ending with, "But I'm scared. I'm afraid of her, afraid she'll find out I told on her. Could you move me to another room?"

Not only did they move her to another room, they sent her roommate to another part of the hospital without giving her a reason.

It warmed Seana. They had protected her.

Just like Barth did.

෴

Barth carried on as best he could under the difficult circumstances. Seana's stay at the Behavioral Health Center stretched past a week. The church folk rallied round him and encouraged him as he worked with the choir and even, because the pastor had a twenty-four hour intestinal bug, gave a brief devotional at the Wednesday Night Prayer service. Though Barth knew his messages touched hearts, preaching was not his primary forte.

Music was.

Today, a sunny January day, he sat in his church office listening to soft music by Dino and tried to wrap himself in peace.

Twice daily, he faithfully spent visiting hours with Seana.

Not easy because Seana was, at best, belligerent and uncooperative.

The rest of the time, he buried himself in music and other church duties. Too, he still regularly researched bone cancer treatments to help Billie Jean – especially holistic approaches, implementing supplements and foods with strong antioxidants that boost the immune system, which, in turn, helps fight cancer. His concern and involvement boosted Billie Jean along, kept her head up, as well as her faith. It was one of the things that validated him these days. Billie Jean's good reports.

Cancer free. Magic, life-affirming words.

Faith. Ahh, now in his case, situational dynamics pulled

and tugged at that fervent five-letter word. He'd never before doubted. Never. Well, at least not for long at a time. But now, with Seana's crash-landing back into the pit, he found himself wondering about a lot of things he'd been taking for granted.

He knew he shouldn't question. But he gazed out the window, into infinite blue littered with snowy cloud puffs ... and saw a faraway flock of birds in V formation, headed by a leader, soaring their way to a divinely ordered destination.

That's the way he'd always lived. Following his Creator to ... wherever. Because he knew it would be the right place and the right thing in the end. But now? He couldn't help himself – he found himself wondering where this would all end? And the whys, once loosed, were infinite.

Why did Seana have to endure such a nightmare? For that matter, why did *he* end up in such a quagmire?

He laid his head back on the plush leather chair's headrest and closed his eyes. How tired he felt. Then softly ... softly his own words floated back to him. *"... why did I end up in such a quagmire?"*

End up. End up ....

An inaudible voice said, *"It's not the end."*

His eyes sprang open.

The impact of it stunned him. Its veracity. He blinked and shook his head. And surrendered to the wooing presence. A soothing warmth spread through him, amid a holy hush that spoke volumes to his heart.

Barth felt the tension slowly ooze from him.

Then an amazing thing happened.

Barth began to grin like roadkill, feeling like Popeye after scarfing spinach, when superhuman energy invaded him, pumping his muscles, tendons, his very atoms into strapping new handiwork. He recognized the source. He also knew that the days to come would not be easy. But the greatest certainty of all thrilled and stirred to life his long dormant joy.

Whatever happened, he was not alone.

And whatever happened, it would be right.

❧✦

Seana's next roommate was Sophie. She liked Sophie. It was as though, away from her ordinary habitat, Seana's perception altered somewhat. Here, she needed more human contact, even if through conversation.

Perhaps it was the newer meds that slowed down that thing that tinkered with her brain. She didn't know and didn't care. She just embraced the slight breather.

So Seana and Sophie began hanging together and talking, even laughing, together.

"Why are you here?" Seana ventured during one conversation.

"Panic attacks. Monster ones at times." Sophie grinned but Seana could see the uneasiness when she spoke of it. "But I'm feeling better than when I first came in."

"I'm not as afraid anymore," Seana confessed. "Not with you here."

"What brought you here?"

"I took a bottle of Temazepam."

"A whole bottle of – sleeping pills, I assume?"

Seana nodded.

Then Sophie shrugged, one bony shoulder protruding from the drooping neck of the loose hospital gown. "I'm afraid of dying. I sure don't want to do myself in."

Seana tried to wrap her mind around that. She'd forgotten what actual reality-based fear was.

"So – why'd you do that?" Sophie asked, looking bewildered.

"I don't know. I didn't really want to kill myself." She shrugged. "I took the pills to get attention."

Sophie rolled her eyes. "That's a really dangerous way to get attention, honey."

"Yeh," Seana agreed. "It is. But sometimes it's hard."

"What's hard?"

"Living."

Sophie peered at her, then slowly nodded. "You're right. It is. Especially when those panic attacks slam into me. I want to run and hide but ..." Sophie spread her hands. "Where do I run to? I can't get away from *me*."

"Sometimes I want to run away, too," Seana admitted.

"Have you ever tried it?"

"No. Except when I took the pills."

"So you took the pills to –?"

"To see if anybody would save me."

❧ ❧

Barth had saved her. Of that, Seana was certain.

And her cry for help was heeded. He visited her every time visitors were allowed.

When Sophie was discharged, Seana found another friend to hang out with. Her name was Gina, a younger woman than Sophie. She suffered from bipolar disorder and was even more engaging than Sophie. She'd had a rough life and had no compunctions about sharing the sordid details.

Group sessions spiced up with Gina there.

But, even so, Seana refused to talk about her own situation.

Gina's lows were black, black revelations to endure at group sessions. On the other hand, the ups were entertaining. So Seana flowed with them, as she did everything else there that didn't disturb the invisible bubble surrounding her, the shield that, when threatened, screamed *back off!*

Her lengthy hospital stay and Seana's lack of cooperation culminated with her latest assigned psychiatrist, Dr. Worton, getting fed up and releasing her.

"She's no better," she overheard Dr. Worton disgustedly telling Barth the day she went home. "But we can't help her if she's not willing to work together with us toward healing solutions."

The ride home was silent. And that suited her just fine. At home, her sofa beckoned.

Immediately, she sank into it, pulled the blanket up to her chin, and felt her cocoon close tightly around her again, blocking out the outside world's chill and racket and agitation.

Shielding her from sudden, groundless fear.

Protecting her.

❧

Zoe knelt beside her mother and peered into her emptied features. "Mama, are you okay?"

"Yes." But Seana's gaze eluded her daughter's frantic one. Rather, she stared beyond to the ball game playing on the television.

"I don't believe it," Zoe declared flatly and arose to pace to the den window. Barth watched her from the kitchen where he washed his hands after a morning of turning the garden spot on the farm's back corner.

Zoe spun and strode to where he pulled off paper towels to dry his hands. "She's even worse, Barth." She narrowed her cold gaze on him and planted hands on hips. "There's some reason she's not getting better."

Barth looked steadily at her. Then took his glasses off, ran them under the spigot to remove dust, and snatched a tissue from the counter to wipe them clean and dry.

"Sit down, Zoe." He gestured to the bar and slid his glasses back on.

"I don't want to sit down."

"Well, I do. Stand if you want to." He sank tiredly onto a bar stool, clasped his hands before him, and sighed.

He felt Zoe's eyes piercing him but at that moment he didn't care. He looked at her then. "I'm exhausted, Zoe. Yes, your mother is worse. Billie Jean relieved me long enough for me to till the land for our garden. So just go ahead and say what you need to and let's get past it."

Zoe reluctantly took a seat opposite him. "I don't know that I can get past this, Barth," she murmured hoarsely. She looked terrible, unusual for the brunette beauty. Dark circles lay swollen beneath eyes that were red, as though she'd been crying.

Barth's heart swelled with compassion. "I'm sorry, Zoe. I'm sorry that your mother's condition hasn't improved. I don't know why it hasn't. Wish to God I did. I've gotten her the best help available. And she still isn't improving. But I'm not giving up on her. This is but another glitch on the road to recovery."

Zoe peered at him, something dark in her gaze. Something accusing.

"Barth, I wish I could trust you." The words were flat and succinct.

They pierced his heart. "I'm sorry, too, Zoe."

Zoe stood and snatched up her purse. "But there's something you're not telling me. I can read it in your eyes."

Barth watched her spin on her stiletto heel and trump to the front door.

He watched it slam behind her and presently, heard her tires's screech leaving the driveway.

He closed his eyes and surrendered to the onslaught of guilt.

Because, on some dark level, he deserved Zoe's indictment.

∝↺↻∾

Seana felt the disgust from those around her. She knew that she disappointed everyone. But the impact of this against her cocoon was no more than a tiny tap that dissolved instantly and floated away into the mist of nothingness surrounding her.

Yet – something about that thing tampering with her head had changed. It was on duty more now, not taking a shift off like it once seemed to, to allow her meds to take her off into oblivion for short spells.

Seemed now the thing was fighting the meds ... constantly.

Dr. Walton, the doctor she'd been seeing, moved away to

practice in another state. She'd not liked him because he never listened to her when she told him things she considered important.

A new doctor arrived on the scene.

Dr. Jones was nice. He began adjusting her meds and, for a while, Seana seemed to even out.

❧

Zoe felt the world caving in around her.

Her mother's mental state had been the proverbial straw that set off the final implosion. Scott had simply wandered into the line of fire.

The incident would have been funny had Zoe been in her right mind.

Since then, she'd had to admit that she just may *not* be in her right mind.

Today, with another local family bailing out on their dance lessons renewal, she mentally deducted the loss from her monthly budget and wilted a bit more.

Scott Burns still occupied the duplex adjoined to hers, but that was the extent of their current relationship.

Like two ships that passed in the night, as the Manilow song went.

That eventful Saturday night began pleasantly enough. Scott had invited Zoe to his place for an early supper of his famous ravioli, which would precede their evening at Happy Feet Dance Studio. The food had lived up to its reputation.

Peyton had stayed over at school to study for a test with a friend. He would be late getting to the studio that evening. So Scott would take up the slack at the studio's weekly dance party, which this week carried the Saturday Night Fever theme.

"Peyton made me promise to save him a crap-load of this," Scott said as he scooped a bowl full and covered it in Saran Wrap.

He deposited it in the fridge as Seana rinsed dishes and packed the dishwasher. They worked well together, Seana wiping down counters and tabletop with Scott sweeping the floor and putting away spices and condiments.

When finished, Seana said, "I'll scoot and dress for the party." The dress had a '70s soft, floaty, ruffly top exposing one bare shoulder. It was a replica of the one worn by Travolta's female partner in the Saturday Night Fever movie. Scott dressed in a European-cut, white suit and black open neck shirt, a la Travolta.

Despite his buffed-up frame, Seana thought he looked every bit as gorgeous as Travolta, especially since his close-cropped head was way overdue a haircut.

They drove there together in Scott's black SUV.

"Pretty good crowd," Scott noted cheerfully, surveying the eager, early arrivals still lounging in cars in the parking lot.

"So-so," Zoe said in a long-suffering tone.

Scott peered at her. "Zoe, you've got to stop beating yourself up like this. This is a pretty doggone good turnout."

"You're right. Sorry, Scott." She certainly didn't want to pull him down, too.

She mentally tried to yank up her spirits from where they lay puddled at her feet. But there was heaviness in her heart that she couldn't quite adjust. She tried to celebrate those present and not grieve for those who had recently abandoned ship.

Inside, with lights adjusted to transform the place more into a movie set, Billie Jean sailed to her, looking spiffy in a new, fitted dance jumpsuit with loose, billowy legs from the knee down.

Before she could unload what she wanted to say, Zoe spoke. "Say, that peachy color looks great on you, Billie Jean." Zoe turned her around and surveyed her from head to toe. "Matches those neutral dance slippers pretty good. Your weight is just right. Don't be losing any more, y'hear?"

"That's the last thing I have to worry about, Zoe baby." She cut her eyes toward a female newcomer who'd just sashayed into the studio. "Did you see that Cameron Diaz dead ringer just walked in?"

Zoe turned. No, she had not. "I see what you mean." She

touched Billie Jean's arm. "Excuse me. I need to go greet her."

But the woman already migrated to Scott Burns like a moth to a night light. Zoe skidded to a halt as she saw Scott burst into smiles when the woman touched his arm and whispered to him in a decidedly intimate fashion.

When Scott's handsome head rolled back in laughter, she felt her claws emerge.

Whoa, girl. She took a long, deep drag of air, pasted what she hoped was a dazzling smile on her face, and approached the cozy pair. "Why, Scott. I do believe you're holding out on us. Won't you introduce me to your – friend?"

Scott seemed not at all fazed by Zoe's false cheer. She knew, because she was not that great an actress. He would know.

Wouldn't he?

In the next heartbeat, she asked herself exactly *what* would he know?

That she was jealous. Plain and simple.

"Of course, Zoe. This is Stacia Dietrich. She's the new home ec teacher at Paradise Springs High."

Stacia, huh? Even her name was exotic. Zoe's smile stretched wider. "Hello, Stacia. Welcome to Happy Feet. Do you like to dance?"

Stacia's bedroom eyes rivaled Joanie's in sultriness. Without even trying and, Zoe suspected, without contact lens enhancement.

"Yes, as a matter of fact, I love to dance." Perfect teeth behind full, luscious lips.

Scott laughed. "She's too, too modest, Zoe. She's studied ballet since she was knee high, as well as tap and modern. You ought to see her in action."

"Oh?" Zoe's eyebrows almost touched her hairline. "So you've seen her – in action?"

Stacia's husky laugh matched her last name – Dietrich. "I'm working with the cast of the upcoming Gershwin musical at school." She laughed then, and Zoe glimpsed in it a touch of down-to-earthness. Or was it earthiness?

Whatever. It made Zoe uneasy. She wanted her to be a classic witch.

Stacia peeked between fingers at Zoe, fighting down giggles. "I'm sorry. Too much work and no play is making me crazy."

Scott hiked up his broad shoulders. "Well, I have a remedy for that." He marched over to the stereo and put in a Saturday Night Fever soundtrack CD, then returned to offer his arm to the mouth-watering female Zoe had already decided she hated.

She watched them begin the dancing for the evening, doing an intermediate to advanced Latin Hustle to the Bee Gees's "You Should Be Dancing." Others filled in around them while some simply gawked from the sidelines. Arms akimbo, Zoe's right hand fidgeted with her bare neck as she watched Scott and Stacia do a menagerie of positions to the music, all graceful and – she was searching for the word to describe them together.

Breathtaking.

She turned away abruptly. And bumped into a militant Billie Jean.

Those astute hazel eyes pinned her. Then her hands seized Zoe's shoulders.

"Huh-uh. Don't you dare run from this." Billie Jean's order cut through Zoe's mental quandary. "This is business. Get that through your thick head, Zoe. Don't let jealousy ruin –"

Zoe jerked her shoulders free but pasted that stupid smile on her lips, wider than ever. "Jealousy? Hah! I couldn't care less about Scott Burns."

Billie Jean's mouth dropped open, and she took a step back and stared at her as though she'd grown horns. "Who's talking about Scott? I'm talking about glamour puss maybe stealing the spotlight from you for a moment, you know? But I'm also talking about a prospective new dance student. They're not exactly bowling you over right now, case you hadn't noticed. She's teaching all those students at the high school, remember?"

Yep. Zoe was beginning to get her cousin's drift.

Billie Jean continued, "So it's possible she'll attract some of them to come over and take lessons." She shrugged and spread her hands wide. "Just saying." She sauntered away, a study in nonchalance.

Zoe turned and looked again. This time she was able to take in the woman's performance for what it was. Professional. That was another thing – she'd been needing a good dance instructor to help her, hadn't she?

The music ebbed on "How Deep Is Your Love?"

In the next instant Scott seized her hand and tugged on her. "What?" She frowned up at him. Irritated. Not wanting to go anywhere with him, blast his gorgeous hide!

"It's time for our special," he stage-whispered as the first strains of the Bee Gees's "More Than A Woman" drifted from the speakers and they took their positions on the now deserted floor. Softly muted lights transformed the scene to romantic as they did slow, sustained Latin Hustle steps, blending with the movie's choreographic sequence.

The nearness of Scott affected her as always. And as always, she struggled to shut down her response, both emotional and physical. Tonight, the battle was half won by the jock's catering to Stacia-babe's fun-appetite.

Already half-miffed, Zoe revved up her professionalism to new heights as they pseudo-romanced their way through the sensual song, doing boneless dips, sizzling eye contacts, and sinuous hand movements during breaks ... that had the crowd *woo-hooing* at times.

Zoe didn't see it coming. Never expected it to happen. And for a take-control freak, she'd later look back and figure that's probably why she reacted as she did.

Scott dipped Zoe on the last measures of the song ... her body went fluid as it was supposed to as he gazed into her eyes, his face only inches from hers. Then, suddenly, he dipped to kiss her full on the lips.

Not a peck. Nossir. A full-blown kiss that lasted for long seconds.

For those long seconds, Zoe felt herself melt with it, into

it. Then – she realized where they were. And she remembered that just short minutes ago, Scott had held a la Diaz in his arms much like this.

Her eyes sprang open as he masterfully turned and twirled her into the Latin Hustle steps that completed the dance. When Scott waved a palm up at Zoe, deferring to her talent, the crowd applauded wildly.

Then, as silence ascended, she took a step toward Scott and hissed at him. "How dare you do that!"

Shock rippled through the room.

Scott's eyebrows shot up but a glint of humor remained in his gray eyes. "Hey!" His volume also shot up. "What's good enough for Travolta is good enough for me. Wouldn't you say, folks?" He turned to the gawkers, who by now thirsted for some comic relief; Zoe realized this and forced a smile.

Applause accompanied their elaborate bows as Peyton, who'd come in late, rushed to put on some more Bee Gees music, this time orchestrating a line dance. By now, the gathering had accepted that Zoe and Scott's little "scene" was staged.

In retrospect, Zoe was glad. But the stomped-down squeezing around her heart did not let up. That Stacia Dietrich gave Scott a little hug in parting did not help her disheveled emotions.

She stuck her nose up in the air and smiled, smiled, smiled as folks left.

Easy come, easy go. That had always been the case with her heart's issues.

On the drive home, Scott seemed deep in thought and unusually quiet.

Zoe, too, found nothing to say. Flashbacks from her past bombarded her. Her ex-husband had seemed to worship her when they married. She had adored him, too, because, to hear him tell it, he could whip the world with both hands tied behind his back. He'd convinced her that he was invincible.

The first disappointment had been when Zoe discovered that his "affluent" family was poor as desert rabbits. That wouldn't have bothered her, however. Zoe was no status freak. It was the lies he'd sown all along during their relationship that cut her deeply.

Yet – even then, he was lovable in his deceit.

But as soon as Peyton arrived, Wilton began to change. Her greatest sorrow was that he never adapted to fatherhood. He also never adapted to responsibility.

He'd unapologetically handed all that over to her.

Wilton's braggadocio cockiness slowly fizzled when reality crashed in upon his handsome, empty head.

Now, she blinked back the pain and acknowledged shamefully that, even then, she'd not sent him away.

He ran out on her.

"What are you thinking about?" Scott's voice cut into her angst.

She took a deep cleansing breath and blew it out. "Oh. Just some dark happenings I experienced in years gone by." No use in being evasive. She refused to become a liar on top of being a pushover.

He cut her a glance. "Like what?"

"Things I'd rather not talk about."

"Is that why you reacted to me like you did tonight?" The words were low. Even.

"Probably." She shook her head. "I'm not sure."

"Exactly where do we stand, Zoe?"

She studied him. His demeanor was calm. Strong. Confident. Unlike the Scott who had pursued her so relentlessly over a year ago. That Scott would have slain dragons for her.

Just like Wilton in the beginning.

Where did they stand?

For the life of her, she didn't know.

"I need an answer, Zoe. I think you owe me that much."

And Zoe heard in his voice that he meant it. He probably wanted his freedom to pursue the new teacher.

"Scott, I'm grateful for all you've done for me." She shrugged listlessly as he pulled into the duplex's driveway. "I have lots of things going on right now. My mother's situation being at the very top. She's no better and I'm afraid of what may be causing her problems."

Scott turned in the seat, relaxed, watching her closely. "Are you still feeling suspicious of Barth, Zoe?" he asked. She could hear, feel the incredulity in his voice.

"Let's just say I don't entirely trust him to be who he says he is."

"Zoe, I can't believe you're saying that." He frowned at her, disbelieving. "I've never seen a more devoted husband than Barth is to Seana. You can't mean ..."

"Scott, we've had this conversation before. Please, I repeat, please do not tell me what I mean. Or what I should think. Because you have not walked in my shoes. Consequently, you have no right to dictate to me how I should feel."

With that she wrested the car door open and climbed out. "I've got to go."

"Zoe!" Scott slid from his side and locked the car. "Wait. So you've already told me that I have no right to counsel you. And you've not answered my earlier question. An important one. Where, exactly do we stand?"

He took her arm, walked her to her door, and watched her unlock it. She turned to face him, feeling trapped. His eyes told her nothing. They were, in the night light, steady and head on.

"Do I have to answer this very moment?" she asked in a long-suffering tone.

Scott's gaze never wavered. "Yes. I need to know."

She sighed heavily. "Scott, at this very moment, I don't know that there is a 'we.' I don't know. I guess it's the trust thing. I've been burned too many times. Too deeply." She shrugged. "You're a great friend. I can't even begin to thank you for ..."

"Stop." Scott gave her a grim little smile. "You've answered my question. G' night, Zoe." He turned on his heel and walked away.

Zoe watched his white *a la Travolta* form disappear around

the corner and presently she heard the door to his duplex open and firmly shut.

She looked up into a star-studded sky and belatedly felt her heart drop to her feet. And she was shocked at the keen sense of loss that swamped her.

What have I done now? she wondered.

❧❧

Seana liked Dr. Jones, her new psychiatrist. And for a few months, he seemed to help her. He was different from Dr. Walton; he wanted to hear every detail of her life. He was delighted with her progress.

That was great at first. But then, like a leaky tire, she began to feel her strength begin to ebb.

"I don't feel like I can stand long enough to take a shower," she complained to Barth.

"Then I'll run you a bath, honey."

He did but had to assist her when her arms grew too weak. She saw that his concern grew as he witnessed her defenselessness.

"She's nearly helpless," Barth explained to Dr. Jones on the next visit. "I have to assist her in most things now."

The good doctor exploded. "What? You mean you're actually bathing her?" He shook his head in disbelief then chewed Seana up one side and down the other.

"I cannot believe that you're so – so lazy. Your sense of entitlement is beyond anything I've seen recently. Get up and wait on yourself. You'll never get better until you take some responsibility for yourself."

"And Barth," he turned his disapproval on Barth, "you've got to stop this. Do *not* help her do another thing!"

Then he marched over to Seana and got in her face. "You are an adult, Seana. You do *not* need your husband's help. Do you understand me?"

Seana nodded but felt too weak to truly react. Even if she'd wanted to.

To react would have been to *feel*.

Which she did not.

Barth was silent all the way home. Looked angry almost. But he gently helped her from the car and into the house. Then he tucked her into her bed on the sofa, making sure the blanket swaddled and warmed her, easing her chills.

She heard Billie Jean come clomping in later that afternoon and sit with Barth in the kitchen. "Been playing with Brutus," she told Barth, out of breath from the excursion. "That dog would chase a stick till Jesus returns if you let 'im. He'd never stop bringing it back for another toss. Look at 'im, standing there, panting and begging me to go back out. No way, Brutus!" She laughed and soon Barth's deeper chortles joined in.

Presently, Seana felt Brutus's tail brush her arm as he padded to his bed, on the floor next to the sofa. And a wet lick on her arm, drippy from his frantic lapping of water to quench his thirst. He still panted when he plopped down into the soft bed. There, he lay all during his daylight hours now. Not being intrusive. Simply lying there, near Seana.

But he knew every move Seana made. She knew because several times, during her dark days, she would feel his tongue soothing her hand or cheek or a foot protruding from beneath the cover. Or she'd feel his snout nudging her hand that held the TV remote.

She would see those soulful amber eyes watching her with concern.

But she had no affection to give. She remained empty. The nothingness was worse than ever before. It yawned like a bottomless chasm, pulling her down, down, toward a black pit, onto whose precipice she clung with white knuckled fingers.

Clinging ... clawing. No one saw. But she felt it with every fiber of her being.

She was so tired. So very weary.

Tonight, Seana watched the clock hands reach eight o'clock. "It's time for my meds, Barth."

⊷⊶

"Zoe's having an anniversary celebration at the dance studio. Remember your daughter?" Barth's joke fell flat. Seana, snuggly buried in her soft sofa, already shook her head in succinct refusal.

Barth tried again. "The entire family will be there. Even Billie Jean, Joanie, and Chelsea. Wouldn't you like to see your girlfriends, sweetheart?" Seana's irritation bled through as she angled her head to see around him to the TV screen where a Braves game blared. Not that she cared, he thought to himself.

She was just being aggravating.

As usual. He felt instantly guilty for thinking that. He sighed, slapped hands against knees, and arose from the ottoman he'd pulled up to the sofa. He moved it back to its regular spot and went to the bathroom to brush his teeth.

He grabbed his navy-blue jacket and pulled it on over his white silk blend Villini pullover and bent down to kiss Seana's cheek. He noticed an exceedingly belligerent cast to her features. "You okay, honey?"

She didn't reply. But that wasn't unusual. Her connection to him was like a temperamental old car. Unpredictable. When he turned the switch, it sometimes sprang into action, others it whined and whirred. At others, like now, it idled.

"I've got my cell phone if you need me. Okay?" He gave her another kiss on her crown. Outside the late April air was balmy, and he could smell early blooming spring flowers. Budding red azalea bushes flanked the curving driveway in vibrant embrace.

All this warmed Barth and he felt thankful for his bounty … regardless of his home situation. He took a deep, steadying breath. He must not let it get him down.

He pushed past the heaviness that hovered. The weariness. *I must go on.*

Resolutely, he joined the family at Happy Feet Dance Studio for the twentieth anniversary of the business.

Peyton's smiling face was the first he spotted. Barth's heart lifted at the warm affection he felt as the young man he now considered his own rushed to embrace him.

Yes, indeed. He was blessed.

❧

Zoe checked the soft drink supply again and mingled with friends, family, and clientele. "Hi, Chelsea," she traded hugs with her friend. "Thanks for coming."

Chelsea's kohled eyes shimmered and her onyx, bobbed hair glistened beneath the dramatic lighting. "Wouldn't've missed it for the world. This place has been my hangout for twenty years, doncha know?"

Zoe's eyes unexpectedly misted. "Yes, I do know. Thanks." She sniffed back tears and moved on.

Her steps paused as she spotted Scott Burns. He was engaged in a serious powwow with Stacia Dietrich in a secluded corner. She was looking at him mighty sweetly and at one point reached to touch his hand.

Zoe turned away and clashed into Joanie. "You okay, honey bun?" Joanie peered into her face like a concerned mama.

"I'm okay." Zoe pasted on her got-the-world-on-a-string smile. "Thanks, Joanie."

"For what?" Beneath piled high, sequin-anchored blonde curls, jade-green eyes widened curiously.

"For celebrating with me." She shrugged, barely managing to rein in her agitating emotions. "Couldn't've done it without my friends."

Joanie brushed hands over saucy hips to unnecessarily smooth her fitted green slacks. "That's what friends are for, Zoe."

Zoe patted her shoulder and moved away. "I'm just beginning to really get that," she muttered under her breath.

Barth and Peyton sat at a table together, laughing and talking, as comfortable and contented as two old hound dogs gnawing on ham bones. She almost smiled at the Norman Rockwell scene. Almost.

Billie Jean grabbed her by the arm, startling her. "Hey girl! Why don't you make some kind of grandstand announcement here? All these folks turned out just for you." Then the spiffed-up version of her cousin wrapped her warm hands around Zoe's and smiled gently. "Just let it go, Zoe," she said, her eyes misting. An unusual thing for the tough as nails woman.

Zoe felt her nose burn and pressure sting behind her eyes. "What're you talking about?" she croaked.

"Aw, you know all right." The words were soft. "I've known you since you were born, Zoe. You're the child I never was able to have. So listen up." She gently squeezed Zoe's fingers.

"Your mama can't counsel you now. But –" She snuffled and squared her shoulders, "I don't know exactly what's going on in that head of yours, but just know that I love you and am praying that whatever's got your clothes in such a wad will soon be resolved."

Zoe narrowed her eyes. "I'm not –"

"Nuh-uh. I *know*, Zoe. Can't fool ol' Billie Jean. You just know that I love you. Y'hear?" The astute hazel gaze brooked no arguments.

Zoe nodded and watched her feisty cousin's departure.

"Mama!" Peyton's cry set off an alarm in her as she pivoted in his direction.

Bart was rushing to the exit like his feet were on fire.

Peyton reached her, his eyes wild with – fear?

"What?" she cried, dreading the answer.

His hands clutched her shoulders. "Oh, Mama," he moaned. "Nana's tried to kill herself again!"

❧❧

"No arguments," Scott all but shouted. "Get in my car, Zoe."

They stood outside the studio. Zoe had left Billie Jean in charge of shutting the place down.

She'd seen the pale, shocked faces upon the news of Seana's latest suicide bid.

After another moment's hesitation, she complied. "You, too, Peyton," Scott called out the window.

Peyton jumped into the backseat. The drive to the hospital was tense. Awkward. But Zoe's main thoughts were with her mother. Dear, precious – *demented* Mama. Oh *God*, when would it all end?

A chill brushed over Zoe. *Not like this! Please. Not like this.*

Tears appeared of their own accord. And Zoe didn't care. *Hang* being in control. Hang being cool and competent. She was desperately tired of it all. She savagely rummaged in her purse and found wadded Kleenexes.

"You okay?" Scott ventured softly.

"No. I'm not." She blew her nose.

She felt Peyton's hand slide over her shoulder and squeeze. "She's gonna make it, Mom," he said. She heard the doubt, the fear in his voice. She also heard the courage.

"She will," Scott echoed. In his voice she heard – conviction.

"Thanks," she whispered and snuffled back a fresh rush of tears.

At the hospital ER, Barth looked like death himself. His red eyes and soda cracker paleness pronounced his grief. Peyton engulfed him in his arms, weeping softly. "It'll be okay," he murmured brokenly.

Barth snuffled and patted his shoulder. "Let's pray it will, son."

Scott, too, embraced Barth, his muscular arms swallowing up Barth's lean frame. Zoe admitted to herself that it had grown even thinner in recent months. Scott's embrace ended in shoulder-clapping encouragement. "We're hanging in there with you, buddy," Scott husked and unashamedly whisked out his handkerchief and wiped away tears.

"They're working with her now," Barth grimly informed them. "She said she took thirty Clonazepams." He shook his head and bit his lip so hard, Zoe saw it turning white at teeth pressure points.

They'd no sooner got settled in waiting room chairs than Billie Jean stormed in the waiting room. Still in her dress-up clothes, she looked around at them, frowning. "How is she?"

She addressed Zoe because Barth was sitting with elbows on knees, face in hands.

"Alive is all I know," Zoe said, sounding even to herself like a zombie.

"That's all that counts." Billie Jean planted hands on hips and her gaze swept over the lot of them. "Ya'll sitting around here as gloomy as a bunch o' undertakers. Stop this whiny mopin' right now." She moved over to take the seat next to Barth. There she laid a gentle hand on his shoulder.

"Now's not the time to give up." Her words were soft yet firm. Zoe felt a bit of strength rise up in her. "Now's time to pray like crazy, folks. We gotta drive back that ol' death angel, doncha know? 'S no time to pine."

Within moments, Pastor Keith and Louann arrived.

Immediately, the whole caboodle of them disappeared down the hall, into the tiny chapel there.

And got down to serious business.

❧ ❧

"She didn't take thirty Clonazepam," the on-duty ER physician insisted. "If she had, she'd be dead right now."

Barth scratched his head and blinked sore, swollen eyes. Now weary beyond words, he seemed to exist in blurred slow-motion. "That's what she told me." He shrugged limply yet his body remained on alert. His nerves sizzled with apprehension.

Dread.

"Couldn't have." That was the doctor's final comment on the matter.

"How is she?" Barth croaked, bracing himself.

"She's coming around."

Barth felt himself cave with relief.

Zoe zoomed in. "She's coming around? Will she be able to go home?"

"No." The doctor looked grim. "We're admitting her."

❧ ৶

Seana was assigned to the geriatrics ward because it had the only available room at that time. The psychiatrist on her case was Dr. Moore. He was a very caring man.

The staff refused to allow Seana to vegetate in her room. So she would sit in the common room area. She didn't talk to anyone. She wanted to go home.

Dr. Moore treated her with different medications and then sent her home.

Her next appointment with Dr. Jones, her most recent psychiatrist, rolled around. Seana began to tell him about her suicide attempt. "I took –"

"I already know about it because the hospital sent me the information." He glared at her. "Let me tell you one thing, young lady. That act was like a slap in my face. After all I've done for you?" He dragged in a deep breath and continued. "If you ever try anything like that again, I will not treat you anymore. Do you understand?"

Seana nodded. Untouched.

"Will you give me prescriptions for my sleeping pills?" she asked.

"No. Absolutely not."

"How am I supposed to sleep?"

He stood abruptly, a definite dismissal. "That's your problem."

chapter seven

"What do we live for if not to
make life less difficult for others?"
– George Eliot

arth was at the end of his rope and could not, for the life of him, find a way to knot it. He was royally befuddled. Seana was worse off than she'd ever been. In the past years, she'd been hospitalized a total of six times in psychiatric facilities.

And she was no better.

Today, Zoe appeared mid-morning, in Cruella mode. "What's this I hear about you putting my mother in a nursing home, Barth?" She swept past him, stiletto heels clicking rapidly over the hardwood to the sofa until she stood before Seana, peering down into her wan, pale face.

"Mama? Are you going to just lie there and take this insult?" she commanded, hands on hips.

Seana simply shrank deeper beneath the blanket, her forehead corrugated with irritation.

"Zoe, I have no choice," Barth said dispiritedly. "She's so depressed she can't do anything for herself anymore." He paced to the kitchen, then back. He shook his head and shifted his glasses. "I can't handle it anymore."

Zoe looked a little uncertain as she peered at him. "I know she's difficult at times but to put her away –"

Barth spread his hands. "I'm not putting her away. At least not like you're perceiving it. I'm just – burnt out, Zoe." He sank into a leather chair, feeling as defeated as he'd ever felt in his life. "I've got to have a break." He laid his head back and closed his eyes.

"Do you really love her, Barth?"

The analytical tone snapped his eyes open and he was on his feet in a heartbeat.

"Yes, I love her more than anything in this world," he all but shouted, hands planted on hips. Barth peered at Zoe, shaking his head. "How can you even ask that? Of course I love her. Look" – he spread his hands. – "if you want to take your mother home with you and care for her 24/7, have at it."

Zoe blinked and her set features went blank. Then she slid into the other leather easy chair, ruminating in earnest. Silence stretched out as Barth sank into a chair and folded his hands across his midriff. Having dealt with Seana throughout the crisis-riddled years, he'd developed patience. So he waited out Zoe's silent internal dialogue.

Finally, she took a deep breath. "I can't do that. Peyton is away most of the day at school and I have my work at the dance studio all throughout the day and late into the night." She sighed heavily. Then she gave a limp shrug. "I still don't like it but – do what you have to do, Barth."

She stood. So did Barth. They peered uncertainly at each other, and Barth knew they'd reached a sort of impasse. A vague, fuzzy truce. But at least this magnificent female offspring of Seana's standing before him was not spewing anger today. She's progressed to negotiable.

In fact, Barth felt something from her he'd not felt before. Empathy. Not a tsunami. But it was a start.

He walked her to the door. When he opened it, June sunlight spilled in and over the highly polished wood floors. Zoe stepped out onto the inlaid rock entrance, hesitated, then turned back. "Bye, Barth."

"Bye, Zoe."

She seemed about to say more, but, in the end, she simply walked away, slid into her car, and drove off.

Barth expelled a rush of air and scratched his head.

When he returned to the den, Billie Jean was there, planted in an easy chair.

She'd overheard some of the conversation. "Didn't mean to eavesdrop, Barth, but you know how it is when you're coming up those stairs and catch a serious powwow in session. I caught enough to know that Zoe's just as disturbed over the nursing home decision as we've been."

She crossed her denimed legs. "However, like Zoe said – she's not willing or able to take up any of the slack here. So –" She smacked one hand against the chair arm. "That's the way it is. And, like I've been saying, I feel it's the right decision for now."

Barth felt right weak from relief at hearing Billie Jean's confirmation. Oh how he'd wrestled with the decision. Fought it. But fatigue had won out.

"Thanks, Billie Jean." He removed his glasses and snatched a tissue from the coffee table to clean them. "Couldn't have made it at times without your reinforcement."

"Shoot," Billie Jean huffed a dry laugh. "Barth, you're the strongest person I know. Bar none. We've both come through the worst of times and are still in one piece. We're gonna make it through this, too. Just you wait and see."

Barth gave a weak smile.

He hoped she was right.

❧

Seana saw Barth's aggravation when she didn't flow with life's happenings. But the weird thing that tinkered with her brain just kept on a' tinkering. It wouldn't let up, and when, in her last hospital stay, she refused to get out of bed for five days and attend classes, Barth seemed to cave in.

His desperation did not impact her. The invisible shell wrapping her deflected any outside stimulus. The warring inside her played out in a private isolated arena.

"Seana, I have something to tell you," Barth addressed her the day he took her home. She lay on her sofa bed and he'd dragged up the ottoman to sit on, planted elbows on knees and gazed into her eyes. He looked very sad. "I'm going to have to put you in a nursing home."

He seemed to expect some response from her. Which irritated her.

"Just go ahead. I don't care." And she didn't.

So Barth called Rosewood Manor, a nice facility just outside Paradise Springs's town limit, within short driving distance for all Seana's family and friends.

The lady at Rosewood Manor helped Barth with the arrangements.

She heard the confrontational exchange between Barth and Zoe that next day. She also heard Billie Jean's conversation with him. Oh yes, she heard. She wasn't deaf. But it was all just words that held little to no significance for her.

Nothingness abounded. The only things that *whooshed* in to punctuate it were sporadic, dreaded spurts of fear and a sense of dread. But for the most part, the white, vast nothingness spread about her like the Mojave Desert, with no beginning and no end.

Seana "moved into" Rosewood Manor within three days of leaving the hospital, following her last suicide attempt. Her roommate was Bess, an elderly lady who couldn't, without assistance, get up or dress herself.

Each day, a Certified Nursing Assistant got Bess up, bathed, and dressed her. Then off she went in a wheelchair to attend activities the facility provided for the patients, such as games and Bible studies.

Seana was awakened each morning by a CNA, who brought her a pan of hot water, wash cloth, and soap with which to bathe herself. When the CNA left, Seana would immediately dump the water into a sink, dress herself, un-washed, and crawl back into bed until time to go to breakfast.

Once a week, certain days were assigned in which patients went to the shower for a more thorough bath. Seana would shampoo her hair then.

Oh how Seana hated that day.

She would return to her room, dressed, with hair still drippy wet. The nurses would come in, see it, and make her dry it. Seana would blow it haphazardly and let it fall where it may.

She didn't care.

Fact of the matter was, Seana didn't care about anything.

❧ ৯

Zoe visited her mother on her second day. Seeing Seana in the nursing home did something to her solar plexus. It was a thudding, agitating thing that spread up to push behind her throat and eyes.

The visit went just as she'd expected. It was like sitting with a comatose person except, every once in a while, the person moved. Zoe decided to chill out and read from the display of magazines on the bedside table, a rare treat nowadays since she'd had to take on more of the dance studio business single-handedly.

Lordy how she missed Peyton's shoulder to the plough.

"Did Peyton come by to see you yesterday?" she asked Seana, who remained curled up on her hospital bed. Dressed, but still in bed.

"Yes."

"Did you enjoy it?"

"Yes."

Zoe heaved a great sigh and plopped her book down on the table. It was a Reader's Digest. No time to get into novels these days. Crazy as it seemed, she felt guilty not trying to at least engage her mother in small talk.

Stupid, huh?

Like banging her fingers with a hammer over and over and not expecting blood.

"Did you talk to Peyton?"

"No."

"Why not?"

A vertical frown line formed between Seana's eyebrows.

"I didn't want to," they spoke simultaneously.

Zoe made a scoffing sound. She stood up and began to roam restlessly around the room. Bess, the roommate, was out playing Bingo. Why couldn't her mother get out of the blasted bed and do *something*?

"Mom, won't you please get up and let's do something together? Just walk or sit in another room, or anything to have you moving. You're like a knot on a log lying there. Vegetating."

Seana clicked the remote and presently Zoe heard the familiar sports-related cacophony blast from the television.

Zoe threw up her hands and rolled her eyes. "I give up."

"Hi," Barth said as he entered the room, walked over to the bed to lean over and kiss Seana's cheek. "Sit down, Zoe," he invited as he took one of the chairs and settled in for a spell.

"I'm just leaving," Zoe said, relieved that she could depart without feeling that splintering sense of guilt over leaving.

Abandonment. That's how she perceived it today as she left the Rosewood Manor and drove away.

"Nonsense," was what Scott had called it. "Zoe, you have a life to live, responsibilities. Your mother, in her right mind, would be the first to tell you to get on with your life. I remember what a fabulous person she is underneath this psychosis. That version is very, very wise. She wouldn't want you to beat yourself up over unrealistic expectations of yourself."

Scott.

She missed those heart-to-hearts. He'd not been there for her lately. She knew she'd hurt him by denying her feelings for him. She'd driven him away, just as she had the others.

Oh well; she snuffled back the threat of tears.

No room for melancholy now. Not ever.

That lapse with Scott had been utterly stupid. How could she forget that she could not depend on another soul to rescue her?

She must be strong.

❧ ❧

Seana lay in bed the next morning. She felt her stomach contract. Growl.

"Breakfast time." The CNA poked her head in the door and smiled at Seana. "Get up, sleepyhead."

"Okay." She'd already poured out the hot water without first bathing. Had dressed. So now she headed for the dining room.

Her breakfast consisted of scrambled eggs, toast, and a half cup of black coffee. That's all she wanted. She carried her tray to a table where several other ladies were already seated. Seana took a seat there.

"You can't sit here," one of them, a squinty-eyed female, quickly insisted. "This is our table."

Seana arose, picked up her tray, and wandered around the room until one friendly lady beckoned to her. "Here, you can sit with us." Another woman sitting there smiled at Seana as she took her seat. At the end of the table was a blind woman.

The seating arrangement became routine for Seana in coming days. Comfortable.

She decided that day she didn't want to go to supper.

"Would you please bring my supper to my room?" she sweet-talked the CNA. "I don't feel so good."

Her winsomeness had not totally deserted her, she discovered, because the CNA liked Seana and would always give in to her wants.

❧ ❧

Night times at Rosewood Manor were something else.

Seana's roommate was nice enough during the daytime. Unlike Seana, Mrs. Hyde, though dependent on assistance, faithfully participated in the facility's activities. So during daylight hours, Seana was queen bee of the domain.

Come sundown, Seana's meds rendered her groggy and in search of slumber. Just when she wanted the television turned off, Mrs. Hyde wanted to play it.

Seemed that loud volume soothed the roommate while it blasted Seana's senses to Hoboken and back. And the noise roared into the wee hours.

One night, after midnight, Seana lay in her bed listening to the woman's snoring. Her nerves were jumpy. Quietly, she slid off her bed and tiptoed to the television set. She turned it off.

Immediately, Mrs. Hyde roared, "What do you think you're doing? I was watching that!"

"You were snoring."

"I was not snoring. That's my TV and if I want to play it, I will!"

Seana turned back to the set. "I'll turn it back on."

"No!" she shrieked. "Don't touch it again."

Seana crawled back into bed.

What had just transpired became the extent of conversation Seana and her roommate had the entire time she was at Rosewood Manor.

❧❧

Mother's Day dawned bright and fair.

Sunlight spilled into Seana's room with excruciating cheer. After a dismal breakfast, Seana burrowed into her bed and began to sink into a slumber pool.

"Hey, hey." A deep female voice scattered the drowsy mist. Seana blinked and peered into the caramel-y features of Eartha, a patient down the hall who'd decided she was Seana's voice of conscience, rescuer, and nuisance.

The full lips smiled, showing pearly whites that stretched forever. Seana groaned and tried to cover up her head.

"Ah, ah." The cover was wrenched from her hands. "Ain't you gonna get all dolled up for your chirrun?"

"No." Another wresting match over the cover, which was over in a breath because Eartha was taller, bigger, and much stronger.

"I think you are," Eartha insisted firmly.

Before she knew it, Seana was on the floor, being propelled toward the bathroom where Eartha stuck her head under the faucet and unceremoniously shampooed her hair. She then beat the wet strands dry with hot air from a hair dryer and used searing curling irons to finish the transformation.

"Stay put," she ordered and left the room.

Seana was afraid to move.

Presently, Eartha returned with makeup. Seana sat as still as a Greek statue while the humming woman applied masterful strokes to her features. When finished, she stepped back, crossed her arms, and examined Seana closely. She smiled and nodded approval.

"Mm-hmm."

One more pat to Seana's hair and she pronounced, "Now you're ready for your sweet chirrun and husband to come see you." She took Seana's arm and propelled her this time to a pleasant visiting room with lots of sunlight and vibrant greenery.

Within minutes, the entire Sunday-clad tribe piled in, Barth, Zoe, Peyton, and Billie Jean, followed by Tim, Sherry, and Ashley. Seana heard them say they'd just finished lunch at the Sunday Mater and Onion Buffet.

At the commotion, Seana felt herself draw inward like a startled turtle. At least she wished she could draw her extremities into a shell. She was already exhausted by the time everyone hugged and greeted her.

"Mama," Zoe gushed. "You look beautiful."

Barth gave her an exceptionally long embrace and while nuzzling her cheek whispered, "You look good enough to eat."

Seana pulled away and sank stiffly down into a comfortable chair. Eartha had dressed her in loose navy slacks and a white pullover top. Barth and Billie Jean had refused to pack her beloved, bedraggled striped pullover to bring with her. She missed it.

"I want to lie down," Seana said.

"Mama, don't you feel like sitting up for just a little while?" Zoe coaxed.

"No." Oh how she wanted them to leave so she could lie down.

"It's okay, Nana," Ashley said, reaching to squeeze Seana's hand once more.

"Yeh, Nana," Peyton said, "it's okay. We're not going to stay long, so you can go lie down soon."

"We just wanted to see you on Mother's Day," Billie Jean said. "You're not my mama but you've always been there for me, just like my own mother."

"You're not my mother, either," Barth said, ignoring the stifled laughter throughout the room. "But I had to see my sweetheart. And just look at you. You look like a homecoming queen."

"Hey! She *was* the homecoming queen of Paradise Springs High in her young days, doncha know?" crowed Billie Jean.

"And she's just as lovely now." Barth pulled his chair next to Seana, leaned over, and gave her a big kiss as close to her lips as he could get. Seana scowled and promptly swiped it away. "That's okay," he chuckled. "You can't get rid of my love that easily."

Everybody got a big kick out of that and laughed appreciatively.

All except Zoe.

∞

Zoe finished shining mirrors and polishing furniture at the studio. She still needed to dust mop the floors but she needed a break. A cold drink. How she missed Peyton's help with the cleaning.

She pulled a chilled bottle of water from the fridge and took a long, cooling swallow. How good it felt sliding down her parched throat and into her stomach, cooling her all the way down. She closed her eyes and took another pull of it and set it down atop the stereo cabinet.

Her fingers moved over the music selections, then halted. She slid in a disc and let the smooth, cool music of Barry Manilow fill her up until she was floating and began to dance barefoot over parquet floors awash with late afternoon sunlight.

Sparkling mirrors reflected long legs encased in jeans, gliding and swaying her lithe form in liquid motion as she drowned in the mellow notes and lyrical message of someone else's pain. She dipped and swirled as it somehow made her own hurt diminish for a few blessed moments.

This was why Zoe loved dance. At that precise moment, she wished she could choreograph herself away, into oblivion, into another musical realm where she could dive into it and never again come up for air.

Where she could disappear and never again have to come back and face what a mess she'd made of her life.

Manilow's "Even Now" pulled on her heartstrings. Groaned like the strings on a cello, heavy and melancholy. It spoke of lost love ... one that did not go away. The heart still felt it. Still grieved.

The song ended and Zoe started to turn it off. But another started playing.

Her hand stilled as the words bombarded her. "Ready To Take A Chance Again" snared her like a booby-trap in those childhood Tarzan movies where the prey was caught by a looped rope and ended up hanging upside down from a sky high tree.

Dangling helplessly.

Only thing, she'd never really taken a chance with Scott, not for the first time. So adding "again" was ludicrous.

Scott.

Just his name rearranged everything in her senses. Jolted and shook them up.

She danced, soaking up the words ... *you remind me I live in a shell ... safe from the past, and doing okay but not very well* ....

Oh yeh. That was her, living in a shell, safe from the past. Doing okay – but not very well.

She slid to a halt, face in hands. What a coward she was.

"Are you okay?"

His words spun her around. Scott approached from the entrance area, his long strides briskly eating up the parquet. "Zoe" – his voice vibrated with concern – "is something wrong?"

She took a deep breath and shook her head. "N-no. Just tired." Her attempt to smile fell flat.

He now had her by the shoulders, those steel-gray eyes assessing her. "You sure nothing's wrong?"

If she didn't know better, she'd think he was worried about her. But she knew better. "I'm sure." She frowned. "How did you get in?"

Scott loosed her and stepped back. "I've got a key. Remember? I helped Peyton on several occasions when you were down with your hip injury."

"Oh. Yeh. But ..." She didn't mean to sound shrewish, but for the life of her she couldn't seem to soften her attitude. "What are you doing here?"

Scott's smile didn't reach his eyes. "I left my cell phone here last night after the clog rehearsal." He moved to a corner table. "Here it is. Right where I left it."

He tucked it into his little belt holder. "How're we doing?"

Zoe was having trouble breathing with him so close. "W-what?"

"The clog number for the festival. How're we doing?"

"Oh." She sucked in a deep breath. "Great. Just – great."

"You sure?" He looked closely at her.

"Of course," she said more sharply than she intended. So

she smiled to soften it. "You and Stacia are doing fabulous." How she hated to admit it. But it was the truth. Act like an adult, she silently told herself.

Scott chuckled. "She's excited because she'd never really done the clogging thing before. Totally out of her league, she said. But she really caught on, didn't she?"

"Yup. She did." Zoe's mouth was hurting from smiling.

He watched her for long moments, as if expecting her to say more. When she didn't, he turned to leave and she noticed how much thinner he looked.

"Have you lost weight?" she asked.

He turned back and gave her a little crooked smile. "A little."

She thought, more than a little. But he still looked terrific.

"How's your mother?"

The words were so soft, so sweet that she teared up suddenly. She tried to gulp back the emotions that swam to the surface, along with the unexpected tears that stubbornly pushed their way out to puddle along her lids then spill over.

How she missed her mother being there.

"S-she's about the same," she croaked. Then held up a hand as Scott reached out for her. "I'm okay," she whispered and proceeded to cry like a baby as he slid his strong arms around her.

Manilow's music still played on the darned automatic Discmaster. Romantic, sad songs. "Can't Smile Without You" finished and the revolving selections just had to land on a replay of "Ready to Take a Chance Again."

Scott's big hand swallowed hers as one arm slipped around her waist, and they began to dance together as her weeping subsided and she lay her head on his shoulder. He smelled wonderfully masculine, a mixture of Lifebuoy soap, spicy cologne, and just a hint of outdoors.

"I'm sorry I upset you," he murmured into her hair, raising goose bumps all over her, the delicious kind. "Seems with you I can't get anything right."

Zoe looked up at him. "You didn't upset me. I was already wired tight as a hamstring." She shrugged and gave him a tight smile. "It's not you, Scott. I'm the one who doesn't get anything right."

In that moment, with his clear, gray eyes gazing into hers, she wondered if he sensed the turbulence in the atmosphere surrounding them. And if he felt her confusion, her failure to categorize this thing between them. Because it was something powerful to her.

When around, he sucked up the air so that she could hardly breathe.

"Tell me what I did," he said softly, taking her hand and leading her to sit at one of the small, intimately placed tables. He took the seat opposite her and gazed at her. The soft, slow Manilow love song, this time "Looks Like We Made It," drifted from the stereo speakers.

Zoe blinked and took a deep breath. "Why haven't you kissed me again?"

Instantly horrified, she felt her face begin to heat with embarrassment.

Scott's eyes rounded and then he, too, dragged in a deep, long breath and blew it out. "Because ..." He raised his hands, those wonderful, beautiful hands, and spread them wide. "Because I didn't think you would welcome that again. Remember you told me – in front of everyone here that night – that you didn't appreciate my gesture." He shrugged and gave her a rueful lopsided half-smile. "I don't push myself on anyone, Zoe."

Then he leaned forward and planted elbows on the table. "I screwed up, Zoe. Big time. I'm sorry for that. Every time I think about that stupid, dramatic gesture, I cringe, especially when I recall your look of disdain afterward. I've had to step back and reassess my feelings for you. I don't want a replay of that night."

Zoe's heart plunged to her toes. "Are you saying – ?"

"I'm saying I need to step back and take time to process the pain and shame of the ..." His gaze dropped to study his hands, now clasped before him. "Of the breakup, so to speak." He shrugged again and looked at her. "Only thing, what did we have, Zoe?"

Zoe sat frozen, a sense of déjà vu gripping her. She opened her mouth to speak but couldn't utter a sound. Because for the life of her, she did not know what they had, or for that matter, if they had anything beyond friendship.

She knew what her heart was saying, but her heart had tricked her before. Done mutiny on her. Did she dare utter her love for him? That in itself caused a quick intake of breath. She was in love with him. How could she have let down her guard?

Scott stood in that moment. "That's what I thought," he muttered and turned on his heel.

Zoe rose to her feet and took two steps. "Scott?" she called.

He halted and slowly turned, his face unreadable.

Again, she opened her mouth to declare her love. But the words jelled in her throat, undelivered.

"Yes?" he prompted, a slight edge to his voice. His long muscular, thinned-down form tightened with what seemed to be impatience.

"Are you and Stacia an item?" She heard the words slip out as though discharged used oil.

Scott actually smiled. "What do you think?"

On that, he pivoted and strode through the exit.

❧

Joanie and Chelsea tiptoed into Seana's room.

"Is she asleep?" Joanie whispered, peering at the stillness of the lumpy form beneath the blanket. The television was off because Mrs. Hyde, the roommate, had hidden her remote from Seana.

It wasn't an ethics thing with Seana. She simply didn't care enough to venture from her bed to search for it. At times she did, when she knew Mrs. Hyde would be gone for hours. But mostly, she simply lay there, staring out the window, letting the nothingness carry her nowhere.

Today, Joanie leaned down, in her face, so to speak. "Hi

there, Seana," she said gently and leaned to kiss her cheek. Chelsea loomed behind her, dark hair and colorful makeup zooming in like the blast of a dark freight train.

"Hi, sweetie," Chelsea crooned. "I brought you a present." She pulled from a Sassy Rags shopping bag a turquoise, soft velour two-piece lounging outfit. "Here." She and Joanie resolutely pulled her up and onto her feet to change her into it.

"When's the last time you took a bath?" Joanie asked, wrinkling her cute nose.

"This morning," Seana blatantly lied with nary a twinge of conscience.

Chelsea and Joanie looked at each other and rolled their eyes.

"Here, let's put some of your perfumed talc on you." Joanie knew where it was because she'd brought it during another visit, weeks before. "And some deodorant. Raise your arms." She sprayed profusely underneath each arm. Then with a fuzzy, plush puff, liberally dusted under each with Estee Lauder bath powder.

Chelsea sniffed appreciatively. "That's better."

Together, the two tucked Seana into the outfit. Then Joanie combed her hair, which resembled damp hay. "When did you last wash your hair?" she asked.

"Yesterday."

"Yeh." She sniffed. "Right."

Joanie worked a little magic on her head, though it did not impress Seana. She wished them away.

They forced Seana to go to the darned visiting area. There, settled between them in a comfortable chair, Seana only spoke when spoken to, and then reluctantly. She couldn't wait till they stopped gabbing and returned her to her room, where she immediately crawled back into bed. She endured their good-bye hugs and endless words as they departed, all smiles and cheer.

Finally, she was alone again.

From her bed, she looked out the window into space. Then when she heard someone enter her room, she quickly slid her eyes shut. But curious, she cracked an eye and peeked. The man looked familiar. It was Bud Carter, from church.

She closed her eyes again, not moving a muscle. He took a seat and sat there for a long, long time while she pretended to be asleep.

Then, he silently wrote her a note. He left it on her bedside table along with a beautiful ceramic butterfly. And she remembered indifferently that his wife, Nell, who owned a ceramic business, knew Seana collected butterflies. Seana had, at one time, attended evening classes there and made several for her collection.

But that hobby had been a long time back.

Forever.

It no longer appealed.

Nothing appealed to her.

Seana no long knew what "appeal" meant.

☙ ❧

Therapy came every day at two. It never altered.

For a while, during the first two to three months, Seana went faithfully. She did everything they told her to. Simple enough. But very quickly, she grew resentful of its intrusion.

Fact was, Seana was resentful of being at Rosewood Manor.

She resented everything about it because, in the first place, she felt she didn't need to be there. In the second place, she wanted to be home. She couldn't put her finger on any one thing that she missed of home, but she felt drawn there.

Then she had an idea.

"I have a stomachache," she told the therapist one day.

"Okay. You just rest," was the sympathetic reply. So she continued complaining of ailments.

It worked.

At first.

Then the therapist caught on. "Tell you what, Seana," she said. "I'll bring some things for you to do right here. You don't have to leave your room."

And she did.

Seana felt more trapped than ever.

❧ ❧

"Come in, Zoe." Pastor Keith stepped aside for her to enter his plush but comfortable church office. "Hold all calls, Nell," he told his secretary before closing the door.

"Have a seat." He indicated a smart padded chair across from him. He lowered himself into his leather chair behind the large executive desk. "How may I help you, Zoe?" His voice resonated with care.

Zoe's eyes immediately misted. "I've really messed up, Pastor. I – I don't even know where to begin." She shrugged and snuffled back tears while snatching a Kleenex from his desk that he'd pushed within reach.

Pastor Keith folded his hands across his midriff and allowed her long moments to collect herself enough to proceed.

"I couldn't think of anyone else to talk to about – things." She shrugged limply.

"That's what I'm here for."

She smiled tightly at him then lowered her head to study her hands as they wadded and plucked at the tissue. "First, I really screwed things up with Scott Burns." Her gaze slid to gauge his reaction.

The pastor's mouth seemed to twitch a little but Zoe felt she imagined it when his features settled into solemnity. "Anyway, at one time he seemed to really care for me."

"And now?"

"Now?" She began to shred the tissue. "He doesn't have hardly anything to do with me."

"Why do you think he changed?"

"Because I embarrassed him in front of my dance studio crowd when I scolded him for kissing me during a performance." Her voice choked off on the last word and she plucked another Kleenex from the box. As she blew her nose soundly and snuffled, she missed the amused spark in the pastor's eyes, which he quickly wiped away.

"So he's backed off, has he?" Pastor Keith asked matter-of-factly.

"Yes. Extremely." Zoe looked straight ahead, mortified for feeling so needy. Then she bucked up and squared her shoulders.

"Look," she addressed him more firmly, more in control. "I'm sorry for being so whiney. It is so not me."

Pastor Keith cleared his throat. "I know, Zoe," he said gently. "But it's okay to seek counsel. The Bible encourages us to seek wise counsel; it gives us a safety net."

Zoe smiled crookedly. "I guess I should have come sooner, huh?"

He chuckled. "It's never too late to seek help. Why don't you share what you're feeling right now?"

Zoe took a deep breath and plunged in feet first. She shared the way she felt about her past and her inadequacies when it came to holding a man. "They always leave," she said flatly. "No matter how hard I tried to be who and what I should be, they always left."

"How was your relationship with your father?"

"Oh." She transcended quickly from gloom, smiled a dazzling smile. "It was wonderful."

"So he thought you were pretty neat, huh?"

"He thought I was a perfect little princess." Nostalgia prickled over her. "At least that's what he always called me, his princess."

"Do you feel that your father was a wise man?"

Zoe sighed. "The wisest man I've ever known."

"Then his opinion of you was one you valued?"

"Of course – oh, I see where you're going with this, Pastor." Her smile vanished. "But that relationship was different. It wasn't a romantic one." She exuded a huff. "In *those* I bomb."

"So," Pastor Keith steepled his fingers before him, deeply in thought, "you're still trying to figure out who and what you're supposed to be."

"Pretty much."

"Tell me about your feelings for Barth, the new man in your mother's life."

Zoe bristled instantly. "No offense, Pastor, but I'd rather not talk about Barth."

Pastor Keith leaned forward, elbows on desk. "But he's a new father figure in your life, Zoe. How can he not be important in your quest to find yourself?"

Zoe glared at him. "He is *not* a father figure in my life. He is my mother's husband. Period."

The pastor settled back in his chair, studying Zoe. "That's strange. Barth addresses you and Tim as his children. He also claims grand-parentage to your offspring. Barth's very proud of his family. And Tim – as well as the rest of the family – seems to accept him affectionately. Why do you feel differently, Zoe?"

Zoe seemed to partially wilt. Then she shrugged, lowering her gaze. "I don't know exactly. There's just something about him – I feel he's hiding something. And I don't trust him with my mother's care since she's so vulnerable. So helpless."

Pastor Keith looked at Zoe for long moments, seeming to weigh something on his mind. Then he shifted and Zoe felt him turn loose of that something. He pulled a pad and pen from his desk drawer, jotted down notes for her and said, "Zoe, here are some scripture references I want you to study. I want you to pray about your feelings in all these areas we've discussed. And if circumstances have not changed by next week at this time, come back to see me. Okay?"

She nodded, disappointed. She'd hoped for a miraculous, instant cure. "Okay."

Then he added, "In fact, I want you to come back regardless. One week?"

"Sure."

He reached across the desk for her hand. "Let us pray."

❧ ❧

"Thanks for seeing me, Pastor," Barth embraced his friend. "We play dodge here at the office and we're both hard to catch. What with daily visiting Seana and all ..."

"How's she doing?" Pastor Keith motioned for Barth to sit as he took his desk seat.

"Not good." Barth shook his head. "She's not cooperating with the staff. They're pretty much fed up with her." He rubbed the back of his neck. "Can't blame them."

"Are you thinking of bringing her home?"

"It's the only thing I know to do. She's biting at the bits wanting to leave there. Don't know as home makes her any more at peace, however. But at the moment? It's the best solution I can come up with."

"Zoe was in this week."

"Oh?"

"She's not changed her mind about you."

Barth sighed deeply. "I know."

"Why don't you level with her?"

"I can't." He shook his head slowly. "I can't handle that particular thing at this time. There's too much going on, Keith."

"I know." Silence stretched out. "But you can't continue to blame –"

"I can blame myself." He stood and headed for the door, turning to address his closest confidant and friend. "I'm the reason she's dead, Keith. All the reasoning and justification in the world won't change that."

"What about forgiving yourself?" The desperation and caring in those words did not escape Barth.

The dark head already moved from side to side, eyes behind thick lenses tear-blurred. "I can't, Keith. I just – can't."

Shoulders sagged, he left, shutting the door softly behind him.

❧

Seana was going home. Barth came to pick her up. All her

belongings were ready when he got there, and it took only a few minutes to load them. She didn't bother to say goodbye to anybody, though some of the staff gave her a smiling send-off.

"Do you have pimento cheese?" she asked on the drive home.

Barth looked at her, disbelieving. "No."

"Well, I want some."

Barth reached for his cell phone and punched in Joanie's number. "Hi, Joanie. I know it's a bad time to ask, you busy at work and all, but do you have any pimento cheese around your place? I'm taking Seana home right now."

"I'll make some as soon as I get home at four. Can you hold out that long? I'm finishing a perm."

"We'll have to. Thanks, Joanie. I owe you big time." He clicked the phone shut.

"Does she have any?" asked Seana, staring dully at the passing landmarks … Fred's Grocery and Deli, Church, Chelsea's Sassy Rags Dress Shop, Happy Feet Dance Studio, Joanie's Homecombing Queen Salon, Mater and Onion Buffet … they all went by in a blur.

"She'll bring some by later. In time for supper."

Seana wasn't hungry. She'd had lunch before leaving Rosewood Manor. She'd not eaten much because she didn't like what they had. Today, she'd not liked fried chicken legs. She'd eaten some mashed potatoes, a little of the roll and butter, and two servings of cherry Jello.

"You hungry?" asked Barth.

"No."

They arrived at the house within minutes and Seana headed straight for the sofa. "Where's my blanket?"

"I'll get it." Barth took her bags to the bedroom and retrieved the soft blue blanket, her favorite, from the closet shelf. She was already curled up on the sofa when he got back to the den. He gently spread the cover over her.

"Cut all the lights on," she muttered. She'd missed the bright lighting amid the dull hospital setting.

Barth did as she asked. Then moved Brutus's bed over the

floor to the head of the sofa, where the pet could see Seana.

His phone loped into a Bach movement and he snapped it open. "Barth here."

Seana heard the one-sided conversation and knew that it was Pastor Keith.

"Yes – I think I can make it, Pastor." He looked at Seana. "I'll see if Billie Jean can stay with her long enough for me to come. I feel sure she won't mind. So I'll see you tomorrow at five."

Seana reached for the remote Barth had placed near her head on the sofa arm.

She heard Barth's footsteps as they disappeared into their bedroom to unpack her belongings. She clicked on the television to the Braves game, and Brutus's gallant head lifted to lick her hand.

She snuggled under the cover and felt her cocoon close in and tighten, soothing, shutting out the world once more.

⊷⊶

Barth arrived at the pastor's office five minutes early.

"Ah, you're here." Pastor Keith met him at the door. Barth stopped short when he spotted Zoe already seated in one of the office chairs.

Zoe, too, looked equally taken aback at his appearance. "What's going on, Pastor?" she asked and jerked her dark head toward Barth. "What's he doing here?"

"Look, Pastor," Barth took a couple of steps backward, hand stretched out, "If I need to come back, I can."

"No, no." Pastor Keith caught his arm and tugged. "Come on in. Take a seat. I promise both of you, this won't be that painful. Sit down, please, Barth."

Feeling extremely uncomfortable, Barth complied, sinking into the matching leather chair near Zoe. She avoided looking directly at him and he felt put out at his friend for choreographing this confrontation. And he knew beyond doubt that had anyone else except their pastor pulled this shenanigan, Zoe would have disappeared in a heartbeat.

He took off his glasses and cleaned them, for something to do with his antsy hands. Then he slid them back on. He sensed Zoe's tension as well. She looked as rigid as an ancient Cyprus tree.

But she at least didn't spring up and stalk out the door.

Progress? Probably respect for Pastor Keith.

Maybe, he thought, they would get through this – this *whatever* Keith had in mind. Barth tried to relax as Pastor's secretary, Nell, brought them coffee from the next room.

"Here. Chill out, you two," Pastor ordered as Nell placed the tray on his desk within their reach, then quietly left. Barth was the first to reach for his cup and then Zoe.

"Cream?" she asked Barth.

"Sure." She poured some into his coffee, then added some to hers and sipped.

"I guess you wonder why I called this meeting," quipped Pastor Keith, his blue eyes twinkling above an unsmiling mouth.

"Definitely," Zoe snapped.

Barth just tightened his lips so as not to say anything he might later regret.

Pastor's features relaxed into serenity, helping Barth to unwind just a bit. Yet he sensed something momentous hovering. Something he did not look forward to. All this perception came from having known the man called Pastor since boyhood, thus being able to read him pretty accurately.

"I can understand your apprehension," Pastor addressed them both. "But I've listened to each of you airing your slant on – family."

Zoe's gasp was audible as she rose to her feet. "I don't think I want to –"

"Please." Pastor's hand reached out in entreaty. "Please sit down, Zoe. Hear me out. I promise not to embarrass either of you. But this situation must be addressed for the sake of family solidarity. Your mother needs that to get better."

Dirty pool, thought Barth. Yet it warmed him.

Zoe reluctantly sank back into the chair, but quickly crossed her arms and legs in staunch defense mode.

Pastor Keith began relating how each of them had sought his counsel in recent days, avoiding anything that sniffed of betrayal on his part. "I needed to have you two together here for this session because, you see, you're both important to me. Zoe, may I speak openly with you?"

Zoe rolled her eyes and began to swing her foot in agitated movements. "You're going to, regardless of how I feel."

"That's fair. But you're convinced that Barth is hiding something from you, aren't you?"

Zoe looked him squarely in the eye. "Absolutely."

Pastor sighed and laced his hands together across his abdomen. "And, forgive me, Barth – but Zoe, you're correct in assuming that."

Barth was on his feet. "I can't believe you would betray my confidence!"

Keith stood too but remained calm. "Barth, you ask too much of Zoe. Please ... you're always the level head in the bunch. Always have been. Remember you taught ol' hothead me to hold my tongue and listen to the entire story before reacting? That concept changed my life. And I want to thank you for the lessons – some of them hard." He grinned then and Barth took a deep cleansing breath and reseated himself stiffly into the chair.

Barth realized he'd been had by his old buddy. Keith had used Barth's own wiles to conquer. What could he say? It worked, by George.

But at the same time, his breath seemed to be cut short as he faced the moment of truth. "You're right, Keith. But I don't like it."

"What's going on here?" Zoe demanded. "What don't I know?" Her eyes narrowed into slits as she turned them upon Barth. "What?"

Barth returned her gaze evenly. "I was very much in love with my first wife, Betty. We could never have children, which was a grief to her. To me, too. But when I told her it didn't make a difference to me, it was true. I loved her, with or without children. We could adopt or whatever." He shrugged limply.

"But I think that's what played into what happened when I was working as music director at Kei – Pastor Keith's church in Nova Scotia that year. At the same time, I also worked for Postal Services – which now pays me a small pension."

He looked at Zoe and smiled crookedly. "So I'm not quite destitute on my own."

Zoe looked away but stopped swinging her foot.

"Anyway," Barth continued, "my wife, Betty, became involved with a man at the church. A policeman. Handsome guy, divorced." He shrugged tightly. "Hard to admit but he was quite winsome. At least, he got Betty's attention."

Barth stopped and cleared his throat. Snuffled and took off his glasses and cleaned them as he attempted to blink back moisture. Zoe was watching from the corner of her eye. Barth felt her skepticism, but he had to finish this once he'd started.

He slid his glasses back on. "I didn't know about the affair until months later. Actually, not until she told me." He shifted in his chair. "I never suspected. Trusted her with my life, I did. Literally."

Barth cleared his throat again and snuffled.

"You're doing fine, Barth," Keith gently urged him on and slid the Kleenex box within his reach.

Another snuffle. "Then one day Betty sat me down and told me she no longer loved me and that there was someone else." He rolled his watery eyes upward and gave a dry huff. "She said she had to be honest with me and that she didn't want to hurt me." Another dry laugh. "Hurt? She was *killing me.*"

Zoe shifted in her chair to look at him. "What did you say, Barth?"

He cut her a teary glance. "What could I say? I said I loved her with all my heart. I groveled, Zoe. I begged her like a dying man for water. But she – didn't love me anymore." Tears now coursed down his cheeks. "Sorry."

"Hey." Zoe's hand reached out to touch his. "It's okay to cry, Barth."

"Sorry," he repeated, snatching a Kleenex from the table, shaking his lowered head. Embarrassed beyond words. "I still have difficulty talking about this."

"It's okay, Barth." Keith spoke encouragingly. "You need to do this to heal. Now, tell the rest."

Again, Barth felt Zoe stiffen and go on alert.

"She went on to marry George, her policeman. And from what I heard from church friends, they seemed to do okay at first."

"How about you, Barth?" Zoe asked and Barth felt her antennae rise even higher.

"I forgave her. I prayed to be able to and God gave me the strength to – let go. It was as simple as that. Not easy. I won't lie. But I did it."

"He's telling the truth, Zoe," Pastor Keith inserted. "They remained friends."

Barth resumed. "Oh, we didn't see each other much after the divorce, but then – a year or so after they married, when George began being emotionally abusive, Betty began calling me when she grew desperate."

Zoe asked, "What would she say?"

"Oh – needing advice on how to handle his domineering ways."

"What did you tell her?" Zoe now leaned toward him.

He shrugged and looked down at his tightly clasped hands in his lap. "I told her that she'd have to decide for herself. But that she didn't have to stay in a situation like that. See, Betty and I always respected one another. I never, ever dissed her for any reason. Never had reason to." He shrugged. "She was a wonderful woman."

Pastor Keith broke in then. "Move ahead, Barth. To her decision."

Barth's head rolled back and he closed his eyes. "Betty,

after a time, realized what a tragic mistake she'd made in ending our marriage. 'I was such a stupid fool' she repeated over and over."

He took a deep breath and exhaled, lolling his head forward. "She wanted me back."

Zoe's eyes widened. "How did you handle that?"

"I loved her." He shrugged. "I had no choice but to take her back. My heart rejoiced at the prospect of our reconciling."

Zoe waited. "But?"

Barth felt like his blood began to drain out but he pushed on. "I told her she must tell George of her decision to reconcile and file for divorce. I wouldn't interfere until it was final and we could be remarried."

Keith spoke up. "We had the wedding all worked out, Louann and I," he said solemnly. "Down to the songs to be sung."

"What happened?" Zoe demanded, clearly impatient to hear the outcome.

"Well," Barth cleared his throat again and swallowed soundly. "She told George about us, and he wasn't happy about it, of course." Barth grabbed another Kleenex and blew his nose.

"And?" Zoe prompted.

Barth looked at the wall and dragged in a deep breath. "Betty disappeared one night. George put out an APB on her, had the entire police force looking for her. She turned up days later in a pond a few miles away. She'd been shot through the head."

Keith injected. "The police – mysteriously guided – seemed to think Barth had done it. And wanted to arrest him."

"Why didn't they?" Zoe asked.

Keith again jumped in. "Because he had an airtight alibi. He was with us, Louann and me, at an out-of-town ministerial conference, doing the music, during the time forensic tests showed Betty's probable time of death. Weeks passed before all the results were in. They told the truth."

"During that time," Barth resumed, "seemed every time I

turned around, I was confronted by PIs and police detectives, digging, digging, treating me like a criminal."

"Remember here," Keith inserted, "Barth was going to remarry this woman who was found murdered. He was a basket case, and that's putting it mildly."

"Then who killed her? George?" Zoe asked.

Barth huffed angrily. "I knew from the beginning it was him. But seemed he had some hold over the investigation that –" He shrugged. "Anyway, I was finally cleared."

Zoe sat back in her chair, mulling over everything.

"Did they ever find any other suspects?" she asked.

Keith sat forward, elbows on desk. "I got the news several months ago that George had become the number one suspect, finally. When it all began closing in on him, he simply locked himself in his house, wrote a suicide note, and used a .38 revolver to finish himself off."

Zoe sighed. "The suicide note was a confession."

"Yes." Keith watched them both. "I tried to get Barth to update you on it then, but he got this aversion to talking about those times after he and Betty split."

Zoe turned to him, disbelieving. "Why, Barth? The note cleared you. You could have trusted me to have a different perspective once I knew."

"Yes, why, Barth?" Pastor Keith asked, seeming puzzled, too.

Barth looked at him, tears pooling again behind the thick lenses. "Because, had I not counseled Betty to be open with George about our wish to reconcile, she wouldn't have been killed. Don't you see? It was my fault she died." He buried his face in his hands and wept openly while shaking his head in shame for doing so.

"Barth." Zoe slipped from her chair and knelt before him. "Please don't – it wasn't your fault. That man was evil. She had to escape him. Don't you see? You were only doing what was right by her. You had no choice. Please don't cry."

Zoe reached up to slide her arms around his shoulders and began to weep with him.

"I'm sorry, Barth," she sobbed, "for all those times I was unkind to you. I d-didn't know."

"I know," he said, by now returning her embrace. "I know. I just want you to know that I love your mother with everything in me." He leaned back to look at her as she arose to snatch a tissue from the ever-ready nearby box. "Keith and Louann begged me to move here and begin anew. I finally agreed."

As Zoe sank back into her chair, blotting her eyes, Barth continued. "I thought I'd never be able to love again after Betty. But that night I saw Seana at Happy Feet Dance Studio, I fell head over heels. I'd always scoffed at the notion of love at first sight, but that made a true believer out of me."

Zoe suddenly chuckled, and then burst into belly laughter.

"What?" both men said simultaneously, looking at her worriedly.

She finally got her breath. "Barth, I know you love my mama. Nobody else could put up with her!"

Like dominos, laughter erupted from her just as Barth's exploded.

Then Pastor's joined in.

The mirthful cacophony continued until Scott Burns, early for the 6:30 choir practice, stuck his head in the door.

"What's going on?" he asked, curiosity lighting up his gray eyes.

"Private joke," Zoe croaked, wiping at her eyes, then burst into fresh laughter.

❧

Later that evening after choir practice, Zoe slipped into a sweater. "Where you going, Mama?" Peyton called from the kitchen where he foraged through the fridge.

"To talk to Scott," Zoe admitted.

"Great!" He poked his grinning face through the door. "Good guys don't grow on trees, ya know?"

"I know," she muttered and slipped outside into the mild

October air. Her courage began slipping, but she squared her shoulders as she approached Scott's apartment door.

She'd spent the past hour in her own duplex gathering nerve to come here. The last few steps from her door to his seemed endless.

With trepidation, she raised her fist and knocked softly. Her breath felt labored and her hands icy as, after a few moments, she rapped again, this time harder.

"Just a minute," came Scott's deep voice as muffled footsteps grew near.

The door swung open.

"Zoe." Her name spilled softly, breathily from his generous lips. She couldn't figure out if it was disappointment or awe. She prayed it was the latter.

"Hi, Scott. May I come in?" She attempted a tight smile.

He blinked and stepped back. "Sure, come in." He scratched his head. "Excuse the mess."

"It's not messy," she replied. And it wasn't. A magazine lay on the floor next to his La-Z-Boy, and his milk glass still sat on the coffee table, but his neatness bled through.

Very courteously, Scott gestured toward a worn but comfortable easy chair. Zoe wished for the old easiness they'd once shared. She grieved over it in that heartbeat as she lowered herself into the chair.

Scott slid his hunky bulk into the upright La-Z-Boy. His thinned-down version still looked mighty good to Zoe in that moment, clad in low-rise, boot-cut jeans and school pullover.

"What's happening?" he ventured in his generic way of opening a conversation, crossing bare feet at the ankles and clasping hands across his slim abdomen.

Or, Zoe surmised, it could mean *what the heck are you doing here?*

An unsettling thought.

"Well …." Zoe suddenly felt like an actress who'd forgotten her lines. "Uh, I want to know what you've got against being nice to me. You know, hanging out with me sometimes?"

She lifted her chin and tried to forget that her heart was tripping along at 120 mph and that she was drowning in oxygen.

He grew still, his features shrouded in mystique. "Hanging out? As in a purely social context or something more romantic?" He shrugged nonchalantly. "Clarify, please, what you have in mind."

"You're being obtuse, Scott." Zoe's nostrils flared in effrontery.

"You're going to have to explain yourself to me, Zoe. I don't exactly know how to respond to you. There's a vast difference between socially hanging out and romantically hanging together."

"You're opposed to being romantic with me?"

"I didn't say that, did I? Those are your words."

Zoe felt like screaming with frustration. "This was a bad idea. I think I should go."

Before she could rise, he had her by the arm, pulling her to her feet and into his arms. Against his hard strength as his mouth trailed from her neck to her mouth and back again, taking her breath.

This time the kiss was deliberate and thorough.

I fit perfectly into his arms, she thought, romantically giddy and knowing beyond doubt in that moment that she'd been waiting all her life for this man.

"Is this better?" he murmured against her ear, scattering goose bumps all over her.

"Mm. Much better," she murmured.

Then suddenly, he pulled back and led her to the sofa and deposited her there. He sat beside her, angled toward her. "Now, tell me what brought this on?"

Still feeling the disappointment of his abrupt withdrawal, she dragged in a deep, shuddering, steadying breath. "Yesterday, during the counseling session with Pastor Keith, Barth shared some really deep, hairy times he'd struggled through. You know, during his first wife's betrayal and her murder?"

Scott nodded once.

She licked her dry lips and continued. "Well, he said some

things that really got to me." Her eyes misted as she looked at him. "Like when Betty left him for another man. And then – he chose to forgive her and wished her happiness."

A tear splashed over and trickled down her pale cheek. Scott reached up to catch it with his finger. "A-and I was sitting there thinking what a coward I am. Oh, Scott. I've been so stupid, pushing you away when all I wanted was to pull you to me and never let go."

Scott began to grin. "Go on."

"I've compared you to the jerks I've known in my life." She stopped and shook her head. "No. I shouldn't feel that way about them. They were who they were." She shrugged. "I wasn't always a prize, myself. Too bull-headed at times. Too – controlling. I saw things differently after hearing how Barth had decided to forgive Betty and love her anyway, even after she'd cut his heart to shreds and stomped on it."

"I can see how that would be difficult," Scott murmured.

"Yes. But he did it. He didn't take it all personally." She shook her head and scowled. "No, that's not what I meant to say. It's just – Barth *knew* who he was. And Betty's rejection of him did not determine how he faced his future. Didn't change his concept of who he was created to be. Does that make sense?"

Scott nodded slowly, his eyes drinking her in. "That makes perfect sense."

"Well, he could have gone off to live in a cave and never looked at another woman." She waved her hands dismissively. "That's the way I reacted to my situations. But he didn't."

She looked at him. "Barth later met Mother and – you know the rest. He even put up with my hatefulness and still showed kindness and love to me."

She sighed and gazed at him, heart in deep blue eyes. "Scott, I've been such a coward. And so despicable." Her voice broke and she began to quietly weep.

"Ah, honey," he gathered her into his arms. Zoe felt something she'd not felt since her courtship days with her ex. And that had proved to be only temporal.

No, what Scott gave her was permanent. Somehow, she recognized it.

Haven.

Then a niggling little thought splattered against her brain. *Will it last?*

What about Stacia?

Never one to withstand suspense, Zoe pulled back and locked eyes with Scott. "What about Stacia Dietrich?"

Scott, dadblamed his hide, had the audacity to grin. "What about Stacia?"

"You jerk." She slapped at his shoulder.

Scott hauled her into his arms again as she struggled to get free and pummel him. He was laughing so hard he nearly lost his grip on her.

"Stacia is engaged, Zoe," he gasped, catching his breath while gripping her flailing hands. "She's just a friend who's endured my Zoe-angst during these past months."

Zoe grew still but still angled him a look of doubt.

"She's as whiney as me, with Joe away in Afghanistan right now. He's a buddy of mine. I'm gonna be best man at their wedding next year."

Zoe pulled back again to gauge his truthfulness.

He looked as guileless as a newborn lamb.

Only then did she snuggle back into his arms, sighed contentedly and said, "Put something sweet on to play."

He moved to his stereo and slipped in a selection.

And as he returned and pulled her up and into his arms to dance, Zoe was suddenly certain it was not by chance that the tune was Manilow's "Looks Like We Made It."

chapter eight

*"Death is a butterfly in its cocoon,
waiting to fly."*
– Maria Housden

*L*et's have the Thanksgiving meal at Mama's house," Zoe suggested as they milled around after the Happy Feet Dance Studio's Friday night party. "We used to have it there and it was always special."

"Great," Barth agreed, obviously pleased.

"Super!" Ashley's clasped hands pressed to her blossoming bosom as she twirled with joy. "Like old times."

Peyton, busy with cleanup, raised his dark head from trussing up and tying a packed garbage bag. "What?"

"We're going to Nana's for Thanksgiving," Ashley supplied.

"Neat," he said, giving a thumbs-up, and finished carrying the bag to the back dumpster.

"I think it's time we started giving you an appropriate tag, Barth," Zoe said, taking him by the hand and tugging him to sit with her at a table already tidied up.

"Like – Papa, or Pops or –" She shrugged. "Whatever."

"Y'know," Barth looked thoughtful, "I kinda like the sound of Pops. Sorta fits."

234 emily sue harvey

"You got it, Pops," she said grinning. Then her features fell solemn. "How much medication is Mom on presently?"

He sighed heavily. "A lot."

Zoe nodded. "I thought so. I want to get her doctor to provide me a list of everything she's taking and give it to me to study. I want to look up everything about each drug. You know, side effects and such."

Barth nodded. "Sounds good to me. I've never believed that pills cure everything. Some, in fact, can hinder. And, in Seana's case, they haven't helped enough to move her toward any improvement. I've been so frustrated at times." His head lowered in despondency.

Zoe reached out to touch his hand. "You're not alone anymore, Pops. We'll even get Billie Jean involved. That ol' pit bull is just what Mom needs to help shake her loose of overmedication and underactivity."

Barth roused, then laughed, as Zoe had hoped. And she felt Scott's arm slide around her shoulder from behind. He leaned to kiss her neck. "Count me in, too," he whispered.

And Zoe felt that kiss warm her from head to toe. But what she felt the most was his caring. His support. Oh how she'd needed it. And lo and behold, she wasn't ashamed to admit it.

They were a team now. And she laughed with joy.

What a wonderful turn of events.

લઉજી

Barth frowned at Dr. Welton, the latest physician to handle Seana's case.

"What do you mean Seana will never drive again?" They stood outside the office door, out of Seana's ear shot.

Dr. Welton looked at Barth, eyes filled with sympathy. "Exactly that. You're going to have to face reality at some point. She's never going to come out of this state she's in. Remember her memory tests indicate she's in early stages of dementia."

Barth drove home sinking to a new low. Feeling as though he'd been punched in the gut and hadn't yet gotten his breath back. Seana didn't seem to notice, and he was glad, for once, that these things drifted unnoted past her.

Later, he called Zoe. "That's what he said?" she exclaimed.

"To the word."

Zoe was quiet for a long time. Finally, she spoke. "I'd like to go with you the next time she has an appointment. Okay?"

"Okay," Barth replied, already feeling some of the terrible weight lifting from his tired shoulders. "Sounds good."

Two weeks later, Zoe stood outside the office door, in the quiet hallway as the doctor passed along more dark tidings. Barth stood beside her, his nerves quaking like a war survivor.

The prognosis was grim. "Your mother is dying a slow death, Zoe."

"No way," she croaked, covering her mouth with her hand. Beside her, Barth felt the iciness of shock splice through him.

Dr. Welton nodded solemnly. "I'm afraid so. She won't survive this."

Zoe blinked back dizziness. She swayed.

Barth caught her by the shoulders. "You okay?"

She took a deep, shuddering breath and slowly shook her head. "I'm okay. Just a little dizzy."

"Would you like to lie down inside for a few minutes?" asked Dr. Welton.

"No. But thank you," she said weakly. Barth was feeling pretty wobbly himself, but it was truly an out-of-left-field experience seeing Zoe's vulnerable side.

"Would you please give me a complete listing of Mom's medications and the purpose of each?" Zoe requested, squaring her shoulders.

The physician nodded. "Of course."

They returned to the waiting room, where Barth's gaze immediately flew to Seana, who sat watching the clock. A death sentence? He tried not to let his mind wrap around it. It was too horrible to entertain. He blinked back the horror of it and saw Zoe struggling, too, for composure. The two of them kept silent as the doctor returned with the data for Zoe.

Quiet prevailed on the drive home. Except when Seana kept looking over her shoulder at Zoe, who sat in the back passenger seat. "Why're you crying?" she repeatedly asked.

"Just hay fever, Mama," she kept saying, but Barth, too, kept shooting worried looks at her in the rearview mirror. He was concerned at this fragile side she'd exposed today. As long as she didn't go into hysterics, he could handle it all.

Suddenly, he was astounded at the paternal feelings surfacing inside him.

At the house he left Zoe in the kitchen and settled Seana down on the sofa, turning on the television. He joined Zoe in the kitchen where they could keep their voices down below the ball game racket.

Zoe phoned Billie Jean to come up for the powwow. "Be right up," was the welcome response.

Barth put on a pot of decaf green tea as Billie Jean plodded up the steps, Brutus on her heels. The red Lab stayed with her sometimes when Barth and Seana were both gone. Other times, too, when Billie Jean pined for his company.

"So?" she prompted as she took her seat at the bar. "Hey man, this looks serious."

"It is," Zoe replied. "Need any help, Barth?"

"No. I've got it." He efficiently poured three cups of hot water and placed them on the bar next to tea bags, sugar, honey, and cream. They each added tea bags. Zoe was the only rogue amongst them, adding artificial sweetener, which she carried in her purse, knowing she'd not get it at her mom's house anymore. Barth and Billie Jean both spooned a small amount of honey into their creamy, steaming liquid.

Zoe quietly informed the two of them what the good doctor had said, fighting tears the entire time

"Huh." Billie Jean's bosom heaved and swelled with indignation. "What does he know?"

Zoe caved in, fresh tears puddling her lower lids. "I keep telling myself that but –" Her voice faded into a quiet sob. Barth reached over to pat her shoulder.

"But nothing." Billie Jean lowered her voice but not its intensity. "You've gotta get a grip, Zoe. Now's not the time for the faint of heart. She needs us."

Barth went into the den, gauged Seana's alertness as he picked up the Kleenex box. Her eyes were as vacant as always, staring unseeing at the busy screen.

He returned, pushed the box toward Seana, and snatched one himself to blow his nose.

Zoe did the same. Billie Jean's features blazed with purpose. "We all know that doctors are just people. They don't have all the answers. Look at me. I'm still cancer free after four years. And they didn't think I'd last out a year in the beginning. Remember, Barth?"

Barth nodded, hands nursing the warm cup.

She addressed Zoe then. "You got that list of medications, did you?"

"Sure did." Zoe sipped her tea, sounding stronger and looking more confident with Billie Jean's reinforcement "It's in my purse." She slid from the stool and went to fetch the list.

Pushing their cups aside, they spread out all the medical data of Seana's treatment for the past four years.

"Now." Billie Jean took charge. "We've got our work cut out for us."

∽∾

At first the task looked like a jungle maze. What to do first?

"First order of business is to get Barth some time off," Zoe insisted.

"I second that motion," echoed Billie Jean. "We tried that before but we weren't militant enough about it. This time, we'll get all the family involved."

They held court that day at Zoe's duplex, three days before Thanksgiving. Scott made coffee and, with the holidays upon them, Peyton was home to help sort out important goals.

Zoe had tried to lighten up on the dance parties to set aside some time to help in the care of Seana. Scott had jumped in like a trooper to assist. He not only treated Zoe like royalty, he regarded Seana with utmost respect, even when she reacted to him as she would a meddling cockroach.

"It's okay, honey," he repeatedly told Zoe. "I understand. Things'll soon get better."

Oh, how Zoe hoped it was true. Billie Jean, Scott, and Peyton kept pounding that it would happen. And Barth was picking up on the litany. But at face value, Seana was not showing any signs of change.

"We've got to get an extreme agenda going," Billie Jean insisted today as they sat circled around Zoe's heavy cedar coffee table, four sets of bare feet propped atop it.

"Yeh," Scott agreed. "I know I'm no expert at this thing. Not even close. But in training athletes, you – you know, drill them in what they need to do. At first they don't feel like they can reach each small goal. But we, the coaches, nag them into doing more difficult and painful things that strengthen and equip them to move progressively on to their ultimate goal."

He shrugged. "Could it be that Seana could benefit, too, from being forced to act normal?"

Peyton brightened. "Yeh. Like when we teach people to dance. They're awkward and embarrassed at first. Then little by little, they develop this –" He held up his hands, searching for the right word.

"Capacity? Aptitude?" Billie Jean offered.

"Close enough," Zoe declared. "Hey, guys," she shook her head slowly, her eyes misting. "We've got to do something. If not, Mama's going to die."

"Hey!" Billie Jean boomed. "Don't even go there! Don't even think about it. But I do agree that for us to sit around and just let

Seana vegetate is sinful. She's wasting away before our very eyes."

Scott sat forward, elbows on knees, champing at the bit. "We need to organize and get this thing rolling."

"Right," Peyton joined in, his eyes sparkling with challenge. "We need to work in shifts to relieve Pops, first off. Then we need to take turns doing things with Nana that will somehow bring her back."

Zoe smiled through her tears. "Y'all are sweet to rally like this. It's been so heavy at times for me. And I know that for Pops, it's been like Mt. Rushmore sitting on his shoulders. I'm ashamed I've not done more."

"You did all you could, Zoe," Billie Jean reminded her. "You had a job to run and a son to support." She slapped her knees. "That was then and this is now. A new start."

"Yeh," Zoe sighed tiredly. "We'll do what we can do."

She looked at them, her heart in her blue, blue eyes. "But the rest is up to Mama. In the final analysis, she's the only one who can bring herself back."

❧❦

No Olympic event was ever more organized and carried off than the care of Seana in those next months. News spread of the effort and soon, friends got involved. Sadie Tate's little twisted fingers got great workouts Smartphone-updating the populace of Paradise Springs.

"I think Sadie's mellowing lately, don't you?" asked Billie Jean as she, Joanie, and Chelsea sat at Fred's Johnson's Deli one Wednesday evening following the church prayer service. "You know" – Chelsea lifted a thoughtful red-nailed finger – "I believe you're right. Her dialogue now seems more ..." – she waved a hand, searching – "more ...."

"Generous," supplied Joanie. "She's not as critical. I do believe this drive to help Seana is doing more than we ever imagined."

"Huh." Billie Jean sniffed. "It's doing all it's supposed to do." She pointed upward. "We've got a great navigator."

"The best." Joanie took a bite of her ham and Swiss sandwich. "I'm going over tomorrow to take her to lunch and pamper her."

"I'm down for Friday," said Chelsea as she snatched a chip from Joanie's stash.

"Hey!" Joanie smacked at her hand. "Buy your own."

"Can't," Chelsea said and grabbed another. "On a diet."

"You and your freakin' diets," Billie Jean grumbled and stabbed her fork into her Caesar salad.

"Hi, girls." Fred Johnson slid into the booth beside Billie Jean. "How's the sign-up going with For Seana's Sake?"

"Great. We can only use so many folks for hands-on care. But the prayer sign-up is just as important. By the way," Chelsea said, pointing a pickle spear at him, "thanks for organizing that."

Fred's face flushed with pleasure. "Least I could do." Then he leaned forward, his ruddy features alight with purpose. "See, here in the grocery store, I see lots of folks from both here and the town outskirts, those not on our church roll." He shrugged. "So I hit 'em all with Seana's story."

Billie Jean added, "Peyton, Ashley, and her mother have all contacted Facebook friends to spread the word." She grinned and shook her bouncy, auburn curls. "Man, with the element of compound interest here, there's gotta be hundreds of folks out there in cyberspace praying now for a miracle."

She slapped the Formica table. "Holy moley, guys! Something's gotta give."

Immediately, three more hands slapped and stacked atop hers. And the laughter spilled like popcorn popping as the girls pealed their motto, *"One for all and all for one."*

This time, shoppers gawked at the usually matter-of-fact proprietor, red-faced with laughter, hands tangled with three ditzy females giggling like adolescents.

❧ ❧

Zoe had begun her stealthy attack against overmedication right away. Because if Seana was dying a slow death, the meds weren't helping anyway. Could actually be hastening her demise. All Zoe knew was that she had to do something.

That something was to contact her friend, Dr. Frieda Awe, who dealt in natural healing substances. She and her husband, Jim, were dance students of hers who were well-acquainted with Seana's medical history.

"Frieda, if I slowly wean Mom off certain meds, shouldn't I offset them with other healing substances?"

They sat at the Happy Feet Dance Studio between dances that Saturday evening. "By all means." Frieda smiled and gave a high five. "That's great deductive reasoning, by the way." She took out a pen, and Zoe provided a business tablet for her to list all Seana's current meds.

"I'll stay in touch and provide you with names of replacements. You know of course to do this gradually and monitor your mother's progress or lack thereof? And if there's the least problem call me right away?"

"Yes. I'm a little nervous, but I feel in my bones it's the right thing to do."

"Then go with it, Zoe. And stay in close touch. I'm always here for you. So remember that if anything really uncommon arises, call me."

Zoe felt much, much better having a medical doctor standing by. One who actually supported her instincts. Who knew the ins and outs of meds and side effects.

She was in business.

≈ঌ৯

Zoe knew that Seana suspected her of doing something to her meds.

Zoe was cunning in her efforts, using her sharp scissors to whittle the pills down gradually without her mother seeing her in action. But those blue eyes watched more as Zoe divvied up dosages. What Seana didn't know was that Zoe took her extra med supply home with her to do the dirty work.

This task was now hers exclusively.

Barth had been happy to turn it over to her.

"These pills look smaller." Seana grumbled each day. But Zoe simply smiled and watched her take them.

Of course, capsules were no problem. She simply pulled them apart and slowly reduced the amount of powder in each. And with Dr. Awe overseeing the mixtures in the dosages, Zoe would replace the discarded powder with the recommended natural substances.

One big challenge came when Zoe followed Dr. Awe's instruction on how to heal Seana's stomach after the long siege of meds. One main combatant was homemade yogurt, made fresh daily, from a Mediterranean store. To this, Zoe added and mixed in some finely ground supplemental greens she got from a health store.

"Yuck! That's nasty!" Seana grumbled, screwing up her face. "It tastes awful!"

Barth had learned to flee to the outdoors during med time.

Zoe got in her face. "It will help get your digestive tract back to normal after all those pills, Mom. Eat up."

Twice a day, Zoe stood her ground, forcing her to eat every bite of it. Sometimes she felt kinda sorry for her mother when she shuddered and gagged. Kinda. But not enough to back off.

Miraculously, the stuff stayed down.

Zoe figured the mixture was too danged mean and stubborn to come back up. It was a good match at facing down her mom's own obstinacy.

Oh yeh. Those were challenging days.

But Zoe was in it for the long haul.

❧

Billie Jean looked at the new bottles Barth and Zoe brought in from the latest trek to Dr. Awe's place. "What are those?" she asked, curiosity brimming.

Zoe poured decaf coffee for the three of them, then sat down at the bar.

In a quiet voice, muffled from Seana's ears in the nearby den by baseball racket, she replied, "This one is Plus, which is an herbal amino acid supplement." She pointed to another. "This one is a multivitamin/mineral supplement, and the other is Ambrotose, which is a glytonutritional dietary supplement. She needs them all twice a day."

"Good luck." Billie Jean chortled.

Zoe laughed. "After the yogurt mixture, honey, these will be gravy."

Barth chuckled, shaking his head. "Thanks, Zoe," he said softly.

"For what?" she exclaimed, rolling her eyes. "Piece o' cake."

"Yeh, right." Billie Jean burst into laughter.

"She's gotten awfully paranoid about the size of her pills," Zoe said, sniggering. "They're so tiny you can barely see them. She narrows those blue eyes at me like a charging bull every time they shrink a little more."

They all burst into laughter, the nervous, overpowering kind that must be expressed regardless of the moment's solemnity.

But, Zoe figured, as the old saying goes: better to laugh than cry.

※

Seana watched the folks come and go. Today was Joanie's shift. She knew that much because it was so regular, the turnover. But regardless of the action stirring around her, she still occupied her cozy little soft dip on the sofa, to which her thin body molded perfectly.

The blanket still swaddled her and drove away chills.

The cocoon remained firmly in place.

Then Joanie asked her to go for a walk.

"No."

"Come on, Seana." Joanie tugged her from the sofa, refusing to take no for an answer.

She coaxed Seana around in the house, in a circular path through the rooms and back to the den and when Seana headed for the sofa, Joanie gently tugged her on "one more round."

Seana was quite tired after three or four laps, and Joanie let her settle back on the sofa. "But don't lie down," she said smiling. "I have a surprise for you."

And there on the warm sofa, legs crossed tailor-fashion, Joanie gave Seana a manicure and painted her finger nails a lovely shade of pink.

When she finished, Seana looked at her fingers and wanted to smile. She didn't, but it made her feel – pleased. "Thank you," she murmured.

"You're welcome," Joanie said, grinning from ear to ear.

Seana realized again how tired she was.

"I'm gonna lie down."

She slid down into her little dented sofa niche and curled over into fetal position.

&⫯&

Billie Jean was, by far, the most militant caregiver, at least in Seana's opinion.

"Come on, Seana," Billie Jean said that Saturday, "let's go get some lunch."

"No. I want a pimento cheese sandwich."

"I didn't give you a choice, did I? Come on, put on your shoes, and go get a clean shirt from your closet."

Seana didn't like to be bossed around. More to the point, she didn't want to leave her sofa. But she knew that, like a pit bull, Billie Jean would not let go. So she put on her slippers, went to her room, and pulled out a long sleeved Braves pullover.

Her favorite striped shirt had disappeared weeks ago. New

slacks replaced her old, baggy ones, ones that fit her whipcord thin shape. She'd grumbled but nobody paid any attention.

On the drive to Fred's Deli, Billie Jean said, "This is the scenic route."

"Same as always."

"So you noticed. Huh." Billie Jean grinned, obviously enjoying the sunny drive. It was again autumn. "Lordy how the seasons fly these days," she said.

"We're getting too far from home," Seana grumbled.

"No, no. We're not far at all. We can be home in the shake of Brutus's tail."

At Fred's, where Seana got a rousing greeting from most everybody there from the customers to the bag boys, she managed to slink to the booth with Billie Jean without being cornered.

Sadie Tate dropped by a minute to say hello. Amazingly, her eyes teared up when she spoke to Seana."I've missed you, Seana."

Seana turned her head away and mumbled, "Hello."

Sadie fidgeted. "Well, take care of yourself, now. We're all praying for you." Then she left quietly.

Billie Jean ordered her a hot dog all the way. "I know you can eat this because you eat them at Petee's." She plunked the sandwich and water before a scowling Seana and tucked into her own healthy fare of salad greens, tomatoes, peppers, and onions. Added to that were bean sprouts and Fred's own specialty, his Power-Punch Healthy Blend Salad Dressing.

Seana glowered for long moments at Billie Jean, who ate her meal with gusto. Seana finally began to pick at the hot dog and managed to finish most of it before their trek home.

There, Billie Jean hooked her arm and said, "We're going on an outing today. Outdoors."

Before she could resist, Seana felt herself tugged out the door again into mild but pleasant autumn air. Brutus followed and loped along beside them as they walked around at least half the back property, a good fifteen-minute jaunt.

Seana was panting nearly as much as Brutus by the time they got back indoors, gaining absolutely no sympathy from Billie Jean.

Seana went to the fridge, filled a large, chilled glass with water, and drained it. Then, on the fridge door, seeing the magnetic pad with Barth's To-Do List For Seana, she yanked it off.

"Look what Barth wrote for me to do," she said indignantly, hoping to recruit a smidgeon of sympathy from Billie Jean, since Seana had done so much walking.

Billie Jean took the pad and began reading it. "Walking ... dusting ... reading Bible ... washing and drying dishes. Doctor said if you don't use it, you lose it."

Seana migrated to her sofa, already feeling it closing warmly around her.

"Ah-ah." Billie Jean's reprimand halted her. "Let's get some of these things done so you can check them off. Won't Barth be proud of you?"

Seana didn't care beans if Barth was proud of her or not. "I don't want to."

"Oh, but the doctor ordered it," Billie Jean said sweetly and fetched the duster and stood over Seana as she dusted furniture.

Next was dishwashing time. There were only a few glasses and cups, but Billie Jean hovered until the last one was dried and put away.

To the sofa Seana staggered, but Billie Jean had other ideas. "Let's read the Bible together. You can sit to do this."

And so the day ended with Seana reading from the book of Matthew. Billie Jean told her they would read straight through the New Testament as they went along.

When Barth came in from a long day at the office and extra guys's activities with Peyton and Scott, Billie Jean showed him the list of checked-off activities.

Barth's face brightened with each accomplishment.

Seana? She headed for the sofa, dived in, and covered her head.

❧

Chelsea brought a Rummikub game with her and made Seana

play it for long spells. "You need to exercise your brain, Seana. It's been on vacation and needs stimulation."

The game's required manipulation of legal number groupings rattled something inside Seana. Not pleasant. "This will help you, Seana," Chelsea repeatedly told her during the game.

So, much as it agitated her, Seana complied.

The same compliance happened with other caregivers parading through Seana's house. Ashley and Peyton took turns overseeing their Nana's activities, which, to everyone's surprise, expanded in coming weeks. Ashley's crossword puzzles and Peyton's Scrabble board were both agony and – if not ecstasy, then something akin to pride – for Seana.

And slowly, she morphed into doing laundry. Or baking cookies. Or taking walks on her own with Brutus tagging along.

Christmas found her stronger and ready to help decorate the tree. She, Zoe, and Billie Jean got in the kitchen and cooked for the family Christmas gathering at her house. Barth, of course, joined in, doing delicious new veggie dishes to add to the traditional fare.

Christmas Day was sunny and cold. Perfect yuletide weather.

Zoe's gift to her mother was a basket chocked full of Bed and Bath and Victoria's Secret bath supplies and fancy, dainty underwear.

"Mm-mm." Billie Jean sniffed extravagantly. "That smells good enough to eat."

"Yeh, Nana!" Ashley piped up. "You're gonna be one foxy lady."

"Thank you," Seana said, uncertain of how to feel.

"You've come a long way, Baby," Barth purred in her ear.

She pulled away and everybody laughed. She wished she felt normal.

But she didn't. Hard as she tried, she could not feel – normal.

"I'm sorry," she mumbled and went to her bedroom and closed the door. The sofa was too public now. She needed this total isolation to shut out the world.

She felt stronger. She could almost touch reality.

Almost.

But something was still terribly wrong in her brain.

The blasted thing still tinkered with the wiring.

It was worse now, because she was slipping from the stark white nothingness and brushed it for an instant at a time. She seemed in a netherland – in between two worlds.

And it was terrifying.

chapter nine

"Just like the butterfly,
I too will awaken in my own time."
– Deborah Chaskin

Zoe, Peyton, Barth, Scott, and the entire Paradise Springs Cloggers drove to Nashville, Tennessee in October for the Southeastern Cloggers's Competition. Ashley and Geena, a close friend and classmate of hers, volunteered to stay with Seana.

Seana found herself doing things for the two girls, like laundering their clothing and fixing them snacks. She didn't take too much note of it because it just happened.

She kept hearing Barth saying things like, "Time is flying. Can't believe it's autumn again already."

Seana didn't agree or disagree. Time was the right now of her existence, not especially connected to life's continuity.

They took a long walk around the back property. The girls oohed and aahed over the changing leaves, all shades of gold, brown, rust, and red and made big fun of crunching the dried ones beneath their feet and watching Brutus chase squirrels.

Seana even watched a movie with them, all three piled onto the sofa, though she got little from it.

At bedtime each night, Ashley came into her room to

give her a big hug. "I love you, Nana. It's so good to talk to you again."

After she left, Seana lay in her bed and tried to wrap her brain around the words's significance.

She could not.

But at least Ashley could.

Somehow, she knew that it was momentous to Ashley.

And on some obscure level, she wished that it was to her.

Thanksgiving was to be at Seana's house again. This time she would cook the entire meal with no assistance. She did some preliminaries while no one was there. It gave her something to do.

Something to do was becoming more important, though she couldn't elucidate why.

Walking became her primary pastime. It made her feel stronger. Cooking also gave her something she sensed was weighty. Only indication of that was her family's delighted response.

Physically, she was better, in that she was mobile and could endure and sustain some normal activity.

If only the blasted thing in her brain would let up. It kept tinkering, toying with it, sliding her back and forth on that blurred edge of reality.

Thanksgiving Day arrived. Everything was ready when the family arrived. Seana was tired, but it was a good tired. One that made her sigh and relax when she sat at the opposite end of the long dining room table, facing Barth, who asked God's blessing on the bountiful spread of food.

That was the extent of solemnity for the remainder of the evening.

Billie Jean crowed, "Did we cream those guys in the Clogging Competition or what?"

"*Yahoo!*" cried the others along with a little foot stomping until Seana scowled at them.

Zoe and Scott were lovey-dovey throughout the meal. Peyton and Ashley kept teasing them about being calf-eyed over each other, and they just laughed along with everybody else.

Seana, not plugged into the conduit of celebration, began to feel herself disconnect even more.

To withdraw toward that white mist. It crawled over her skin, trying to penetrate. Its tug was hypnotic. She made herself resist its pull.

She forced herself to sit through the meal, and only when Barth arose did she leave the table. The younger crew took over cleanup. No one seemed to notice Seana's lack of engagement in her surroundings.

On some level she realized that in itself was a change. Folks weren't reacting to her as much. There wasn't anything profound in her discovery. Just fact.

"We've got an announcement to make." Zoe harnessed everyone's attention by rapping a spoon against a glass. "Scott and I are engaged."

Woo-hoo choruses broke out as they applauded the turn of events.

The words bounced off Seana, but she remained in the den as they all swarmed in around her, with Ashley plastering to her side as Peyton went to the piano where he started playing Nana's favorites.

They did not appeal to her today. Did not touch her.

Barth could not long resist and joined Peyton on the stool, playing an octave higher or lower as they did their famous switch-places act.

Seana began to grow impatient for them to leave.

Oh no.

The whiteness grew brighter and enveloped her like a thick fog.

Her eyes closed and she nudged Ashley aside as her body began to slide into proneness. She felt Ashley move away, giving her the space she needed to burrow into her sofa niche.

She sighed.

Slowly, the gaiety subsided.

The house grew silent as her family left, one by one, whispering goodbyes and kissing her cheek.

At last, she once more slid into her snug cocoon.

అఇ

The Christmas lights blinked greetings each time Seana entered the den. The nine-foot spruce was from their forest, as was their tradition by now. This year, Scott joined Barth and Peyton on the established tree-cutting team.

Decorating it now involved Barth, Seana, Zoe, Scott, Peyton, and Ashley. Billie Jean joined them sporadically to critique and fill in gaps. Bing Crosby Christmas music wafted from the stereo. Crosby was part of Barth's tradition during yuletide, and the entire family joined in singing "White Christmas" and "The Drummer Boy" as they worked.

All except Seana.

Seana had helped with the decorating, and even from her remote perch, she recognized that the result was colorful and engaging to her family. It did not reach that spot inside her that *felt*. That *responded*. Like the music, it did not penetrate that blasted white nothingness.

Seana knew it was there. Knew it did not belong there.

"Mama?" Zoe called. "Didn't you hear me? I asked if you want me to bake pecan sandies for Christmas Day."

"I don't care," Seana muttered and continued cleaning up the tinsel that had missed the tree during the wild tossing contest. The others joined in and took inordinate care in hanging the silvery strands just so, for Seana's benefit. In that activity, she was meticulously accurate with getting uniform dangles.

Seana finished hanging the last strands and immediately embarked on her standard walk path through the house. She timed this daily activity to see how long it took her to go from the den to the back bedroom.

One minute, five seconds.

She always circled the route several times during her regular trek. She could hear her doctor saying, "If you don't use it, you lose it." And that prodded her in some mysterious way. "Lose" was not a good word.

When she finished, she sank back down on the sofa, tired.

On Christmas Eve, Seana asked Barth, "When can I get my driver's license back?"

It had expired during her illness. Barth would not let her have car keys, but Seana knew it wouldn't be a great thing for her to drive.

Barth turned from the counter where he chopped onions for squash and cheddar casserole. His eyes teared from the onions. He sniffled and took off his glasses.

Snatching a paper towel to dry his face, he asked, "Why?"

"Because. I want to get my license again."

He laid down his knife, washed his hands, and came over to the bar to sit across from her. She was garnishing potato salad with olives, quite precisely.

He wiped his glasses to a sparkling shine and slid them back on. "We'll wait till you're able to drive again and then we'll see about your license, okay?"

He gazed into her eyes, and for a moment she thought he looked sad.

"Okay."

Then he smiled. "Want me to make us some hot chocolate?"

She'd just recently acquired a liking for it. "Okay."

He hustled about putting milk in the microwave, then measuring out a special health store chocolate mix into cups. When the microwave pinged, he added the mixture to the steaming milk and stirred.

"I'm tired," Seana muttered and arose to Saran-wrap the potato salad and slide it into the fridge.

"Do you want to try a marshmallow on top?" Barth asked, wiggling his eyebrows like a silly school boy. He dangled the puffy white marshmallow over her cup.

"Yuck," she said and headed for the sofa.

Barth chuckled. "I figured as much. I'll bring yours to you."

He sat hers on the coffee table as she folded herself onto the sofa. Brutus's head lifted from his bed nearby to sniff the aroma. Barth tossed him a small treat before taking his seat in the easy chair.

Seana saw Barth close his eyes for a moment and bow his head. He looked so sad.

Seana picked up her cup and sipped.

It was good.

❧ ❧

After the holidays, Barth fell into a routine of working at the church office more. He needed the distance from the house, from the frustration of having Seana so near, yet so far away.

Besides, the regiment of friends and family committed to Seana's caregiving was as staunch and organized as the armed forces. He would actually get in their way if he didn't regularly disappear.

"She's really come a long way in the past year," Billie Jean declared one night at Happy Feet Dance Studio. Ashley had volunteered to sit with her Nana tonight and let Barth come and stretch his legs for a spell.

They sat at a table with candlelight, apart from the brightly lighted parquet dance floor. "So have you," Barth reminded her.

"Yup." The curly head nodded vigorously. "Thanks to your help. And Zoe's. That gal's turned out to be a regular Dr. DoRight when it comes to holistic medicine."

"She's quite a smart cookie." Barth reflected on the changes in Zoe, and his heart stirred with gratitude that the family situation had done an abrupt 180-degree turn.

"Have you checked with Fred Johnson on the For Seana's Sake prayer list progression?" Barth asked.

"Fred says that the prayer list has grown to thousands."

"Wow." Barth blinked and shook his head. And something inside him floated up like a helium balloon aiming for the galaxy.

Hope.

"It's gonna happen, Barth." Billie Jean shot him a thumbs-up.

And for the first time in a long time, Barth felt a distinct flutter of faith. Not the "what if" kind.

The "when" kind.

"C'mon." She grabbed his hand and tugged him toward the dance floor. "Time for a line dance!"

And so, for a few feet-stomping moments in a four-wall line dance to Marcia Griffith's "Electric Boogie," Barth forgot to be sad.

❧ ❧

Seana refused the marshmallow in her hot chocolate again that night and saw Barth's coaxing smile vanish and the weariness return. But the *why* of it did not ripple her opaque waters. It either sank into endless depths or floated away into infinity.

When she lay down to sleep, Barth prayed with her as he always did then joined her in bed. He no longer snuggled or spooned up to her as he once had. She'd been too prickly about it. "Like a cactus," was the way Barth had referred to her persnickety rebuffs.

So when she sank into slumber, it was a dark, dreamless, bottomless venture. Normal for her now.

Hours later, Seana awakened suddenly – fully awake with no transition from sleep.

This was, for Seana, unusual. In the silence, she could hear Barth's deep, even breathing. It was an exceptionally dark night. No doubt the skies were overcast, she thought.

A sliver of light appeared beneath her bathroom door from a nightlight put there to insure she wouldn't stumble through the night.

Later, Seana would tell Barth that she didn't know when she became aware of the light. It came like her awakening, without transition. It was different from the sliver beneath her door or even moonlight – tonight nonexistent – which normally spilled through her windows.

No, this light was more an illumination than light with a defined path.

There was something extraordinary about this light: it had, somehow, a center of consciousness. Seana felt a prickling of something.

Not fear.

Awe.

She was not afraid. Instead, it was like seeing an old childhood friend who'd changed, but she still recognized its totality rather than compiled features.

"Hello?" she murmured under her breath.

The light moved slightly. Actually, not really moved, just was suddenly closer to her without leaving where it was.

The prickling over her increased.

"Christ?" she whispered.

The light moved again. This time enveloping her. She looked down and her entire physical form was illumined. She wiggled her fingers and the light remained. She felt the warmth then. A pleasant, soothing sensation that relaxed her into a near giddy puddle of peace.

Yet … it went beyond that. Seana felt an overwhelming sense of – what?

It hit her like a brick up the side her head.

Love.

The thing she felt in her very pores was love. She knew because she'd been without it for so long that its advent was astonishing.

Seana knew its source.

Barth tossed restlessly, moaning in his sleep. Did he do that often?

"Would you please help, Barth?" her lips moved soundlessly.

The light did not leave her, but in some mystical way, it moved over and covered Barth, who sighed and settled bonelessly on his side, sleeping like a newborn.

"And now," she whispered again, "would you please, please go to Billie Jean's bed downstairs? She needs you, too." She sighed. "Oh yeh, and give her a double whammy, please?" The light moved again, and without leaving her, made its way through the wall in the direction of the stairwell that led downstairs.

Seana lay there for a long time, marinating in the presence.

And then, the light was gone. Her bedside clock said three a.m.

Seana lifted her head from the pillow to search the room but saw only the sliver of the nightlight from beneath the bathroom door.

The room was as dark as before on this moonless night.

She lay her head down and closed her eyes because, in that instant, she felt as relaxed as she'd ever remembered feeling. A deep tranquility overtook her and lulled her into instant, deep sleep.

Sunlight awakened her. Barth was already up. She heard him puttering in the kitchen. No doubt fixing coffee and breakfast. She sat up and took a deep breath that tingled in her senses, all the way out her fingers and toes.

Something astounding was taking place inside her.

She blinked and turned her head this way and that. The sound of birdsong outside her window beckoned to her. Barth came to the door, stuck his head in, and said, "Breakfast is ready."

His smile pierced her in a delicious way.

Seana slid from the bed, buoyant as a child.

The nothingness was gone. She felt light as a feather in the wind. Felt like twirling and leaping. But somehow managed to walk into the kitchen, right up to Barth, who turned from the stove holding her plate of scrambled eggs.

She took the plate from him, deposited it on the counter, and then slid her arms up around his neck.

"Barth, I'm back."

His mouth fell open, and his eyes, after a long, dumbstruck

moment, filled with tears. "Really? Are you really back, Seana?" his voice cracked with emotion. "I'm not dreaming am I?"

She smiled then as the burn of tears pressed behind her eyes, a long forgotten sensation. "Yes. I'm really, really back, honey."

His arms seized her, and he buried his face in her hair as they both wept and laughed, gazing at each other in wonder then coming back together, even closer.

Thumping, rapid footsteps from the stairwell intruded on their intimate celebration. Billie Jean's trumpeting voice called, "Hey! You guys!"

Presently, she rounded the corner into the kitchen and skidded to a halt, her eyes round as donuts. "Sit down. You'll *never believe* what happened to me at three a.m. this morning!"

∽∾

Seana had an appointment with Dr. Welton several months later so she kept it.

"How are you doing, Seana?" he asked, making notes. Barth sat beside her, silent this time, leaning back to watch the exchange with an amused detachment.

"I'm doing great, Dr. Welton. I have my driver's license."

His hand stilled and he looked up at Seana, expression stunned. "How –"

"Oh, Barth bought me a new car, too. He'd sold the other one to Peyton, our grandson, awhile back when he needed a good car to travel back and forth to school. No, I like the new one better anyway and –"

"How did this happen?"

Seana looked at Barth to see if he wanted to add to the conversation. He smiled, his eyes glowing behind the thick lenses, and nodded a silent *go ahead.*

Seana shrugged. "I'm well, Dr. Welton. Simple as that."

The good doctor stared at her, aghast. "To what do you attribute this – healing?"

"A miracle," she said. "A God thing."

Clearly skeptical, the doctor made more notes. "I want you to continue your meds –"

"Oh but I'm not taking your meds anymore. And I'd like you to dismiss me." Seana smiled, feeling completely at peace with her decision.

"B-but," blustered Dr. Welton, his face reddening, "You cannot discontinue Abilify or Lexapro because you might be right back where you were within six months."

Seana shook her head, still smiling. "I haven't taken them in two months and am doing just fine. I know you're skeptical, and I know what's happened is not normal. But I want to be released because I know I won't be sick again."

Dr. Welton, face still red, took a deep breath and exhaled. "Okay, Seana. I'll dismiss you – however reluctantly – but I want you to make an appointment with my psychologist for another memory test."

"Okay."

Seana left feeling free as a butterfly ready to explore all the velvety, fragrant flower petals of creation. She kept the promise to Dr. Welton, making an appointment with the psychologist, but after a week cancelled it.

There. Her conscience was clear.

Now, she would stretch and flap her beautiful wings!

epilogue

*"A butterfly could flap its wings and set
molecules of air in motion, which would move
other molecules of air, in turn moving more
molecules of air – eventually capable of starting
a hurricane on the other side of the planet."*
– Andy Andrews, *The Butterfly Effect*

Five years later

*T*he months following Seana's awakening rang with triumph and wonderment. At first, Barth watched her closely, cautioning her against overdoing things, such as cooking huge meals and taking on too much responsibility.

Seana knew he feared a relapse. Each time she saw the fear in those Cocker Spaniel eyes, she would reassure him. "Honey, I'm not going to go there again. Trust me. I know. I feel it" – she would place her hand over her heart – "here."

So, little by little, Barth's apprehension eased and he grew more confident that what had transpired that night in their bedroom had truly been a supernatural visitation.

Paradise Springs, said more than one resident, would never be the same.

"And it should never be the same," said Pastor Keith from the pulpit on this five-year anniversary of Seana's miracle. "Something of this scope happens maybe once in a lifetime. We've heard this story over and over, from many sources but never from the recipient. And now, I want to ask Seana to come up here and – in retrospect – to tell her version."

Amid applause, Seana arose and made her way to the front and up into the pulpit. She laid her carefully prepared notes on the podium and looked out at the expectant sea of faces. She smiled.

"First I want to thank each of you who carried me along all those years in prayer." She looked at Joanie, Billie Jean, and Chelsea sitting in the congregation, all three dabbing their eyes and blowing their noses.

Seana cleared her throat. "And then there were those of you who literally carried me in your arms. You were hands on, believing for me even when I could not believe for myself. Thank you from the bottom of my heart."

She went on to recount some of the difficult times, giving examples of her emotional quandary. And she shared in detail the doctor's diagnosis of dementia and early stages of Alzheimer's, citing the chart readings and all the medical "proof."

"One doctor told my family that I was slowly dying. Another told me I'd never drive again." She laughed. "How many of you see me surfing all over the place in my little white Accord?"

Hands went up all over the auditorium as emotional laughter joined hers.

"What do doctors know?" shouted Fred Johnson in a croaky voice.

"Yeh!" called Sadie Tate from across the room. "They don't know everything."

Seana shook her head slowly, reliving the wonder of it all. "Seemed they were right until that night I had a bedroom visit around three a.m."

The congregation fell so silent Seana could have heard a sigh.

"That was ..." She choked up. All over the place, folks snuffled and coughed.

Seana blinked back tears and cleared her throat. "I cannot even put into words what happened. It's too sacred. I can only quote from the book of St. John, 8:12, 'I am the light of the world: he that follows me shall not walk in darkness but shall have the light of life.'"

Seana's face glowed. "The light that touched me that night was Him."

Billie Jean, overcome with joy, stood and called out. "Sure was! I can vouch for that because He came to my room, too!"

Applause erupted, then a standing ovation.

Seana shook with emotion but continued. "I thank Him for mercy and grace and healing."

She took a moment to compose herself. "My husband stuck by me throughout all those nightmarish years. I could never have made it without him. Nightly, he read the Word to me. He didn't know it, but despite the cocoon surrounding me, the truth of those passages penetrated and made their way into my heart. Somehow, they did."

She turned to where Barth sat on the platform, his eyes red behind those thick lenses. "Barth, when I was at my worst, any other man would have walked away or let me rot in that nursing home. But not you." She blinked back tears. "Thank you for your faithfulness and unconditional love. No woman is more blessed than I am."

She addressed the congregation, her family, and friends. "Now, I want Scott to sing this song that sums up what I'm feeling right now."

Seana moved gracefully from the pulpit to her seat beside Zoe as Peyton took his seat at the piano and began to play the introduction for Scott, his wonderful stepfather.

The rich baritone voice began singing an old Andrae Crouch song:

> *Through it all ... through it all ...*
> *I learned to trust in Jesus*
> *I learned to trust in God.*

Through it all ... through it all ...
I learned to depend upon His word.

᧕᧚

A week later, Seana and Barth applauded wildly, while the Paradise Springs Cloggers exited the platform following their rousing performance at the annual Paradise Springs Summer Festival. Barth's whistles split the air.

Seana looked at him, grinning from ear to ear. "That's my man," she mouthed at him.

He pushed his glasses back up on his nose and mouthed smugly, "I know."

They watched Danny Day and his Foothills Ramblers Band dash away to raid John Ivey's Tarheel Dog Booth fare. Seana thanked the Lord that her appetite was healthier than ever as she inhaled the mouthwatering aromas wafting through the warm July air.

"How'd we do?" Peyton and Ashley, now dance partners, arrived like gangbusters, out of breath and high on performance adrenalin.

"Wonderful!" Seana and Barth said simultaneously, and all burst into laughter.

Zoe and Scott, still winded, strolled over, arms binding them at the hips. "Good, huh?" Zoe stated confidently.

"Best you've ever done," Barth declared sincerely.

'Would've been better if you two were still dancing," Ashley insisted, miming a pout.

Seana laughed and hugged her, sweat and all. "We older folks like to sit back and be entertained, doncha know?"

"Time to slow down a bit," Barth added. "It comes to everybody at some time in life."

"Aww." Scott cuffed his shoulder, grinning. "You're not old, man."

Barth and Seana looked at each other and burst into

laughter. Barth slid his arm around her and winked at Scott. "Tell me that when you're twenty years older."

Chelsea and Joanie left their partners and made their way to the circle. "Hey, you two, wanna go sample some of that BBQ?" asked Joanie.

"I can't wait to dig into it." Chelsea rubbed her back and flexed her ankle, making her tapped shoes jingle slightly. "I think somebody else might be right behind you in retiring from clogging, Seana," she said, raising her dark eyebrows.

"Hey!" Joanie protested, "not me! I'm a long way from sitting on a shelf." She fluffed her blonde hair, at present becomingly short and bouncy.

They all strolled over to picnic tables set up by John Ivey.

Billie Jean, having taken Seana's empty place on the clogging team, sashayed over in her crinoline-petticoated outfit.

"Dang it you don't look downright pretty, Billie Jean," Barth exclaimed.

Billie Jean scowled at him. "What'd you expect, Barth?" she quipped. "Country ugly?"

Barth back-pedaled, looking sincerely contrite. "No. Of course not. That outfit just –"

"Brings out the feminine beauty in you," finished Seana, by now feeling sorry for Barth.

"Oh shut up, Seana." Billie Jean flung out her arms. "Let 'im get outta this on his own. That's part of the fun!"

They all ordered an array of sausages of every description, hamburgers, hot dogs, and BBQ, along with crisp golden fries. Today, the weather was just right, not hot or humid, just breezy and balmy.

Before long, Sadie Tate arrived, choosing the next table where they could all chat. "You're doing good with the clogging, Billie Jean," she said, smoothing her latest Sassy Rags multi-colored sundress down over her spindly knees as she maneuvered herself onto the picnic seat.

Billie Jean smiled. "Thanks for those great healthy, sugar-free cookies you brought by. You know what I like."

"Was just thinking about you," Sadie said as she tucked into her hamburger. "Wish I was as conscientious about healthy eating as you folks."

Seana grinned, watching the ol' bird scarfing down the fat-ladened fare without a morsel of regret. She also thought how Sadie had mellowed and stopped her gossiping ways. Was, in fact, downright sweet nowadays.

Fred and Elsie Johnson strolled over from their booth, leaving it to one of the high schoolers to manage for a spell. They, too, joined in the feasting.

"Sorry we're late and missed your performance, Zoe." Pastor Keith and Louann rushed up with their all-the-way hot dogs. They scooted onto the bench next to Sadie and the Johnsons. "An emergency came up."

"Nothing serious, I hope," Barth said around a mouthful of BBQ. Today, he and Seana had called a time-out from the health routine and opted for the less hearty but delicious pork concoction.

"Not anymore." Pastor wiped his mouth. "You remember little Harry Woodall?"

"The Sunday School nightmare," Barth said before he thought.

Pastor and everyone else chuckled. "That's him. Anyway, he's in middle school now and had an altercation with another student and got his nose broken."

"Is he okay?" Seana asked, frowning, hurting for the little boy who'd stolen her heart way back during those days she taught him in Sunday School. He'd been a good boy beneath his busy-ness and innocent lightning-rod that drew trouble.

"Yes." Pastor Keith went serious. "Said he tried to talk to this other boy about not bullying smaller kids and girls." He shrugged. "The bully didn't like his interfering and pummeled him."

"Oh my." Seana put down her fork.

"He'll be okay. In fact" – Pastor looked at Seana – "he mentioned you, Seana."

"Me?"

"Yes. He remembered a time you taught the class about doing the right thing, even though it's not the popular thing to do at the time. He said you'd shown him that it's always right to do the right thing. And that's what he felt he was doing by standing up for a small, defenseless girl. Even though he got a broken nose for his efforts, he said he got in a few good licks and it was worth it."

Tears stood in Seana's eyes as she reflected on that.

"Mom?" Tim stood and leaned to hug her. "Sherry and I've gotta run. Still some office work to do. Peyton? You coming soon?"

"Yes sir," Peyton replied. He'd joined the family business since graduating from college. Seana's son Tim was giving nephew Peyton a generous percentage of shares in the family company along with a nice salary, plus commission on all sales. The bequest from her and Ansel had become even more lucrative and kept them all busy. Seana still, on occasion, dropped by to help them catch up during busy seasons.

So did Pops Barth.

Pops.

Barth.

That one decision to marry him.

Even before that, her decision to sign over the real estate business to her son was still gaining momentum. Granddaughter Ashley also would share in the profits. She was already training for future involvement, after college graduation.

Now, Peyton was third generation with the firm. At the same time, he also was third generation in Zoe's Happy Dance Studio business, another bequest from Seana and Ansel.

And the gift went on and on … and on.

Each decision.

No more than a butterfly wing's flap.

"You ready to go, honey?" Barth touched her arm and she arose.

As they strolled to the car, she gazed up into blue infinity. Lord, how beautiful life was. And she viscerally felt it in that instant ….

The cocoon.

The struggle to emerge.

The breathtakingly beautiful butterfly soaring and flapping its wings.

The love bonds that had flourished here in Paradise Springs as a result of her long, dark struggle.

And triumph. A miracle.

And she laughed, a peal of pure delight.

"What?" Barth peered at her, curious.

"Just thinking how a decision can set off a chain of events that affect so many lives."

He smiled then, dimples and all. Those eyes behind the thick lenses lit up and adored her. He stopped right there. In front of the world and Paradise Springs and pulled her into his arms.

His deep voice was husky. "I'm just glad you made a decision – that night we met at Happy Dance Studio – to give me a chance. Just look where it got me."

His head dipped and he kissed her.

And dang if she didn't feel it all the way out her fingers and toes.

And in that moment, Seana was certain she had the power in her to change the whole daggum world!

But for the moment, she would simply enjoy being in her man's arms and float in *feeling*.